Halfwide

A Novel

By

TEDDY JONES

Acknowledgments

Many deserve my gratitude for their encouragement, assistance, criticism, and support in my effort to tell this story. Writing colleagues Martha Burns; Candace Simar; and John Dufresne and the members of his Master Class at the 2010 Taos Summer Writers' Conference (Cully Perlman, Peter Stravlo, Kim Bradley, Jim Scutti, and Jill Coupe) all offered criticism that guided several revisions of the manuscript. Although none of them worked with me specifically on *Halfwide,* mentors and colleagues at Spalding University's Master of Fine Arts in Creative Writing Program provided valuable advice on craft that affected further revisions of *Halfwide* and other developing stories.

Friends and family including Patricia Carmichael, Monica Delatorre, Ouida Jones, Cameron Langford, and Val Overbey read, listened, laughed, and pushed me forward.

And Jim Bob Jones, my greatest source of support and encouragement, deserves more from me than words can convey.

For all those identified above and all I have neglected to mention, my thanks will have to do until you're better paid.

TEDDY JONES

CHAPTER 1

More So

NOTES—Dorothy Faye Bell
Day 1 May 19 10 p.m. Whaley, Texas

This will be a record of some odd things that have happened to me, Dorothy Faye Bell, age fifty-five. I'll admit I'd been out of sorts, irritable, for some time, even before that day the first odd thing happened about two weeks ago. Harold came in and said he was buying a travel trailer and trading the car and pickup in for a new pickup. He had been even quieter than usual for a while, so I figured something was up. But I never would have guessed a twenty-eight-foot Tahoe model trailer and a pickup or the reason for them that he dropped in a little later.

When he first mentioned it, I thought a lot of things, like why spend money buying a travel trailer, just rent one, or no, I don't want to go, or surely this is a joke, but I didn't say any of them. I just kept wiping the kitchen counter. Getting information out of Harold is easier if he tells it his way instead of answering questions. He is so slow about it, I could just scream. Push and he'll just clam up. That I've learned.

I didn't have to wait as long as usual for him to get to the point. He seemed kind of excited and started talking a lot—telling all about the trailer and the good deal he made on the pickup and how he'd get them both the next day.

When he started talking fast, I started putting out the plates for supper. I had to do something because I was getting edgier. That feeling that makes me want to get busy and stay busy got really strong. Managing to get a look at him, without looking directly, I could see his face was different. He looked kind of excited and happier than he had in a long time.

Thinking about that night, I decided I'd do something different this time. I'll write down every day some of what was happening. That's partly because my mother used to say I must have amnesia. Of course she knew I didn't really have amnesia. I never forget things I'm supposed to do or what I go to the store for or what day it is. And I have a good memory for words and definitions. What bothered her was that I'd say I didn't remember incidents she'd mention, like things that happened when my kids were little. She didn't expect me to recall much about my own childhood, but she thought I ought to be able to remember theirs.

She might have been right. I didn't tell her this, but things I do recall about a lot of times in my life are like little pictures—snapshots with the background out of focus. Sometimes I don't even recognize the people, much less the places or what was happening.

I didn't try to explain this to her, but I think part of the reason I forget is that a lot of things seem ordinary when they happen—so why bother to remember? Oh, maybe the first time something happens it might be odd, but pretty soon it'll just be more of the same and then I just put it out of my mind.

Maybe I do put too much out of my mind. I've wondered if later I might be sorry I've left out too much. Maybe there just won't be anything there when the time comes for me to live with my memories, like old people do.

Back to why I decided to write about what's going on. This does seem kind of odd—not bad odd or scary odd—just different. This time, if later it doesn't seem so odd anymore, then I can decide if I want to put it out of my mind instead of just losing it.

Ha! I just read what I wrote. I don't mean losing my mind. That's not what happens. It's losing parts of my life. This is not going to be easy if I keep getting off the track. The other reason I thought I'd write is that if one day I do lose my mind, maybe someone will find this and there'll be a clue in here. More likely, I'll just be able to read it years from now and laugh about how I once took myself to be important enough to write about.

Well, I guess I don't have to do this all tonight. I still have a little more work to do getting ready to leave. More tomorrow.

As she looked across the small space between them, Dorothy Faye was surprised to see Harold was still awake even though it was after ten. But this was the first travel day on this trip, so maybe he was still excited, congratulating himself on his plans. The radio was tuned to the talk station he liked and turned down low. *USA Today* was in his lap. "What's a seven-letter word for integrity?" she asked, not expecting a reply. "It has an *e* in the middle."

It was true; the puzzle she had the book open to did have that clue. Careful not to look pleased with herself, she continued reading from the first page in the little notebook she had in the middle of the crossword book. She'd started writing yesterday, feeling a little silly as she stashed the notebook inside her *New York Times Crossword Puzzles* book. She wasn't certain why she hid it, but it felt good to have a secret, something she hadn't had since she was a girl. Maybe it would be a place for some of the words she knew but seldom had a chance to use except in conversation with Mrs. Ottley.

Looking around the interior of the trailer, she considered how she would describe it in writing. *The interior comprises* (she liked that word and its proper usage) *three areas, the sleeping quarters, the kitchen/bath, and the living area. Euphemism* was the word she recalled when Harold had called it the living area. It was the *back*, as far as she was concerned, where they now sat. There was a recliner where Harold had extended the footrest a while ago and a smaller upholstered rocker where she was sitting. The built-in couch crossed the entire area at the end. If you didn't mind sleeping on top of a sheet of plywood and three inches of foam rubber covered in nubby fabric, the couch could be a second bed. Level with the top edge of the couch, a shelf extended from one side of the trailer to the other. Without time to do any arranging, Dorothy Faye had put the TV on that shelf. Nothing else. The set didn't work in here anyway because they weren't connected to cable and didn't have a dish. She was not unhappy that most of their stuff (that's how she thought of it—just stuff) either had been sold at the garage sale last week, given to the neighbors or Goodwill, or put in the trash. She never had been fond of dusting.

One time, years ago, Harold had said, "I'll never understand why you don't put plastic covers on the furniture and lamps like Janiece does. It keeps everything looking new and you won't have to dust as much."

Dorothy Faye smiled as she remembered that conversation. "I'll think about that," she replied. It was one of the few times she could recall that she had not done exactly what Harold wanted. *See there, Mother, I do remember some things.*

"Integrity?" he asked, voice loud. She nearly jumped. She hadn't expected a response any more than she ever did. The way it usually went, he would say something; she would listen. If she answered with a question about what he had said, he'd look at the TV as if she hadn't said anything. That part was fairly new, since he'd taken up pretending to be deaf. He used to just walk off. She'd concluded that in the interest of conserving his energy, he'd affected deafness. What she had learned over the years was that to him any response that was not an agreement was a potential argument. And she'd concluded he didn't want to argue, not with anyone and especially not with her.

If she started a conversation—well, no, you couldn't actually call what they had conversation. If she made a comment or, like tonight, asked about a puzzle clue, his method was to be very certain. When asked his preference for supper, he'd state, "I want chicken-fried steak and fried potatoes, nothing else." Or if he didn't have a good, final, definite kind of answer, he just didn't answer—deaf again. When he said, "Integrity?" she was surprised.

"Uh-huh," she said, "seven letters with an *e* in the middle."

"I don't know." He pushed down the foot piece on the recliner, sat straight up, then stood, all in two moves, very smoothly. "I'm going to bed. Remember you've got visiting to do in the morning. Don't stay up too late." In four short steps, he passed through the kitchen and arrived in the sleeping quarters, a space almost entirely occupied by the bed.

"Look here, hardly any floor for you to vacuum," he'd pointed out proudly as he had shown Dorothy Faye the trailer the first time, two weeks ago. Two closets, each capable of holding five hangers, flanked the head of the bed. This whole bedroom was up three steps from the other room because it was in the part of the trailer that extended over the gooseneck connector. So as you went into the bedroom, the distance from floor to ceiling changed from about six and a half feet to four and a half. Although he wasn't a large man, at five foot ten and 165 pounds, Harold did some wall-bumping as he undressed. Always neat, he hung his clothes before lying down. No more than ten minutes later, his breathing told Dorothy Faye he was asleep.

Ten o'clock was Harold's routine bedtime. Dorothy Faye was accustomed to staying up another hour or so, enjoying the time to read or work puzzles. She'd had more time to herself before Harold had, as he called it, retired early, about fifteen years ago. Tonight she planned to use the time to write some more in her little notebook. But first she stepped outside.

Even though Lakeview Hospital stood only three blocks from noisy main streets on both north and east, little disturbed the quiet tonight. No one else was visible in the parking lot. Several of the rooms in the hospital had the drapes open. A nurse passed by a window in one of the fifth-floor rooms. The windsock on the helicopter landing pad on the hospital roof hung limp against a backdrop of sparkling stars. A few clouds showed between the buildings west of the hospital. The slightly damp air felt cooler than usual for May. Dorothy Faye turned in a slow circle, absorbing the scene. She noticed a security guard in the parking garage entrance looking her way. *I knew this would happen.* She inhaled a jerky half breath, waved to the guard as calmly as possible, and retreated to the trailer.

Day 2 May 20 10:30 p.m. Lubbock

He said he had it all figured out. "There's no need for us to have this house anymore. We can live in the trailer and instead of staying in one place, we can move around. It will be like one long vacation." I must have looked like a guppy—mouth opening and closing, no words coming out. When I didn't say anything, I know he took it to mean I agreed. It's not that I disagreed; I was just surprised. Although I don't know why I should have been. Ever since we've been married, Harold has had one or another "idea" he's working on. And it never matters much what I think about them. He does what he wants to and I work around it. Adaptable, that's me. I said to myself when he married me, with my two babies, that I'd do what I had to, to make it work. Of course, it helps that most of his ideas turn out so that in the end there's something to laugh about. And he's pretty good-natured about laughing at himself.

She stopped writing to think more about today's trip. They had left the house in Whaley they had rented for more than twenty years and drove with the trailer to Lubbock. It was only a twenty-five-mile trip and seemed even shorter. They pulled into the parking lot here at Lakeview Hospital this afternoon. All the way up here, Harold was telling about how he first came up with the plan. She knew that while he was telling it, he was working out how he would pass along the story to his buddies at the café and to his sister Janiece and her husband, O.D. He always had lots to say when he was telling about his "ideas." That is, until something caused him to have to abandon the plan and wait for another inspiration.

He hatched this current scheme after he heard from someone that people can use trailer parking spaces at the hospitals when they have family who are patients there. "See," he said, "we act like we have family there, and we can stay maybe two weeks, no charge. Nobody checks to see why people are there—honor system, I guess. It'll be nicer than the KOA because there are only a few spaces. No crowds. There's no sewer dump, so we'll have to be careful about the commode. Go inside the hospital as much as you can." He had this reckless grin on his face when he said that. And he kind of leaned over and poked her like it was all a big joke. She asked him if it was against the law to pretend to be something they weren't. He said he doubted it and that they'd figure out all the details as things went along.

She heard a sound outside. She listened a minute longer; it was only a car starting. She resumed writing in her notebook.

I doubt Harold ever suffered the humiliation of public eviction. I remember it too well. Even if a lot of my past is out of focus, that picture remains clear.

All the way up here, Harold hummed "On the Road Again." I caught him at it and said, "You know, Harold, you really are better looking than Willie Nelson."

He looked at me sort of funny for a second and then said, "Well, he should've taken better care of himself." He knew I was going along with the joke—his latest idea.

After Harold broke the news about this plan, I quit the job I had as a care attendant for Mrs. Ottley. I felt bad about leaving her because she's eighty-five and has outlived most of her friends. Her daughter got a replacement for me right away, but I still worried about her adjusting. Mrs. Ottley surprised me, though. She told me I should have a good time, said I should do it while I could, that one day I'd be too old. And although she didn't say it, I think she had the same idea I did, that a wife has to go with her husband. At least that's what I've always done so far.

Big day tomorrow, so I'd better stop for now. What I'm trying to figure out is how to seem like we have family in the hospital without lying about it. Harold's solution to my concern about this being against the law was to say I could go in and visit some each day—didn't matter who I visited or how long. Then we would be visitors. "Solved that little problem," he said.

We'll see.

I've got it! A seven-letter word for integrity is honesty—e in the middle.

After inserting *honesty* into puzzle #97, Dorothy Faye put the puzzle book and its companion notebook in her purse and slid the purse under the edge of her chair. Harold didn't stir as she settled into bed.

Harold does make good coffee. That was her first thought when she woke to the aroma. He was in his recliner, sporting Wranglers, boots, and a plaid shirt. *And he does try to be considerate about noise. He didn't turn on the radio until I got up. Why am I making a list of his good qualities?* She wondered for only a second; she knew the answer. She came up with the exercise about twenty-five years ago. It helped her quiet her mind when she had trouble accepting his schemes. She thought it was better for her than biting her tongue.

Right now she needed another item for the list to offset her worry about getting caught by someone in the hospital. *He seldom expects me to cook breakfast,* was the best she could do as she ate her bowl of Total. *The only thing to do is just get on with it. See what happens next.*

"Tall and graceful," Dorothy Faye murmured. As she walked toward the hospital entrance, she repeated the description she had chosen for herself years ago. Ignoring the fact that she stood only five foot five inches and never had been willowy, she smiled and nodded to a man she passed near the door. When he returned the smile, she stood even taller as she entered the hospital.

Dorothy Faye knew she had an inviting sort of face even if she'd never been a beauty. Never being beautiful was an advantage, really, because now, at fifty-five, she didn't feel a need to dye her hair or use lots of cosmetics to hold onto her looks. Her complexion stayed tan year-round, and complemented her green eyes and short, curly, graying brown hair. As for what was inviting about her, she never gave it much thought. Knowing she always looked pleasant and people responded to her without her saying a word satisfied her.

The only person who ever seemed bothered by the fact that strangers smiled at Dorothy Faye was her first husband. "Whatever you're doing that makes people notice you like that, I want you to stop. It's not safe being friendly with just anyone," he'd said. They were both eighteen and he was shouting at her. Remembering, she sighed and shook her head. For a minute she didn't feel tall and willowy, just sad and a little angry at the eighteen-year-old Dorothy Faye. She wondered why she didn't recall any more about when or where or what else was happening then. *Another fuzzy snapshot.*

She'd come up with a plan that before this was over with, she would go to each floor of the hospital to observe. It had been several years since she had been at Lakeview. Back then she had worked as a sitter doing private duty for patients here. Families sometimes hired a sitter if their patient was elderly or confused or if they thought the regular staff couldn't, or didn't, watch the patient closely enough. Sitting, just being there, was pretty much all the job required, although Dorothy Faye could have done more. Back in 1964, she had completed two semesters of nursing school with very good grades.

She chose the cardiac care waiting room on the fourth floor as her starting place for today instead of the surgery waiting area on second. A volunteer recorded the names of visitors to Surgical Waiting. Dorothy Faye knew that was to make it easier to let people know about their patient's progress. She didn't intend to sign in as some patient's family member. She would not lie to accomplish Harold's scheme, no matter what.

Why am I going along with this? He can park that rig anywhere and pretend to visit as easily as I can. She knew the answer—there was no house to go back to, she didn't want to stay in the trailer all day, and she'd rather not argue with him about who would do the visiting.

Dorothy Faye returned the smile of the room's only other occupant as she extracted the puzzle book from her purse. *That sad young man is going to want to talk if I give him any chance at all.* She began to study the puzzle clues. *Ruse* fit immediately, followed by *eland*. She worked quickly, using a ballpoint pen.

When she glanced at her watch, she had completed the puzzle in fifty-eight minutes. Entering her time below the puzzle, she heard sharp tones from across the room. A second man was talking with the first one she had noticed. Both looked quite distressed. Dorothy Faye concluded it was a good time for her to explore the hospital a bit.

Day 3 Sunday, May 21 10 p.m. Lakeview Hospital, Lubbock

I don't know what Harold did all day. I also don't know, and won't ask, just how long he intends for this "vacation" to go on. But I expect it will be like a lot of his other ideas and not last too long. Something always comes up to change his whole direction. Like that time he thought he'd start doing bodywork on cars. He could have, all right. He's handy when he wants to be. He set up in the garage at the house; bought Bondo and paint in several colors; got a secondhand paint sprayer; and ordered several books on how to do auto body repair. I didn't see much of him for about three weeks, and then one day I went out to the garage and my red Chevrolet was two-tone blue. "Don't touch it 'til it's dry," he warned me. "What do you think?"

He looked proud of what he'd done and I knew the right answer. But what came out of my mouth was, "What will I drive to work this afternoon?"

But I don't think the fact that I wasn't overjoyed with my new paint job stopped that whole scheme. A couple of other things happened. First, there wasn't much business. How many people in Whaley, Texas, population 2998, want to change the color of their car or need bodywork every month? Then the bulldog clinched it.

He'd had the dog for about twelve years. Harold loved that dog. He even traveled with Harold when he was a truck driver. Handsome was his name, but he wasn't. An English bulldog may be a lot of things, but good-looking isn't one of them. Anyway, one day Harold was working on a job in his "body shop." Just to finish it off nice, he decided to clean off some rust on the chrome with steel-wool pads. To make a long story short, Handsome mistook Brillo pads for dog treats and ate at least one. He was foaming all blue around the mouth when Harold noticed him, and he died by the time Harold got him to the vet. Harold closed the shop and ended his career in auto bodywork the next day.

Visiting today was not difficult. No one seems to pay much attention to who's in the waiting room. Since it's quiet in the hospital, I'll probably stay longer tomorrow. It's nice not having to cook. I wonder how many showers I can take in this trailer before he'll have to get to a sewer hookup. I'll just leave that up to him to figure out. I also wonder what the hospital people would do if they realized we're squatters on their land. I guess it's not a felony. But I'd feel better if we didn't have to pretend. I may have to say something to Harold if the other spaces fill up. I can't go along with this scheme if it means someone who needs to be here couldn't get a space. And I will not be evicted, not even to give him a new story to tell his coffee shop buddies.

Speaking of cars, now that he traded in the car, we just have the one pickup for both of us. I suppose he plans to take me where I need to go—or wherever he thinks I *need to go. Not that I ordinarily go that many places other than work, but sometimes I just like to drive myself around. Without supervision.*

The next four days passed much as the first in what she had begun to think of as the "elaborate charade." (That clue had been in puzzle #98 and did seem "apropos"—also in the puzzle.) So far, Dorothy Faye had checked each floor of the hospital, roamed the gift shop, watched a morning quiz show in the outpatient surgery visiting area, explored the cancer therapy unit, and spent some time in the chapel. Not one person asked whom she was visiting.

This afternoon, after talking with Dennis, the young man she'd seen the first day in the CCU waiting room, she paced the parking lot. Thoughts of their conversation competed with questions about herself. The resulting jumble propelled her and obscured the surroundings. She jumped at the sound of a car horn and realized she had jaywalked across Twenty-Fourth Street.

She'd been wondering if there was something wrong with a woman who would just go along with the idea of leaving the place she'd lived for more than twenty years. What's wrong with a person who doesn't feel bad about leaving what's passed for home for a long time? She didn't have a good answer for that question. So she decided to think about something she might be able to do something about. She resolved to make herself a schedule so she wouldn't have so much free time to think.

The pickup was missing when she concluded her visiting and the wandering walk. The formaldehyde aroma of new paneling and cheap carpet greeted her as she stepped into the trailer. Without Harold in the recliner, she could give the place a good look. "Critique is what I'll do," she said, staring at the little refrigerator and then at the nubby upholstery. But before any words of appraisal came to her, she sat down, hard, and shook her head, slowly.

"I cooked supper!" Harold announced as he arrived, carrying a bucket from the Colonel.

As Dorothy Faye put paper plates on the little bar over the cabinet, Harold pulled one of the two stools up to the bar. Eating from paper plates was his idea. "Cuts down on washing dishes so we use less water," he explained. She had put most of their dishes in with the things they gave to Goodwill. She had lingered a minute over the good pottery her mother gave them on their first anniversary, but then decided it didn't matter much. "We're lightening our load," he'd said. So far, even though their load of stuff was much lighter than before, she felt like she was carrying something heavy every step she took. Dorothy Faye studied the extra-crispy chicken breast she'd just bitten into. It seemed to weigh two pounds.

"I went over to Janiece and O.D.'s today," he reported as he opened his pill bottle. "She told me we should have a cell phone, in case something comes up. I think that's a good idea."

"Did she?" Dorothy Faye responded, as she swallowed a gulp of air. It sounded like a hiccup. She turned to the Colonel's bucket and side orders to avoid thinking of his veto a few days ago when she had suggested a cell phone. Offering him the corn and fried okra, both of which smelled like extra-crispy chicken, she searched for another item for the list.

———◆———

Maybe it's the weather making him talkative—a low-pressure system moving in— or maybe it's the fact there's no TV. Harold had started talking right after he took his Glucotrol, while he was efficiently separating kernels from cob. *He still has good teeth.* She cautioned herself to pay attention. He started in on reporting about Janiece and O.D. with corn in his mouth. As she listened, she wondered if his blood sugar was low. That made him act odd sometimes.

Harold made short work of the chicken and was still holding his last drumstick when he opened the door and stepped outside. Looking south, he said, "We could get a big wind or some hail out of this. Might even lose the roof since this rig doesn't have any old tires to put on top of it." He made a little choking sound as he chuckled at his joke about the tires. "Janiece said she'd been out to see Rubyjo the other day and that she's no different."

"Did she expect her to be?" Dorothy Faye asked. Harold's youngest sister was often the focus of Janiece's concern. Rubyjo had never been perky and ever since she was divorced about twenty years ago, she spent most of her time sitting at her kitchen table smoking cigarettes.

"Janiece said Rubyjo probably has a chemical imbalance."

"Oh, has she been to a doctor?"

"No, that was something Janiece had seen about on television. I said to Janiece that all's wrong with Rubyjo is she needs a good man." Harold looked serious as he pronounced his conclusion.

"Could be." As far as Rubyjo was concerned, Dorothy Faye actually thought she was doing what most people do as they pass the years, just getting more so. Rubyjo had started out grim and had acquired an excuse twenty years ago for being that way.

Dorothy Faye watched Harold step back inside. He moved slowly, as if he were wading in mud. She wondered if he was keeping up with his blood sugar.

Day 8 May 26 8:30 p.m. Lakeview Hospital, Lubbock

Maybe I'll go to bed early myself. I don't like listening to the wind and rain. But first I'm going to write about the two things are on my mind. The first one is Dennis and the second one is how irritable I've been feeling around Harold. There's a lot more on my mind. But I'll write about those two since I said I'd write in here about things I might not want to forget.

About Dennis—I knew he wanted to talk to someone. He looked so sad and upset and alone there in the waiting room. He's always been by himself except for that one time I saw him talking to that other man. I was working on a puzzle, trying to find a seven-letter word for "an elucidating glimpse." I haven't gotten that one yet. Anyway, I finally looked up at him. He took that as an invitation. He moved over next to me, said hello, and then stared up at the TV on the wall for a while. Then he said, still not looking at me, "It's so hard just waiting."

I nodded and said, "Tell me about the waiting you're doing." That was all it took. Maybe I remind him of his mother, the one he's here for. She's in a coma since a stroke she had three weeks ago after heart surgery. They've lived together since his father died in '91.

"Since I never married, my brother, well, everyone, expected I would take care of Mother," he said. "So I have." His voice was shaky. Now he was talking directly to me, ignoring the TV. I knew he was ready to cry.

"It's hard waiting and feeling like you're not able to help," I said. I felt pretty helpless myself because the next thing I knew he was crying. And I didn't even have a Kleenex to offer.

Before it was over, he had told me a whole lot of things about his mother, his brother, how mad he was at the heart surgeon, and how he'd realized how alone he was at the age of forty.

After talking for nearly an hour, he took a deep breath and said, "Thank you so much. I feel a lot better now. You helped me. I can stand to go back in there and stay with Mother for a while longer now."

The odd thing was that I hadn't said a thing once he started. I just patted him on the arm and listened to him and felt concerned. I'm not sure why that left me feeling so—guess I have to think about exactly how I felt, feel. I do know it took all I had to sit there and be still. I felt like I needed to be up doing something to make things right for him—or was it to make it okay for me? But I felt good too. It made me stand up really straight when I left. An "elucidating glimpse" might help me understand all of that. Ha! I got it—it's insight—seven letters.

I'll think about Dennis and that feeling some more, later on.

Now, about being irritable toward Harold. Usually, when I get irritable, I check to see if I've been eating right and getting enough sleep. That's because I know I'm better about accepting things when I'm in good shape. Things—what I mean is accepting how he thinks up these big plans and assumes I'll go along with them, accepting how he acts like Janiece is always right and I'm not worth listening to. And he thinks it's funny that the security guard keeps watching me. I saw him twice today, looking directly at me.

That sounds like I'm feeling sorry for myself. As my mother put it one time, "Don't you think you're taking yourself a little too seriously?" I guess maybe I am. I'll try to just keep making lists.

One thing I'm certain of is that it's me that's different, not Harold. Even if he is feeling bad, keeping it to himself isn't different. Fifteen years ago, when he had the back injury, he didn't complain until his left leg went numb and he couldn't walk. Said later he didn't want to worry me. It was the same with his diabetes. He never mentioned being sick until he'd already seen the doctor and filled prescriptions. And this whole vacation scheme is no stranger than any of the other ideas he's come up with. If I didn't think it would make me more irritable, I'd make a list right now of all the schemes he's had since I've known him. He's sixty-two now and he was twenty-nine when we married. So that's thirty-three years worth of big plans. No, he hasn't changed; he's just more so. Guess I'll go to bed now.

———◆———

Around midnight, Harold shook her awake. "There's been a tornado on the south side of town. I got up when the wind got worse and just heard about it on the radio. Get dressed. We're going to leave." Harold operated in his best take-charge mode; no more slow-motion wading in mud. He moved as fast as he ever had. "I'll back the truck up and get hooked. Just be sure all the cabinets are closed." A siren sounded, coming nearer. "Lots of people were hurt at a trailer park and some killed in the parking lot at the mall.

The cloud is supposed to be staying in South Lubbock and moving east. The north side of town is safer. We're heading to Janiece's."

"Why are we leaving?" Half asleep, Dorothy Faye had a little trouble making her mouth work. It made no sense to her to be driving off in this rain and wind and lightning.

"Because," he said, "in no time this place is going to be covered up with ambulances and police. Someone will start asking questions." Seconds later, as Dorothy Faye was thinking about that and trying to wake up, she saw an ambulance, followed by a police car, arrive at the emergency entrance.

He is *a very good driver*. She had the first item for her new list. Harold had the trailer attached to the pickup in less than ten minutes. His backing-up technique was especially impressive. The skills from his years of driving eighteen wheelers were not forgotten.

Dorothy Faye inhaled deeply as she made certain the trailer door was secured. Ozone fragrance, a perfume. She knew better than mention it to Harold or he'd be setting up a lab. As she got into the pickup cab, she knew if he did decide to manufacture perfume, she would probably go along with it. The wind had slowed, and the rain now fell in a heavy, steady shower. Calmer now, she leaned against the seat and closed her eyes. "More so," she murmured. Harold didn't hear her.

CHAPTER 2

What Next?

The trip from Lakeview to O.D. and Janiece's house on Sixth Street took only about ten minutes. Few other drivers braved Lubbock's streets, filled as they were with rainwater and debris. Harold left the trailer connected to the pickup's fifth wheel pivot after he parked in the driveway. "This'll do until morning. Trailer's level enough to sleep in," he said. He and Dorothy Faye hurried toward the back porch.

Janiece opened her back door and pulled Harold inside. "Praise the Lord! Y'all get in here right now. We just came out of the cellar. Harold, you must be crazy to be out driving around in this storm." O.D. stood beside her silently, smiling and holding a large old mantle clock. "O.D., keep a watch on the TV weather so we can get back underground if we need to. Oh hi, Dorothy Faye." Janiece was excited and talking even more than usual, which was a lot.

A Q-Tip! From where she stood, looking toward the voice, Dorothy Faye saw a six-foot-tall Q-Tip. Outlined by the light behind her, her head wrapped in layers of toilet paper, and thin as a stick, Janiece did resemble a Q-Tip. It only took a second for Dorothy Faye to realize that today was

Janiece's beauty shop day. She had a new tightly curled and teased coiffure, sprayed to stay and wrapped for the night. She went in once a week and took care between times not to disturb her hairdo. If you looked under the toilet paper, you'd see a six-week rinse job that conferred a completely uniform dark brown shade, the same color her hair had been for the last forty years. Apparently she was not concerned with achieving a natural look. A while back she had added permanent eyeliner and brows. When Dorothy Faye asked if the tattooing had hurt, Janiece had looked offended and said, "Tattooing is for sailors and hippies. This is permanent cosmetics, so I don't have to worry with putting them on every day."

Janiece seemed to enjoy the excitement of the storm—this one or any storm. Every time a cloud came up, she recounted her mother's deathbed warning. "I'll never forget Mama saying, just before she died, 'Janiece, that clock of your granddad's is for you, now that I'm going. Don't ever let it get blowed away in a tornado.' That was Mama's first coherent words in eighteen months, and then she died." Janiece told it exactly the same each time. Then she'd grab the clock from the mantle and head to the cellar.

Harold had told her that Janiece wanted that clock since she was a child and her rendition of the deathbed scene eliminated any inheritance claims from her siblings. The fact was that he'd never even wanted the clock, but he said that dramatic scene irritated him every time he heard it. Harold looked over at Dorothy Faye and raised an eyebrow.

Janiece, Harold, Dorothy Faye, and O.D., holding the clock, crowded the mud porch. Janiece made sure that anyone who entered the house came through this room and removed their shoes, regardless of the weather. Tonight that made sense. They all had gotten wet on the way to the porch. Janiece's toilet paper was damp. Only the clock, covered in plastic, was dry.

Seeing Janiece and Harold side by side, Dorothy Faye wondered again how a brother and sister could look so little alike. Harold had told her he looked a lot the way he remembered his dad and Janiece resembled their mother, all angles. Their father left when Harold was thirteen, Janiece fourteen, and Rubyjo was just seven.

They heard from some of his relatives that their father died a few years later. The story they heard was that he was in Wyoming working in a new gas field that had opened up. He'd gotten sick with something—they didn't know what—and died quickly. Their mother said his people were surely lying and that he'd probably been shot by a jealous roughneck in a fight over a woman. That was the last thing she ever said about him—the subject of their father stayed closed from then on. Neither one of the girls seemed particularly concerned about his being gone, or later, being dead. He'd been gone, working in one new oil or gas field after another, most of their lives.

Janiece had snagged O.D. and married at sixteen. Rubyjo outdid her and married when she was fourteen. By the time he was twenty, it was just Harold and his mother living together. He'd gotten a job as a swamper for an oil field trucker when he got out of high school and worked around Levelland, where they lived. Then a couple of years later he'd gotten on with a long-haul company.

When Harold was twenty-two, their mother had to be put in a nursing home because at the age of fifty, she'd become what Janiece labeled "dangerous." What that meant was that she'd lost her memory and wasn't able to take care of herself. She just seemed to turn backward and get lost in her past. They took her to lots of doctors, but none of them could help. Today they might have diagnosed Alzheimer's.

Harold said he'd felt bad back then that he couldn't take care of her. One day while he was gone on one of his trips, she put fish sticks in the oven, box and all, and then forgot them. When he got back, Janiece told him about the fish-stick fire and finished by saying, "That cinches it! There's no way I can take care of her. I mean she goes to the bathroom in the closet and then she even forgets to wipe herself. O.D. said we can't have her ruining our house like she's ruined hers."

Janiece often quoted O.D. She would make a statement, "Them Mexskins that are moving in are just ruining the neighborhood." Then she'd add, "Don't you think that's right, O.D.?" He'd nod or say, "Uh-huh." From then on, she'd quote him as having expressed the opinion she'd originally rendered. "O.D. says all them Mexskins are just ruining this neighborhood. Next thing you know, there'll be drive-by shootings." O.D. got credit for saying a lot more than he ever said.

After his mother was in the nursing home, Harold and his sisters sold her little fire-damaged house and he lived in the sleeper in his truck. She died three years later.

Dorothy Faye was working nights as a waitress at the truck stop near Idalou when she and Harold met. He was the only customer at about three o'clock one morning. He ordered coffee and a piece of chocolate cake. He smiled a small smile, more toward his plate than at Dorothy Faye, and said, "I didn't think I could go another mile, I was so sleepy. Now I know the reason I had to stop here was to meet you."

She'd heard a lot of lines in the three months she'd worked there. But for some reason, she thought he seemed sincere. It was probably that and the fact that she was tired of her mother saying, "You need to get out and meet some nice, settled man. Try going to church." Anyway, when he asked if he could call her, she wrote her phone number and Dorothy Faye Carson May next to it on a napkin, smiling a nervous smile, and trying to keep her hand steady.

Dorothy Faye's hand started shaking again when he called a few days later. Her mother passed her the phone and started straightening up the room, staying near enough to hear the conversation. Living with her mother since Ronnie left, Dorothy Faye had gotten used to her nosing into everything. "I suppose that's what I pay for rent and babysitting," she later explained to Harold.

He asked her to go out to a movie. She agreed and invited him to come by before for supper. She thought she might as well run him off right away. He could see the kids, be scared by them and her mother, and that would be that. Later on, when she met his sisters, she realized her mother probably seemed tame by comparison. What really surprised her were the kids. They had just worked him over. Elizabeth, a little past two years old at the time, climbed into his lap, patted his face with her tiny hands, batted her eyelashes, and smiled up at him. Little R.J. jabbered and smiled like the one-year-old he was. Harold was done for.

"I had a real good time. Thank you for supper and for going to the show with me," he said when they returned. He hugged Dorothy Faye at the front door. He didn't try to kiss her. "Can we do this again real soon?" Dorothy Faye forgot what she answered. Her gliding steps were so light, her mother didn't wake up to grill her. Dorothy Faye was sure he was interested in her, but that night she kept it her secret.

They were married in September of 1967. He seemed pleased to acquire a "ready-made" family. The kids hung onto him all the time. Her mother even said, "Well, he doesn't talk much, but he seems to have a lot more sense than that last one."

The fact that Harold wasn't much on talking about his feelings toward her hadn't bothered Dorothy Faye. She was too busy with the kids and work to waste time in conversation. The fact that he'd only said, "I love you" a couple of times in those seven months before they married didn't trouble her too much either. She remembered Ronnie had talked a lot about love and didn't mean any of it. What Harold did was what mattered. What he did was offer to take care of her and her kids. And she promised herself she would make it work. That was what love meant to her, making and keeping a promise to someone you cared about. She didn't let herself be concerned that she felt no fluttery excitement. That fluttery feeling she'd thought was love with Ronnie had been replaced rather quickly by stomach pain and headaches during the time they'd been married. With Harold, she was calm—no aches, no pains.

Harold made enough money as a truck driver for her to quit work a few months after they married. She stayed home and took care of the kids and made sure that when he was home, Harold had good food and clean clothes. He called home every night from the road and talked about his day. As far as the kids were concerned, he was the only daddy they had ever had. And he was good at being a parent. He'd listen to them and play outside with them and discipline them just by talking or sending them to their room.

Their life together had a rhythm dictated by his driving schedule. For seven days he'd be gone and then home for four or five days. During his home times, Harold stayed busy with his projects. But he never ignored his family. He involved them all in carrying out his plans. From the time they were small until they were both occupied with their teenage activities, Elizabeth and R.J. fetched tools and supplies, learned to build and repair things, and gathered information necessary to whatever plan was underway. At school, their reading ability always tested high, which Dorothy Faye attributed to their helping Harold with "research." While other kids their age watched television, R.J. and Elizabeth busied themselves as Harold's apprentices.

The cadence of Dorothy Faye's days was predicted by her awareness of the needs and wants of Harold and the children. She read them expertly. She'd paid attention in the psychology and child development classes when she was in nursing school and now was glad of it. The kids seldom quarreled because she diverted them from conflicts into games. She monitored their diet, taught them hygiene, and made certain they were fully immunized.

She read to them and encouraged them to learn some manners. She kept the house clean but pleasantly messy, and she never moved any of Harold's equipment or project materials. His clothes were clean and ready for his trips. She listened with genuine interest to his ideas about inventions and his plans for projects. She never missed an opportunity to encourage him to elaborate. And he did.

Harold seemed to thrive on the attention. More than once he mentioned to her that whenever one of his friends asked about his new family, particularly his wife, he always told them what a good wife she was. That was enough for her. She relaxed; she enjoyed her life.

Dorothy Faye's mother asked, a few months after the wedding, "Well, are you happy this time?"

"I'm happy. We have everything we need. Harold's always good to me and the kids," Dorothy Faye responded, ignoring the implication of "this time." It was true at the time and for many years after. Harold paid the bills and gave her money for the household costs. She didn't worry about his being interested in other women or being suspicious of her. He seldom drank alcohol or swore and hardly ever raised his voice. Part of that was because it was his nature. The other part was Dorothy Faye's cheerful, watchful way of making everything work out—just the way she'd promised herself.

O.D. and Harold headed out to the garage. O.D. was always glad to have company, particularly Harold. "Come on out to my room," O.D. said, taking his cigarettes out of his shirt pocket. Janiece didn't allow him to smoke inside. From the doorway, Dorothy Faye could see he'd set up two recliners, an end table, a floor-model ashtray, and a radio in the half of the garage not occupied by Janiece's car. She noticed that the Early American braided rug that had once been in the dining room now covered the painted garage floor. O.D. had a regular little retreat for himself. "Harold, I located a dump station for your trailer. Over on West Nineteenth Street at a trailer park," he said as they went out the door.

That left Dorothy Faye alone with Janiece in the room with the television and the smell of some pine-scented cleaning product. "Is there anything good on television tonight?" Dorothy Faye asked, because she knew that the only other choice was to hear about Janiece's latest doctor visit.

But Janiece surprised her. "Don't you think Harold's been actin' strange lately?" she asked. Without waiting for an answer, she said, "This whole trailer thing and moving out of your house and all is the weirdest thing he's ever done. I hope he's not getting like Mama was."

While she was thinking of an answer, Dorothy Faye realized she shouldn't have been too surprised. If Janiece wasn't talking about her illnesses, she was diagnosing others'. "Oh, I think he's fine. His diabetes is stable. He takes his medicine and is pretty good about what he eats. This is just something he wants to do right now," Dorothy Faye said. She smiled in Janiece's direction.

"You're just too easygoing, Dorothy Faye. Always letting him do whatever pops into his head. If it was me, I'd just tell him *no way*. If you want to drag a trailer around, drag it without me. That would stop him in his tracks." Janiece shook her finger toward the garage as she delivered her version of the perfect ultimatum.

Pleased she'd remembered "ultimatum" from a puzzle she'd worked two weeks ago, Dorothy Faye concluded Janiece shouldn't expect an answer to that. Using the same technique she had used with her kids, she tried a change of subject. "Janiece, I noticed you have your new Cadillac covered up out in the garage. Is something wrong with it?"

"No, I'm just protecting the paint," she answered, as if putting a tarp on a Cadillac inside the garage were the only logical thing to do. The distraction didn't work. Janiece persisted, "Now that you've left the hospital parking lot, what I want to know is what's next?"

"Well, I think that next, I'll go to bed. See you tomorrow." Dorothy Faye smiled again and went out to the trailer. On the way out, she realized the trailer's electricity wasn't plugged in. She'd either have to use the battery lamp or go back in to ask about plugging in the trailer's connection. She chose the battery lamp. At lease she could sleep tonight without worrying about being evicted.

She knew Harold and O.D. would stay up late. It seemed like O.D. stored up all he wanted to say until Harold came around. He didn't get much opportunity to talk when Janiece was in the vicinity. He and Harold would talk for hours about the weather and baseball and oil field work. O.D. still worked as a pumper part-time even though he officially retired year before last. And after his accident and forced retirement from long-haul driving, Harold had worked in the fields over near Crosbyton part-time. They could speculate for hours about oil and gas operations and about oil field people they both had known over the years.

Another reason for their long talks was that O.D. was always interested in Harold's projects. He often would offer suggestions, so they usually talked some about whatever the current scheme was too. Sometimes Harold used O.D.'s suggestions, like the time he had suggested putting satin liners in the pet coffins.

Once when Harold was on the road, he noticed a couple of pet cemeteries near Dallas. When he got home, he investigated and found that the burials were usually made directly into the ground, sometimes in a plastic bag, but nothing like a coffin. At some of the cemeteries, they just took the dead animal and put it in a hole and promised the owner to keep the grass cut. Others were fancier. They advertised perpetual care and sold personalized headstones to memorialize Fluffy or Spot—Faithful Companion.

He also found that in Texas alone there were ninety-two pet cemeteries advertised in the yellow pages of different cities. Thinking he'd found a niche, he began making pet caskets in three different sizes and in two different types of wood. He planned to get an inventory established before he began marketing in earnest. About the time that the garage was filling up with the miniature coffins, O.D. stopped by. He suggested they might sell even better if they were lined in satin and had little pillows. The next day, Harold had Elizabeth and Dorothy Faye measuring, cutting, and stitching.

That was one scheme that worked out pretty well. Before he moved on to another interest, Harold sold more than a thousand of those little boxes to pet cemeteries. In the five years, beginning in 1976, that Harold turned them out, he put more than twenty thousand dollars in the kids' college accounts from the income. He even figured a way to avoid shipping costs. He carried them in the sleeper compartment of his truck and delivered them when he was on the road on his regular trips.

The story he told about explaining the boxes in the sleeper to a trooper who pulled him over for a weight check made the coffee shop rounds for quite a while. When the trooper asked for his logbook and Harold had to open the curtain on the sleeper to get it, the stack of caskets was obvious. Of course, the patrolman asked what they were. Harold's reply was direct and truthful, "Caskets for small animals." He said he thought the officer might not be the pet cemetery type, so he told him, "I have a religious belief that all animals are sacred. Anytime I notice roadkill, I stop and give the poor critter a decent burial. Those are the coffins I use, make 'em myself. This trip I haven't seen as much as an armadillo that needed burying." He said the trooper just shook his head and sent him on down the road.

The last three of those boxes were in the things they gave to Goodwill a few weeks ago.

The battery lamp cast only a small halo of light, barely enough for Dorothy Faye to read the last entry in her notebook, the part about Dennis. She concluded that anyone who took the time could have helped him; there was nothing special about her. She thought about how she defended Harold when Janiece criticized him. "Is that really how I feel or is it how I've told myself to feel? What if Janiece's right, that something's wrong and he's not telling me, so I won't worry?" She startled herself when she spoke. Since she was talking to herself anyway, she went on, "Well, I know this, no matter how irritated I might get with Harold, he's a treat compared to Janiece." There was only an occasional flicker of lightning in the east now. The storm had passed.

"Wake up." She opened her eyes, certain she'd heard the words spoken. But Harold was still asleep. *No wonder he's asleep, the sun's hardly up. It couldn't have been him. Besides, the voice was female.* Starting the coffee, she remembered a dream from last night. A pet coffin—putting something in one of them, outside digging a hole, a deep one at the back of someone's yard. Ready to put the casket in the hole, she realized the hole had filled in. She dug again. And again, the hole closed up. "You don't have to do that. It's already taken care of," a voice said. "Just go get ready."

But in the dream she'd felt unfinished. She laughed quietly, thinking Janiece could be contagious. Closing her eyes, she saw a little snapshot. Her father looking at her, puzzled, and her mother beside him saying, "Dreams don't mean anything. You shouldn't have eaten that pie before you went to bed." Although she didn't see herself in the picture, she knew she was a teenager at the time, tearful and afraid. But she couldn't bring the rest of it into focus. *I need coffee. Dreams don't mean anything.*

Harold said, "You beat me getting up. O.D. and I were up late talking. I'm going to do some scouting while he's pumping his lease today. Need to decide about our next step. And I'll take the trailer by the dump station."

Busying himself with combing his hair, he had to stoop a little to see his whole head in the bathroom mirror. Staring at his back, Dorothy Faye wondered when he'd bought the shirt he had on; it was the second new one in two days. She waited to see if he'd ask her opinion about their next destination. After a couple of minutes of silence, Harold turned to her, smiling. That was her answer. "I'll eat some cereal and get dressed real quick so you can go," she said. *He has nice hair, and lots of it.* She added the item to her list.

"Mornin', Dorothy Faye," O.D. mumbled as they passed at the trailer door. He was headed to his pickup, looking a little the worse for wear. Maybe the late-night visiting wore him out. Or maybe Janiece had already outlined what he needed to do today to keep her happy.

She found Janiece in the kitchen, cleaning her cabinets, again. A mop stood in a bucket in the corner, and a basket containing Comet, Formula 409, Murphy's Oil Soap, and Lysol sat on the counter. "O.D. said he'd get back early to help me move the furniture in the family room. You know, the carpet will fade if you don't move things around every month. O.D. said just the other day how nice the house looks. I think it's time we got some new drapes. O.D. said these did smell a little dusty, even after I had them cleaned," Janiece paused for breath. "O.D. was thinking maybe we ought to move. The neighborhood's getting trashy."

"You're thinking about moving? Maybe y'all could try a trailer too." Dorothy Faye said it just to see the look on Janiece's face. Deadpan, she went on, "I'm beginning to think there could be a lot of advantages to trailer living. You know, if you don't like the neighbors, you move. There's not much to clean. If you get tired of the floor plan, you don't remodel, just trade it in for a different one."

"I know you're making jokes because you're upset. Who in their right mind could live like that—almost like homeless people? Why, even O.D. says it's not normal, and he hardly ever criticizes Harold."

Janiece was in high gear, waving her cleaning rag to emphasize her points. And O.D.'s purported points. If a person didn't know better, he'd probably think O.D. held forth on all sorts of subjects, at length, regularly. "I swear, Dorothy Faye, I don't know how you can be so calm. Why, you don't even have any real furniture anymore—just that stuff that came in the trailer. Did you keep anything? I mean, what about Mama's little end table Harold got when she died, and what about the kids' baby clothes and their toys? Surely you—"

Not waiting for Janiece to inhale and rev up again, Dorothy Faye gave a careful answer, a vague one. "Oh sure, Janiece, we stored some things. They're not all gone."

The end table Janiece was talking about had been secondhand in the first place, and of Mediterranean style. Harold had taken it after their mother's funeral because Janiece insisted. "After all," she'd said, "it's only fair. I have the clock."

Janiece had stopped talking. Alarmed by the uncommon silence, Dorothy Faye thought maybe she'd missed a question while thinking about the end table. Janiece was standing on a chair, positioned to scrub the shelves, her head hidden in one of the upper cabinets. All the spices and other items from that cabinet stood lined up on the counter. She had stopped talking because she was engaged in her other passion—cleaning.

Day 9 May 27 5:45 p.m. Janiece and O.D.'s driveway, Lubbock

Without a car, I could only escape the smell of Lysol by taking a walk. I told Janiece I was going to Higginbotham Park.

"That's another thing. Why do you let him get away with leaving you on foot while he's off driving around town? What if you wanted to go somewhere?" she asked.

She seemed to be winding up for more talk, diverted from alphabetizing her spices by my starting for the door. I should have had the sense to just walk out quietly. She'd never have noticed I was gone.

I told her I could use the exercise. I could see her shaking her head as I left. The truth is, I felt like I'd explode if I didn't leave right then. I don't think it's all Janiece either. I don't like to admit it, but I'm even more irritable today than I have been lately. I was even too edgy to be happy working a puzzle after I got over here to the park. This isn't like me a bit. Usually I can settle down with words—a book or a puzzle.

But today, screaming or cussing or crying are all about an inch away. Everything I hear or see or smell or read chips at me, and little splinters break off and start to fall. If I close my eyes, that's exactly what I see. And as the shards of me drop, they turn into pictures. Example: a boy and a girl, about six and eight, were running and laughing near this bench when I got to the park. When I came over to sit down, they took off toward the playground. Now I knew they weren't my kids. I'm not out of my head or anything. But I had to turn away to keep from just grabbing them and hugging them. That feeling, that urge, was so strong I had to close my eyes. That's when I saw pictures, falling into a little pile.

I know what my mother would say about this. "Sounds like you have too much time on your hands." But she was also the one who thought I should be able to remember more about my life. Of course, even when I do remember, what real good is it? What has passed is past. Bringing those snapshots into focus might be nice, but she was the only one who was ever interested in talking about the past, my past. And she's gone.

Harold is always interested in right now or better yet, what's next. Like figuring out this whole trailer thing. Or just waking up and smiling. I'd never complain about him being the way he is. Not really, even though sometimes I have to make those lists. But when I feel the way I do today, it's hard to be a good wife and match his good humor.

Reading back over that, I think my new word may begin to apply to me. It's prolix. Stumped me in that last puzzle, but when I gave up and checked the answers, there it was, just waiting to describe Janiece. Prolix— adj. Wordy and tedious, tending to speak and write at great length. Sounds like the name of a new drug for arthritis!

More later.

She was sitting in the trailer with her puzzle book open in her lap when Harold came in, smiling. Dorothy Faye touched the spot on her hip where she wore the estrogen patch. A crinkly texture under her fingers assured her it was there.

Harold said, "Using the dump station was a snap. Just takes a few minutes. I brought the trailer back as soon as I took care of that little chore. Thought you might want to hide from Janiece. She said you'd been gone on foot for more than an hour. She told me she walks as little as possible, claims it's bad for her chronic fatigue syndrome."

"She has chronic fatigue syndrome? Since when?" Dorothy Faye controlled the urge to raise her eyebrows.

"Maybe that was last month. She probably has something else now. Janiece." Shrugging, Harold conveyed his opinion of Janiece's habit of enjoying poor health. "The main thing I think she has is a yen for one of those handicapped license plates so she can park up front wherever she goes." He leaned on the counter and looked around the trailer's interior like he might be considering remodeling. "What did you do today?" he asked.

He nodded attentively as she gave an account of her exploration of the region north of Nineteenth Street and west of Quaker.

"I'd better be careful. With you walking all over, some truck driver will swoop by and carry you off," said the former truck driver, "just like I did."

Dorothy Faye crossed the small kitchen space to the stool where he sat and hugged Harold from behind. "Well, thanks. What was that for?" he asked.

"Just for me," she replied, still leaning against him. "Where are we going next?"

CHAPTER 3

Thank You, Mr. Sam

They stayed at Janiece's one more night. Dorothy Faye stayed out of Janiece's way by going to the movies, twice, and walking, a lot. Harold didn't say where he'd been, but he stayed gone most of the time too. They moved back to Lakeview this afternoon. As soon as he had the trailer leveled and plugged in, Harold asked if Dorothy Faye wanted to go with him to Walmart.

She followed him into the Fourth Street store and back to the sporting goods section. He stopped to study the display of fishing flies. He said, "The variety is good and the merchandise is neatly organized." From the sound of his announcement and the confirming nod that went with it, he might have been the store manager instead of a customer.

Dorothy Faye agreed by nodding, smiling at his proprietary air. *No wonder he makes a reason to stop in a Walmart at least once a week. Mr. Sam bought our new trailer.* "I'm going to look at the produce. A big salad would be good for supper," she said as she left him deciding between Super Duper and Beadhead Wooly.

This side trip to Walmart was one of Harold's regular excursions. It was their secret. Not that they'd set out to make it a secret; over the years, it had just happened.

Deciding which of two heads of romaine to buy had her attention when Harold turned up at her right elbow. "Find what you wanted?" he asked. "This all looks nice and fresh, doesn't it?" He gave one bright red tomato, then another, the squeeze test. He held one of them to his nose. "They even smell like tomatoes. Now that's good quality."

She was thinking more about what Harold referred to as the Sam Walton Memorial Fund than about vegetables. All these years, they'd only talked about their windfall to each other, never told another soul.

———————————◆———————————

Harold had rushed into the kitchen as soon as he parked the big rig. Fall of 1970, it was easy to remember. "Dorothy Faye, you'll never guess what I did. Go on, just try."

He was so tickled, she played along just for the pleasure of seeing him excited. "Let's see. You were driving through Mississippi, stopped at a roadside park, stepped over the fence stile to use the outdoor facilities, and found buried treasure—three million in Confederate money."

He shook his head, "Nope, it was in Arkansas."

"Buried treasure in Arkansas? I thought all that was in Arkansas was pigs. Okay, in Arkansas, even though you never stop there if you can avoid it, you went by Pig Sweat Lake. You decided to wet a hook and to your surprise, you reeled in the biggest catfish ever caught there. You're famous. Your name is in a record book in Elmer's Bait Shop in Pig Hollow." She was laughing so hard, the kids came to the back screen door to see if she was all right.

"Nope, wrong again. There is no Pig Sweat Lake in Arkansas. Maybe in Louisiana, but not Arkansas." Now they were both laughing.

"Wait, I know. You were tuning around on your CB and got to talk to Elvis, driving to Graceland in the middle of the night in one of his CB-equipped Cadillacs."

Tipping his kitchen chair to balance on its two back legs, hands behind his head, Harold said, "Nope, you'll never guess. I did something a guy like me, an ol' boy from West Texas, doesn't ever do. I invested in the stock market."

"You're right. I'd never have guessed that." Dorothy Faye swiped her dishrag across the table, then sat down across from him. "Did it cost much to invest?" Then before he could answer, "Never mind that. I know you wouldn't have done it if you didn't think it was a good idea. What stock did you buy?"

"This is a good story. You'll like how this happened. See, over in Arkansas, there's this company called Walmart. They have discount prices but sell good quality merchandise, lots of it made in the USA. I've hauled over there a couple of times before to Bentonville where the headquarters is. When I was in Arkansas this time, I was on the CB and heard a couple of local guys talking about Mr. Sam going public. I thought I was about to hear some juicy Arkansas gossip. Then I realized they were talking about Sam Walton, the owner of Walmart. I heard 'em sayin' that a person could buy stock in the company for sixteen dollars and fifty cents a share, and that's when I understood what they meant by going public. That's stock-broker talk.

"Next thing you know, this powerful feeling just overtook me. I just knew I was on that particular road for a reason! To make a long story short, I pulled that big truck out there right up in front of a stockbroker's office as soon as I got to Bentonville. Thirty minutes later, I came out with a hundred shares of Walmart stock."

Until the '80s, they'd only checked on the stock a couple of times each year, content to add the little dividend checks to their savings account. Over the years, stock splits followed one after the other as the company expanded. After each split, the stock price climbed. The dividend checks got larger.

Mr. and Mrs. Harold Bell joined the Sam's Discount Club Warehouse in Lubbock as soon as it opened. By the time the original one hundred shares had increased to 6,400, Harold had begun dropping into Walmart stores a couple of times a week on his trips. He'd peek into the employees' break room to look at the bulletin board where the daily stock price was posted. So far their stock had multiplied eleven times. The dividend last year was more than forty thousand dollars.

They never had counted on anything but the income from their work, and after Harold's accident, his pension and his part-time pumper's pay.

They didn't need the extra money. They just left the stock alone and put the dividend checks in their savings account. Harold said they should think of the dividend checks like getting money from home without writing. "We'll just save it for later. We might need it when we're old or if we get sick." Neither one of them had any health insurance, but until Harold was diagnosed with type two diabetes about five years ago, neither of them had ever been sick with anything serious.

This past year the broker in Bentonville had made a personal call to Harold to suggest he might want to consider selling some of the stock and getting into some other investments. When Harold told her, he said the broker called that diversifying. "That's stockbroker talk for 'don't put all your eggs in one basket.'" The broker had said that at current prices, the Walmart stock was worth several million dollars. After that phone call, they hadn't really talked about whether to take his advice. Neither one of them mentioned the actual number the broker had given them. They were sort of stunned. Besides, they didn't need money and didn't lack anything they wanted. If the stock and the money it was worth disappeared, nothing would be different. Dorothy Faye supposed Harold was still thinking about the broker's advice. Or not.

Back when the stock increased so many times and the price kept going up, they had agreed that none of that money seemed real. Except, maybe the dividend checks, which did sail right through the bank to land in the savings account without a hitch. If Harold gave the stock and its value much thought, other than stopping in the stores regularly, he never let on. Until the broker called, Dorothy Faye hadn't thought about it at all for months.

———◆———

She imagined she didn't think about having a lot of money because she couldn't even come up with words to fit the idea. Staring at the heads of romaine, she worked on that puzzle. Unbelievable—impossible—shrewd investing—incomprehensible—dumb luck—opportunity? But regardless of her remoteness from the idea of wealth, the Walmart millionaire's wife decided to buy both heads of romaine.

As they ambled toward the checkout, Dorothy Faye halted her cart in the middle of the aisle. *Money.* The thought had stopped her. *What if it's money that has Harold acting strange? Maybe he didn't tell me all that broker said.* She had no idea how much they still had in savings, since he bought the trailer. For that matter, she didn't know if he actually bought it. Maybe it was rented. For a minute she considered putting back one of the heads of lettuce. A woman said, "Excuse me" in a loud voice and pushed her cart around Dorothy Faye and her stalled basket of vegetables.

"Forget something?" Harold asked.

"No, I just remembered something I need to do," Dorothy Faye said.

———————◆———————

Salad scraps cleared, Dorothy Faye stood in the kitchen area feeling unfinished. *Well, there's only so much wiping that a person can do. Is choreless a word?* She wondered about that as she draped the dishrag over the faucet. "Harold, I think I'll take a walk, maybe go in and visit. I'll be back by dark." She detected a nod from behind his *USA Today*.

As she approached the hospital door, she hesitated, then turned left and walked across Twenty-Fourth Street to the park. She began walking faster. As her speed and distance increased, the feeling of aggravation she was becoming familiar with was replaced by a close-to-but-not-exactly-calm feeling. It was more like knowing something good might be about to happen. It sure beat being irritated for no good reason. By the time she made two long laps around the park, an hour had passed. Darkness triggered the security lights on the parking lot.

"You're back. Are things okay with you folks?" a voice asked from behind a Suburban at the edge of the lot.

Dorothy Faye turned to locate the source of the question. It was the young security guard she'd nodded to before. "Oh yes, we just left for better shelter when the storm came up."

A young man approached her and offered his hand. "I'm Alan Waters. I work security here. But I guess you figured that out already, from the uniform."

"Nice to know you, Alan. I'm Dorothy Faye Bell. My husband and I are in the trailer over there."

"Yes, ma'am. I know." After a pause, "Nice out tonight, isn't it?"

"It sure is," Dorothy Faye replied. They moved together toward the trailer. She hoped he couldn't hear what she was thinking—*don't tell any lies, don't get caught squatting.* "It must be pretty quiet at here at night. What do you do to pass the time?"

He laughed. "Mostly I try to decide if I'm going to apply to law school like my parents want me to when I graduate. Other than that, I enjoy watching people."

"Thinking and watching are enough to keep a person busy," she said. "Well, thanks for walking me over here. It's good to meet you, Alan. See you again." She could feel her pulse thumping in her neck.

As she closed the door behind her, Harold said, "I thought you'd been busted when I saw you with that security guard. Was he suspicious?" He laughed and folded his paper.

She took a deep breath. "I don't think so. He was just being nice. His name is Alan."

"I'm kinda disappointed," Harold said. "I'd been workin' on a good story to use to get you out of trouble. Guess I'll have to save it for later. Believe I'll go to bed now that you're here."

"Night, Harold." She watched him neaten around his chair, amazed at how little it seemed to take to please him. He was having a good time— just like he'd planned to.

Up and down, round and round, small circles, brush your tongue. Up and down, round and round. The words she had chanted as she taught her children to brush their teeth chattered in her head. Brushing her teeth, watching in the mirror over the trailer's tiny bathroom sink, she wondered how many times she'd done this. Twice a day, 365 days a year since age three, that's 730 times 52. Pausing, her mouth still foamy, she calculated, marking on the mirror with her index finger. The answer, 37,960, was inaccurate, though. There were other uncounted tooth and breath care occasions. Anytime she'd thought sex was a possibility, making herself fresh and appealing included brushing her teeth. She closed her eyes as she thought about how sweet Harold was about making love when they'd first married.

They'd planned a weekend honeymoon. Her mother offered to keep the kids. Dorothy Faye remembered the nightgown she'd splurged on. Something new, for a new start. Choosing the gown had taken a long time. Even back then, she'd seldom talked about sex or anything that might suggest it, to anyone. Excited as she was about getting ready for her honeymoon with Harold, she kept it to herself. *Used* was the word that had come to her mind. *I want to look pretty, and I want him to know this is going to be right for him. I may be used, but for him I'll be good as new.* She'd hoped it would be true because she'd worked hard at being new for him. That meant thinking about a fresh start and a future, and it meant putting Ronnie out of her mind. She told herself if she did that, the sex would come naturally.

The new gown was blue with satin piping around the modest neck and the hem. She packed it carefully with her new plain white bras and underpants. She couldn't stop herself from worrying. She knew Harold had girlfriends before her. At his age and being on the road, he'd had plenty of opportunity for experience with sex. But she'd never asked about that. What you don't know can't upset you, a piece of her mother's general-purpose advice, guided her. Harold hadn't asked her about Ronnie either. She told herself to relax. It didn't work.

The wedding ceremony at the JP's office took ten minutes, including Janiece's hurried effort to shoot a roll of pictures. "I'll have 'em here for you when you get back. Harold, you look so nice in that suit. You too, Dorothy Faye. Y'all stand together." The fact that they were already standing together didn't stop her. "Dorothy Faye, get your mother over there beside you. Do we want the kids in these? O.D., what are you doin'? I need you to help me get them arranged. Rubyjo, stand by Harold and try to smile."

They left for their little honeymoon in Amarillo, sightseeing in Palo Duro Canyon on the way. At the Holiday Inn, he gave her first chance at the bathroom and had the lights low when she came out. Noticing she had her fists clenched to stop the shaking that started when she was brushing her teeth, Dorothy Faye paused for a deep breath before crossing to where he was sitting on the side of the bed. Harold stood, smiling, and touched her lightly on her right shoulder. "Turn around and let me take a good look at Mrs. Bell." Turning a full circle, she felt herself relax a little as he said, "My, but you are fine looking. I don't know what would have become of me if you hadn't said you'd marry me."

He gathered her into a soft hug, rubbing gently the length of her tense spine with first one hand and then the other. "You feel so good to me," he whispered. "Will you let me help you off with that gown so I can touch you all over?" Dorothy Faye could only nod. She took his hands in hers, and together they lifted the blue gown up from the hem, over her head, slowly.

"You seem sorta tense. Why don't you just stretch out here and let me help you relax. We're not in any hurry. We've got from now on." He massaged her back gently.

First relaxing, then warming to his touch, Dorothy Faye turned to him, inhaling a faint scent of Aqua Velva. He was still as she traced the shape of his chest with her fingertips. She was surprised and grateful that, although his eagerness was evident, he didn't rush her. They explored each other tentatively, then with all they had held back. As her breathing and heartbeat returned to normal, Dorothy Faye's pleasure was partly relief. He was nothing like Ronnie.

Listening to his slow, steady breathing, Dorothy Faye was surprised when Harold said softly, his face turned away from her, "Thank you so much."

She wondered if he was dreaming. "For what, Harold?" she responded equally quietly so as not to wake him if he was asleep.

"For marrying me. I love you, Dorothy Faye," was his reply.

<hr />

After the first couple of years, having sex (making love, as Dorothy Faye preferred to think of it) became a little less frequent, but never less satisfying. When her effort to keep memories of Ronnie at bay wavered and comparisons came to her mind, Harold was the winner, always. Even when she'd started making lists to counteract occasional irritations, Harold came out smelling like the proverbial rose.

Toothpaste outlining her lips, she looked at her reflection in the small mirror. *I don't look all that much different than I did then. And I know we haven't had any arguments.* But for quite a while now, toothbrushing had been strictly a part of dental hygiene, not preparation.

She slowly wiped her face and turned out the light. In the dark, the answer to a question she had not asked herself consciously came to her. The last time they had sex was the day before the broker called from Arkansas, the end of December. She was certain. That was more than five months ago.

CHAPTER 4

WWJD?

Dorothy Faye noticed that Dennis's eyes looked desperate, almost frantic instead of sad the way they had before. He whispered in the dimly lit waiting room. The only other person in the room was a large man who was sleeping, spread across the couch near the back.

"The doctors say her condition is stable and that she has to be moved out of critical care to the skilled nursing facility. I think what they mean is that she's going to die, but not soon enough. They can't have her taking up space in critical care. They even showed me how her incision is healed. Like that helps if she's unconscious. Can I tell you something? I dreamed last night I was trying to run away from something. I was scared to death, but I couldn't get away because there were miles of bedsheets tied to my ankle." Dennis barely paused for breath.

Dorothy Faye didn't have to search for words. His continued, his voice urgent. "I don't know what to do. Get another doctor, move her to a different hospital, take her home, get a private nurse, talk to her more so she'll come out of it, call her preacher so those people at her church will pray for her. There must be something I could do. She's counting on me to take care of her. I hate this place. Why can't they do something?" He looked nearer to exploding tonight than crying. Snores from across the room increased in volume.

One concern followed another, all emphasizing his failure—his brother's expectations, his own sense of duty. "You're so kind to listen to me. I tell you things I'd never say to anyone else." Suddenly he was holding tight to her hand. "I hoped you'd be here tonight. Talking to you is the only thing that's keeping me from going crazy." Dorothy Faye shifted and patted him on the back. His breathing slowed and his shoulders slumped.

Looking like a lost pup, he said, "Please don't say you have to go just yet. Should I…" The gush of words halted abruptly. They both reacted immediately to the same sound. The loudest fart Dorothy Faye ever heard had risen from the sleeping form across the room. Two loud snorts followed, and the sleeper flopped to a new position precariously near the edge of the couch.

Dorothy Faye widened her eyes and opened her mouth, miming a silent scream in the way that always had made her kids laugh. And Dennis did. He chuckled, then laughed aloud until a tear ran down beside his nose. Shaking her head, laughing with him, she handed him a Kleenex. Dennis took a deep breath, exhaled loudly, and sat back in the chair. "That pretty much sums it up for me," he said. "I feel better now."

Day 11 May 29 11:15 p.m. Lakeview Hospital, Lubbock

This is odd too. After 11 p.m. and Harold's not back yet. O.D. picked him up around three. I'll admit I was ready for him to go. How can anyone spend so much time fooling around with flies and fishing line? Like he was giving me a gift, he said he was leaving the pickup in case I wanted to go somewhere. I added that to my list—Occasional thoughtful gestures, I wrote. Turns out, a gesture was all it was. I erased that item from the list when I noticed he left the pickup but not the keys.

I suppose I could've gone into the hospital and called Janiece. She'd have been happy to come get me and spend the afternoon telling me what I should do. She always knows just what's best; just ask her. A woman of action, she calls herself. I could imagine hearing another tale of something she did to keep O.D. in line. Who's she kidding? He's never been near the line and wouldn't recognize it if he tripped on it!

They go fishing lots of times. But what's odd is that he's not back yet, and it's after his bedtime. But come to think of it, he only keeps regular hours when he doesn't have a project underway. I've seen him stay up all night working on a scheme lots of times.

———◆———

She heard Harold's voice outside the trailer. "Okay, O.D., I'll see you tomorrow." Dorothy Faye stowed her notebook in her purse and picked up the puzzle book. "Yep, been fishing. Only caught a few and just released 'em. And my wife's too busy with the hospital to be cooking. You fish?"

"Not since I was a little kid," Alan answered. "You folks far from home here?"

"Quite a piece. Sure makes it convenient to see to family, having these spaces for trailers." Harold's voice sounded extra hearty, a sure sign he was either bolstered by beer or feeling guilty, or both. "You worked here long?"

"Several months now. It's a good job for a student. Are you folks…"

Harold interrupted. "Look at the time! I didn't realize it was so late. My wife's probably worried about me. Have you seen her out here this evening?"

"Yessir, I saw her leave the hospital about thirty minutes ago coming out this way."

"Well, I'd better be gettin' in there and see how things are going. Good talking to you."

Harold stepped inside. In the same hearty voice and with a large smile, he said, "Well, hi, hon. You didn't have to stay up for me. I bet you were thinkin' I'd need supper. Me and O.D. stopped and had some real good barbecue on the way back in. You know Janiece only cooks two nights a week now. Says they need to watch their diet, have bran cereal for supper. O.D.'s pretty much starved for some real food."

Since Harold hadn't asked a question, Dorothy Faye said nothing, just watched as he pulled off his boots. He continued his tale while tugging at his left boot. "We fished all over that lake. Had a real good time. But I'm about worn out. Think I'll go to bed." Stepping to the bathroom he said, "I noticed you didn't move the pickup."

"No, I didn't have the keys."

Wranglers in hand, he stood in the bathroom doorway. "Well, I guess you didn't at that. Here they are in my pocket. Night, hon."

Day 11 May 29 (continued)

I was right. Something is odd. He surely didn't want to give me any opportunity to ask questions when he came in. If he'd been with anyone but O.D., I'd think he'd started chasing women after all these years. That might explain some other things too. But it's more likely he's hatching another plan. If I was Janiece, I'd tear into him and tell him how transparent he is. Fact is, if I was Janiece, he'd probably have learned to do a better job of hiding what he's doing. But it might feel good just once to let him know I'm not the simpleminded fool he seems to think I am.

No, that's not fair. He probably doesn't think I'm simpleminded or a fool. He just thinks there's no need for me to know because I'll go along with whatever he wants. Why would he think otherwise?

I'm tired of thinking about Harold. (I just reread that—correction to above—If I WERE Janiece. I will use proper grammar regardless of anything else.)

In addition to correcting my writing, I could spend some time thinking about myself. Plenty of things I could do to make improvement on that person. Let's see, I could have a makeover like those women in the magazines. Then I could buy a lot of clothes and shoes—rent a storage unit to use for a closet. Buy a car. Or maybe I'll take a real trip—airplanes, trains, passport, all of that. There's nothing I can remember that I've dreamed of having or doing, though.

That's sad. When did I give up that kind of dreaming? The kind you carry around with you like a compact in your purse, opening it now and then to peer into a perfect future, seeing wonderful possibilities and hoping for more and better. When did I quit—what's the word? Aspiring. I can't remember. Maybe Mother was right.

Is it that when you get to be my age, you realize you've gone as far as you're going? I don't think it's the age. Look at Janiece. She's older than I am, and she seems sure there's more out there for her. Eyebrow tattoos, excuse me, permanent cosmetics, a new Cadillac, a better neighborhood.

I doubt if I'll find an answer for this tonight. But I know one thing. I did a little good today. Dennis was smiling when I left him.

———◆———

The next morning, Harold was up early. Dorothy Faye poked at her cereal and watched him dress and listened to him talk, faster than usual. "No fishing today. O.D.'s got some work to do over on his lease. I'm going to help. Don't wait on me for lunch or supper. Maybe they'll have something good in the cafeteria here that you'll want." Harold was wearing another new shirt. He buttoned it crooked, one side longer than the other, as he hurried.

She stood at the door and waved to him as he left. She had a destination for the day herself. An escape. Sightseeing might improve her disposition. He hadn't asked, so she hadn't told him. She waited a few minutes, looking around the "living area." She took a deep breath and shook her head. Sure now that Harold had had time to get out of the lot, she put on her walking shoes and stepped out the door.

The Texas Tech University campus was quite a walk, farther than Dorothy Faye had thought when she left the trailer. Even though it was hot and humid, she continued until she had crossed the street at Nineteenth and University. Perspiring, she slowed a little as she angled southwest toward the center of the campus. Laughter called her attention to several groups of students spread across the open areas to her left. The Texas Tech campus teemed, or teamed, with cheerleading squads.

Dorothy Faye examined the groups clustered across the expanse of grass, shielding her eyes in the bright sun. She pretended she was a writer assigned to report.

Cheerleading camp is one of the enterprises Texas Tech employs to generate revenue during the summer lull. The spirit groups are athletes in their own right, executing tumbling routines and precision lifts that require stamina, skill, and strength necessary to any competitive sport. The teams wear shorts and tee shirts, each school's group identified by its shirt's slogan. Team One—Borden County—Go Plainsmen—We're About Winning—Hawks Rule.

School banners scattered across the lawns stake out each group's territory. Coronado —Ropesville— Sundown—Iowa Park—Archer City—Plains.

One group's blue shirts match the washed-denim hue of the sky exactly. Color and teenaged vigor spark the campus like fireworks—a crimson starburst, a brief explosion of laughter, a pinwheel of tumbling bodies.

Meandering (puzzle #92) toward the library, she considered stopping to commit her journalism to paper, but laughed at taking herself so seriously.

The Croslin Room held plants, fountains, and comfortable seating in an area outside the library's entry and exit checkpoints. The word *oasis* came to mind as she chose a seat away from the doors and closed her eyes. Another puzzle word, *irenic*, one she'd had to look up a long time ago, eased into a corner of her awareness. She drifted, welcoming the distraction.

Black and white snapshot again. She's wearing shorts, practicing cheers with two girlfriends in the deserted high school gym. Ronnie, frowning, fists clenched, red-faced, stands alone under the Exit sign.

Two campers chattered their way into the library, taking the place of the memory. Dorothy Faye opened her eyes, frowned. *Must have gotten too hot on the walk over here. Seeing things again.* The tee shirts on the two girls asked

"WWJD?" in letters six inches high. Smaller print on the back explained the acronym's question—"What Would Jesus Do? Highview Christian Academy." Staring at the question, she remembered—Ronnie was having a tantrum about her trying out for cheerleader. "Don't you know everyone will think you're a slut, just like all cheerleaders?" he shouted. To keep the peace, she gave up the whole idea. *What's wrong with me? That was forty years ago. Ronnie and his bad temper are long gone. Walking is the thing to do, walk and observe and stop poking around in the past. Everything I find there makes me sad or irritable.*

Heading north, she dodged a campus bus she'd not even seen approaching. Across the parking lot at the Administration Building; then right, toward Human Sciences and the statues of people suspended in conversation and play, in bronze like ants in amber. She continued walking away from her memories. Without noticing the distance, she rapidly reached Tech's northern boundary at Fourth Street.

Campus buses emitted diesel fumes and students in almost equal amounts into the commuter parking lot, where she turned west. As she squinted into the sun, she wished she had brought a hat. A cluster of trees, as foreign to the High Plains as any of the international students she passed, offered shade. She accepted the shelter and sat atop one of the berms that some landscape architect had had pushed into place near the recreation center. Before the landscaping, the entire campus had been as flat and treeless as the rest of the Caprock region.

She remembered visiting here in 1963, thinking she might attend. The flatness of the campus hadn't affected her back then; she was more interested in which dormitory she might be housed in. None of them, as it turned out; she'd ended up in the nursing school in Amarillo that offered her a scholarship for the first year.

Ronnie had been against her going anywhere to school. "I'll be the wage earner. You won't have to work," he'd said. He didn't intend to go to college either. "I'm plenty smart and won't have any trouble getting a job. You'll see. Just leave it to me. I can't live without you. You know we're meant to be together forever."

That memory was clear and sharply focused. He was dramatic and intense and she was young and confused. She was nearly convinced she should stay. Listening to him and reading those *Ladies Home Journal* and *McCall's* stories showing how to make homelife perfect and collecting recipes from

Southern Living almost made her believe that immediate marriage was her destiny. She recalled that hormones had something to do with it too.

She headed back toward Lakeview. The next time she came over here, it would be without her past.

That evening she'd opened her notebook and begun to write, *WWJD*, when Harold stepped in and went directly to his recliner. He smiled at her but didn't speak. He started reading the paper.

She stared at the back of the paper, the classified ads, for a full three minutes. Without a word, she went back to the hospital to see if Dennis was on duty in the waiting room. He wasn't. Rather than pace the waiting room, she took the elevator to fifth floor and walked the stairs down to the basement cafeteria. The exercise settled her, but only a little. Not in the mood for a puzzle, definitely out of items for the "Harold's Good Qualities" list, she went into the half-darkened cafeteria, sat down, and tried to decide what to do next.

Dennis peered in the door of the cafeteria, then hurried to Dorothy Faye's table. "I'm so glad I found you. I wanted to talk with you again before we leave."

"I looked for you upstairs. Has something changed?"

"No, and yes. No, Mother's condition is no better. She may never regain consciousness. The CAT scan showed extensive damage from the stroke. But she's able to breathe on her own. She's going to be moved to the nursing home with a feeding tube in place. I know she'd hate being there. But for now, it's the right thing to do."

"You said no and yes. What has changed, Dennis?" She touched his arm as she spoke. No other late visitors had chosen the cafeteria. They had it to themselves.

"Me."

She waited for more.

"I realized last night I've done all I could do for my mother and what's happened is not my fault. Not anyone's fault. People get sick and eventually they have to die. I never admitted that to myself before. You know, if you don't let yourself think about things like that, they don't seem real. It's like dying only happens to people you don't know. If you just keep it out of your mind, it doesn't seem real. But that's not the way life is." He stopped to breathe deeply. "I feel different. Not as afraid. I slept all night last night."

"I'm glad. I know this is hard for you. Are you going home for the night now?"

"Yes, and going back to work tomorrow. I'll be here twice a day until we move her to the nursing home. I told her that. I don't know if she's able to hear, but I want her to know I'm not leaving her. I need to get myself back to a routine—try to have some kind of a schedule. Believe it or not, I'm usually a pretty capable person. You've seen me at my worst. I just fell apart when all this happened."

"It's understandable. When will she be transferred?"

"Day after tomorrow or the day after that. Paperwork." He sat quietly, staring into the darkened part of the dining area. "I think the place she's going is pretty good. It didn't smell like urine and no one was moaning. The hospital's case management nurse said it has a good reputation. But I know I'll need to be there every day to be sure they do all they can to keep her clean and comfortable." He inhaled again, slowly, and stood very erect.

Dorothy Faye smiled up at him. He seemed taller tonight. "I know you'll do a good job, Dennis."

"I realized something else last night. In all these times we've talked, I've never asked about your patient. You've been so kind to let me talk and I didn't even think about your concerns."

"Don't worry a bit about that. Everything's fine. I'll walk out with you."

She stopped at the trailer door to look at the stars and across to the park. There was Alan again, staring at her from the edge of the parking lot. He waved. She waved. Once inside, she gritted her teeth. He was onto them, she was sure.

She looked at Harold, asleep again in his recliner, but didn't wake him. She opened her notebook. The next page held only "WWJD," where she'd started earlier in the day.

Day 12 Tuesday, May 30 Lakeview Hospital, Lubbock

WWJD?

Tonight I'm a little worried. Dennis will be transferring his mother to the nursing home soon. He gave me his business card (see below). Made me promise I'd call if I ever need anything. I think he meant it.

Dennis Farley, M.S. Computer Science

Information System Consultant

3428 62nd Street

Lubbock, TX 79413

806.799.2122

Dfar@yahoo.com

What worries me is that security guard, Alan. He passed by inside when I was talking to Dennis. Then I saw him again when I came out to the trailer.

Harold will probably think it's funny if I tell him. He'd think it was an adventure if they evicted us. He'd probably enjoy being on the six o'clock news. Or he'd invent some elaborate explanation and expect me to go along with it so they wouldn't make us leave.

Imagine the story he could tell at the cafés. Something about how he got all these days of free space and how I kept them guessing with my "visiting." It would sound like we were as crafty as spies after he perfected the story by telling it a few times. Or maybe he'd tease me for being afraid. Either way he won't take me seriously.

She stopped writing, her pulse thumping. She stared at the page, then at Harold dozing in his recliner. "WWJD?" she muttered. "What *Would* Janiece Do?"

She stood and opened the door, then pulled it together. Hard. Harold sat up straight, looking dazed. The footrest folded away with a loud snap.

"Get up, Harold. We're leaving. Now!"

CHAPTER 5

Reliable, Like a Clock

"Sorry we wasn't expectin' you folks, or we'd a had the space ready for y'all." The manager wore his KOA company vest over his pajama top. He didn't seem too upset about being called from his trailer at ten thirty. "Number twenty-six will be real nice. There's a little tree over there we planted a couple of years ago that's managed to stay alive. You folks come far today?"

"No, we've just sorta been seein' the sights, takin' our time." Harold wrinkled his brow as he felt his pockets for his billfold. Head down, avoiding further discussion of the sights along their seven-mile route from Lakeview's parking lot, he mumbled, "The wife likes to see...Seems like she's sorta taken charge of our..." After staring a second at the bills he'd counted out, he offered them to the campground manager, chuckled, and raised an eyebrow. "Take today for example. It's been kind of a mystery trip."

"Well, I've been married twenty-nine years, and my wife's never given me a day's grief. She's reliable—feeds me regular, keeps things clean, don't talk too much, no surprises. Yep, I can count on her, just like a good clock. Course, I guess people can change." He completed a receipt and offered it and an understanding grin to Harold. "Yep, I've heard it said that people can change."

The digital clock behind the manager blinked 12:00, as it had for the ten minutes Harold had been at the counter. Harold blinked back at it, folded the receipt, and nodded in agreement. "I suppose that's possible."

***

Harold drove toward the back of the KOA campground. He said, "Number twenty-six, right back there by the fence. I'll have us set up in no time. You okay?"

"I'm fine," she said, surveying the lot, not looking at Harold.

The two words were her first since she'd almost blown him out of his chair by slamming the trailer door. And then she hadn't said much—only that they were leaving. When he made the mistake of asking where to and what's wrong, she had just glared at him.

Harold had searched his pockets for the pickup keys, snuck a look at her, then started toward the door. "I guess we can go back to Janiece and O.D.'s."

"No. I know what Janiece would do."

Thirty minutes later he'd pulled into the KOA on Clovis Highway.

***

Several times during the night he woke to sounds of passing cattle trucks and to the syncopated clicking of freight trains traveling the tracks just beyond the highway. Each time the sounds snapped his lids open, he stared at the ceiling three feet above, alternately envying those truck drivers passing alone and peaceful through the night and berating himself for not telling Dorothy Faye the truth. Other people always were drawn to her to tell their troubles. Her kind eyes told them she would understand. Why couldn't he tell her? Could she understand him being afraid? And each time Dorothy Faye's steady breath sounds replaced the questions at the edge of consciousness and guided him back to sleep.

———◆———

The next morning Harold left, saying he was supposed to help O.D. on the lease. He met O.D. at his house and as they got into O.D.'s pickup, he said, "I'm ready for some breakfast."

"You didn't eat yet? I thought they told you that you had to eat real regular with your medicine."

"Didn't want to push my luck."

O.D. nodded and headed toward the Levelland Highway.

At the café, Harold finally gave O.D. a short version of the sudden change in location last night. Then he asked, "What do you do when Janiece gets like that?" He hadn't finished his scrambled eggs. He stared at the mess he'd made on the plate, a mixture of hash browns, catsup, and eggs too confusing to eat.

"Usually I just let her sort of talk on and on till she kinda wears herself out. If she wants me to do something, I do it and keep quiet till she gets on another subject. If that doesn't satisfy her, there's always work I need to get done on the lease. By the time I come back, she's forgot about whatever started her up." O.D. got busy polishing egg yolk off his plate with the last bit of his toast. After a minute he grinned and said, "There's lots of days I've thanked God for that lease. I won't ever stop workin'."

"Well, Janiece's always been like that. Dorothy Faye's a different story. She's always been cheerful and ready for anything I'd think up. Like she was waiting to see what was next and ready to help. Last night was different than I've ever seen her."

O.D. pushed back his cap and frowned a while before answering. "You think she was mad about you comin' in late night before last?"

Harold shook his head and pushed his plate away. "She didn't say anything about it that night. Just smiled like always and went on working her puzzle. The door-slamming thing happened last night after she'd been over at the hospital visiting again."

"You don't reckon something happened at the hospital, do you? Or maybe she's goin' through the change." O.D. sat forward and spoke with a hand cupped to one side of his mouth. His voice was so low, Harold could hardly get what he was saying. "I'm not supposed to mention this to any-one. But since it's you." O.D. hesitated, looked around, then replaced the hand near his mouth. "Janiece had a spell a few years back. She'd complain about being hot and not being able to sleep. I swear she was gettin' com-pletely unreasonable—throwin' off the cover in the middle of the night, getting up and taking showers, talking even more than usual. She went to one of her doctors and come back saying he told her she was going through the change. I didn't notice anything else different except her foolin' with the thermostat a lot. I took to wearing an extra undershirt so I wouldn't catch pneumonia." He looked around as if someone could have overheard. "Dorothy Faye say anything about being hot?"

"No, she's already done with that change business." He stood and grabbed their breakfast ticket from O.D.'s hand. "My treat. I feel better since I ate. Let's go get your work done. I imagine everything will blow over by this evening."

CHAPTER 6

Revolutionary?

After Harold left, Dorothy Faye took her time getting dressed, moving around the tiny space of the trailer tentatively, as if she were in foreign territory. She finished eating her cereal and opened her puzzle book. Favoring revolutionary change, seven letters—_ _D_ _ _ _ _ . Dorothy Faye stared at puzzle #101, trying to concentrate. *Distracted* didn't fit in the puzzle blanks, but her mood qualified. "Now I know why people watch daytime TV. It's so they can't hear themselves think." She spoke to the nonfunctioning television set. No answer.

Day 13 May 31 KOA Campground, Clovis Highway near Lubbock

Maybe there's a reason I'm not Janiece. Doing what she would have done got me away from one problem and into another. The good thing is that nice young security guard at the hospital won't know for sure that I was an impostor. But now I'm out here with no vehicle. If I wanted to go somewhere (where?), I'd have to hitchhike or hop a freight. Neither one of those would be difficult to do because the highway and railroad tracks are about all there is out here except for a few other trailers. I could probably find someone here to talk to, but I'm not fit company today. And taking a walk round and round this trailer park would make me feel like a hamster—getting nowhere.

Quit being pitiful (pitiable?) [check that—I need to get a dictionary].

I planned to write about things that seem odd. Talking to the blank television set probably qualifies. Even stranger is how I just became Janiece last night, or someone else. It was as if I was trying on new clothes, something flashy and low-cut, not my usual style and nothing I even liked. There I was in a red dress, wearing makeup and new permanent eyebrows and long rhinestone earrings, and yelling orders at Harold. I went to bed in the whole costume too. Never said another word to him and slept straight through without ever waking up. But this morning was a different situation. Those clothes didn't fit! And to be fair to her, Janiece never did wear long rhinestone earrings. But remembering the whole episode, I think for a little while I enjoyed telling

Harold what to do and acting just the way I felt, without thinking it over and without considering his feelings.

All this time I've been concerned about Harold's blood sugar—maybe I should be thinking about mine. That would be a convenient explanation for my behavior. But I don't think it's true. The other thing that is odd is that Harold did exactly what I said to do. I expected...I don't know what I expected. But I didn't care at that moment. I was afraid we'd been discovered, and I was upset that he'd made this big plan and then left me to do the dirty work. But he didn't balk. And I'm still mad. No telling what I would have said if he hadn't left early this morning.

Could be he's planning again right now—how he can take me off somewhere and leave me now that I've turned into Janiece. Or maybe he'll tell people I've been possessed, not by the devil, but by his sister.

After she read what she'd written, she shook her head and put the notebook inside the puzzle book. Focused now, she considered #101 again. Soon, she inserted R A D I C A L in the open spaces that had stumped her.

Thinking about what to do for supper, she sat on the floor in the "kitchen area" and began sorting through the cans stored in the lower cabinet.

"Hi, hon. You okay? I just got in from helping O.D. out on the lease. We..." He stopped midsentence, his eyes wide, and moved in three quick steps from the door to where Dorothy Faye sat. "Why are you on the floor? Are you hurt? Here, I'll help you up."

Dorothy Faye made herself smile up at him and took his hand, held on to it even after she was standing. "No, I'm fine, just looking for something to make for supper. Did you boys have a good day?"

Nodding, he said, "Don't you worry about supper. I'm gonna take you out. In fact, I'll take you out every night from now on if that's what you want. Would you like that? Yeah, I think that's just what we'll do—me and Mr. Sam."

She turned away and said, "I'll change my clothes."

CHAPTER 7

You Could Have Called

T he next morning, banging on the door stopped Dorothy Faye in the middle of a search for a particularly difficult word, *Q _ _ I D _ _ _*, in puzzle #144. That was all she had when she was interrupted. She concluded the second letter was probably a *U*. That was before she opened the door. Elizabeth. Dorothy Faye immediately remembered she hadn't called her daughter before they left Whaley.

Elizabeth's first words were, "Mother, you've gotten smaller. Do you feel all right?"

How do you reply to that? I still wear a size ten? My shoes still fit? I was never very tall? Not attempting any response, Dorothy Faye stowed the puzzles and hugged her daughter. Almost immediately Elizabeth got her wind and started questioning her.

"Where is he anyway?" Elizabeth stood in the living area, hands on hips.

"O.D. picked him up early, didn't say where they were going. I didn't ask. He'll be glad to see you whenever he gets back. Sit down. Let's talk.

How's everything at work?" Words crowded out as she tried to settle her daughter down.

Elizabeth could be intimidating when she got on a tear. Those hands on her hips suggested she was revving up for a good one. If you didn't know better, you'd think she and Janiece were blood kin.

Dorothy Faye struggled to think of a distraction, but only came up with, "I didn't know you were coming to Lubbock. I'm so glad to see you. Are you here for business?"

"Of course you didn't know I was coming. You moved and didn't leave a forwarding address. I was frantic, thought about calling the police. It was like one of those bad jokes about sending your child out to the grocery store, and when she comes back, you've moved, furniture and all. I thought I was a thirty-five-year-old orphan."

She dropped into Harold's chair and shook her head, the way a parent does when a child misbehaves. A brief pause and then she started again. "I can't believe you didn't even call me and tell me you were leaving. I can understand if you didn't tell R.J. He's oblivious anyway. But me?"

"I'm truly sorry if you were worried. How did you find us?"

"I won't go into all the things I tried, but let's just say I now know your credit rating, your driving record, and when you had the utilities turned off. Also, you don't have a criminal record. Your neighbor in Whaley said you'd had a yard sale and you left in a new pickup pulling a trailer. She thought you were on vacation. I didn't want to, but I finally called Aunt Janiece's house. Thank goodness O.D. answered. Well, are you?"

"Am I what?"

"On vacation." Elizabeth sighed as if making herself understood had never been this difficult. She peered at her mother.

Dorothy Faye was sure she was trying to see if she was coherent. *Next she'll be asking me the day of the week and the name of the president.* Dorothy Faye answered, "I guess you might say that. I'm not sure what we're on. Harold says it's an adventure. He came in about two weeks ago all excited about a new idea."

Elizabeth raised a hand. "Never mind, that explains it—a new idea. So you just went along with it. Did you really sell your furniture? What about my cheerleading outfit?"

"Going along with it seemed like the right thing to do. He was happier than I'd seen him in a long time." Dorothy Faye wondered how much sense she was making as she tried to explain. She also wondered if she could succeed in avoiding the cheerleading outfit question. The little girl who bought it and the letter jacket that went with it seemed thrilled that she got the whole costume for ten dollars.

"So how long is this adventure expected to take? Where are you really going?"

"Not too far, it looks like. We've made about thirty-five miles, by my calculation…" She stopped with a little laugh and a shrug. "Did you come all the way from Dallas just to look for us?"

"I came to find out what's going on. When O.D. said you were living in a trailer, at least I knew that you weren't dead or homeless. I had visions of you in a double-wide in some mobile home community." She made "double-wide and mobile home community" sound only a notch above tenement or hovel. "Knowing Daddy, I thought he'd probably already have the thing tied down and have a skirt around it. But this is worse. No address, no television, and no telephone. And this trailer—it's not even a double-wide—it's a half-wide. Do you even have a cell phone? What if I needed to talk to you or if you had an emergency?"

"We're just fine. Don't worry. Harold just wanted to have this adventure. He's been a little odd lately, so I thought we might as well do it." Watching Elizabeth, Dorothy Faye could almost see her developing her next list of questions. Thinking she was a bit slow from lack of conversational practice with her daughter, she talked fast, filling every potential breath of silent air between them. "You're right about one thing. I do need a telephone. Let's go to town right now and get one. And a dictionary. C'mon, I'll drive."

As they started toward town, Elizabeth asked, "What are you going to do with a dictionary?"

"I've moved up to more difficult crossword puzzles. Sometimes I need to look for a word. Once I start looking for one word, I find other interesting words on the same page. Working on a puzzle this morning, I needed a dictionary when I got stuck on a nine-letter word. Begins with a *Q* and means commonplace or recurring regularly. I don't have any idea what the word is, but since a *U* usually follows a *Q*, if I had a dictionary, I could browse through the *QU* words."

They rode silently for several minutes, Dorothy Faye relieved that the interrogation about their poor behavior seemed to be ended.

"Quotidian," Elizabeth said.

"New word. Quotidian. I'll have to look it up. Thanks. But I think I'll still get an American Heritage dictionary—for when you're not here." After a few seconds, she said, "I knew I could count on you."

Day 14 June 16:00 p.m. KOA, Clovis Highway

Taking Elizabeth for a drive did the trick. Just as she did when she was small, she settled right down as we rode along. On the way to town she told me about her boyfriend. He works at the same computer company she does. They've been dating long enough for her to have begun renovation work. So far she's gotten him to change his haircut, to quit dressing like a college geek (her words), and to open a savings account. He probably doesn't realize yet that the whole thing is doomed. As soon as she has him improved, she'll be tired of him. By then he'll be well-groomed, charming, and have money in the bank. Girls who never even looked his way will be after him. It'll work out fine for both of them. She's done it before—broken three engagements already. She'll be thirty-five this year, so she may not want to marry anyone. If she ever tires of selling computer hardware, she'd probably excel at home remodeling. That girl's a fixer.

The only person she hasn't had much luck at changing is her brother R.J. Oblivious, she calls him. I think he's pretty sweet. He reminds me of Harold. Besides, he doesn't ask her for money, or us either, for that matter. And he always has a job and has never been in any real trouble. He's not ambitious in the same way as Elizabeth, and she doesn't understand that. She's a little short on tolerance for a lot of things and a lot of people, particularly if she thinks they're not as intelligent as she is or if she disagrees with them.

She wasn't that way until she was about fifteen. Until then she'd always been eager to give any idea a try. That year Harold had decided to raise some fighting chickens. Game bird breeding was what he called it. She decided it was an indecent enterprise, unfair to fowls, and threatened to set free his breeding stock. I think he agreed to close the operation more because he was onto something new than because of her arguing with him. Regardless, from then on she began to argue about a lot of things, with almost everyone.

Just to be fair to Harold, he never participated in the actual cockfighting, just had a lot of those cranky birds strutting around the backyard. I guess I could add that to his good qualities list—doesn't engage in cockfighting.

This isn't supposed to be about Elizabeth. I began this to write about things that seem odd. Her finding us and coming out to check on us really isn't. She acts when she's concerned and all those involved should just stand back. She delights in identifying and solving problems.

But there are two odd things to write about. The first one was buying the cell phones today. I felt like I was watching someone else examining all the different brands and asking about features and calling plans. My stomach felt queasy and I concentrated so hard, my shoulders hurt considering all the possible choices. I finally settled on one that was prepaid, had no monthly bill. I got Harold one too. I couldn't quite locate what pained me until I tried to compare making that decision with other decisions I'd made.

As hard as I tried, I could only come up with two big decisions I ever made on my own—marrying Harold and before that, marrying Ronnie. I didn't even decide to leave Ronnie. He left me. Had I gone through all those years without making any other important decisions? Why did buying a cell phone qualify as a major decision?

It's not that I haven't done things that required some decisions, but none of those seemed to actually be my decisions. Someone else always had set the plan, made the real decision, even though I made some small choices along the way. Had I been so attached—so much a piece of my husband, either one of them, all this time—that when I do make some decision that is out of the ordinary, and in this case, maybe contrary to what Harold wants, that it seems MAJOR? It's only cell phones, after all.

I'm glad I have a dictionary. I can probably find my own picture in there, listed under "quotidian, consumed by."

More later, about the second odd thing.

——————◆——————

Harold opened the door just as she put the notebook into the center of the puzzle book. "Come on outside, hon. It's nice and cool and not too breezy out here. O.D. stopped so I could get Long John's. We'll have a picnic on one of these tables. I promised you—you'll never cook again if you don't want to."

"I appreciate not having to cook, but I'm concerned we shouldn't eat so many fried things. Not on your diet. And it's expensive."

She might as well have been whistling. He opened the bags of food—fried fish with crisp crumbles, coleslaw, French fries, and malt vinegar—and made a show of placing them on the table. He was a waiter and she was his only customer. He laid one of the napkins across his arm and showed her to her seat.

"No, no, waiter, this seat won't do. I want to sit with that nice-looking man who bought me this meal," Dorothy Faye said. She couldn't help going along with his little show.

"As you wish, ma'am," he said, sitting down next to her and giving her a one-armed hug. "How was your day?"

"Interesting. Elizabeth's here. Well, not here, but at a hotel. She'll be back in the morning. All disturbed that she didn't know where we were, so she tracked us down," Dorothy Faye said.

"How is she? Did you two have a good visit?"

"When she got through working me over for not keeping her informed, we did. She's renovating some new boyfriend."

"What did y'all do?"

"Talked, mostly. And went to the mall. I got a dictionary and cell phones for you and me." She hurried on to say, "I didn't spend much on anything."

Harold paused, examining a French fry, then staring a minute into his wife's face. "Did you tell her we'd probably be leaving soon?"

"No, I didn't know we were. Where are we going?"

"I thought we'd try Consolidated Medical Center. You know, staying at the KOA can eat up money in a hurry."

Dorothy Faye felt her smile stiffen. She stared off to the right, toward the setting sun, which was visible only as a fan of rays above a line of storm clouds on the distant horizon.

He moved into her line of vision. "Honey, you know I'm kidding. It's just more fun to do something that's a little risky. Kinda like gambling. We can stay here a couple more days so Elizabeth can visit before we go."

Still studying the clouds, still wondering about money, she said, "I'm concerned that we might take up a space at the hospital that someone else needs. I mean, maybe the parents of some terminally ill child or something."

"I'll tell you what. If there's only one space, we won't take it. Does that seem better to you?"

"I guess so." She cleared their trash, bagged it neatly, and closed the lid on the metal trash can tightly, with hardly a sound.

CHAPTER 8

Different, Not Smaller

E lizabeth would turn up right on time. Dorothy Faye knew she needed to be prepared. She had thought it out by the time she finished her bowl of Total. She wasn't going to tell her daughter anything about those snapshots or how irritable she'd been. Everything she said and did would show Elizabeth that her parents were normal, at least not any different than usual. She didn't want her worrying about them. Harold had left early, going somewhere with O.D. She hadn't asked where. He said he'd be back by noon.

As promised, Elizabeth arrived at nine o'clock and parked in the sliver of shade cast by the scrawny elm tree on the territory assigned to space twenty-six. Dorothy Faye felt good just looking at her—so pretty in her tan linen pantsuit, Chinese red silk shirt, and brown pumps. The only frill was her jewelry—a rope of big red stones for a necklace with matching stud earrings. No rings. A businesswoman ready for business, from all appearances.

"Have you tried out your new phone?" Elizabeth asked. She probably had a list prepared.

"No, I haven't needed to call anyone. You know I'm not fond of talking on the phone. But I've put your number in the contacts section, and Harold's, of course, and R.J.'s."

"I hope you'll call him. I think he ought to know your number, even if he doesn't call often."

Dorothy Faye half paid attention to what Elizabeth was saying. The other half she devoted to listening to her daughter's diction. If you didn't know better, you might think she was from Nebraska, not West Texas. Never a dropped consonant, never a nasal twang.

Elizabeth paused. Before she could begin again, Dorothy Faye asked something she'd been wondering since yesterday. "The first thing you said when you saw me yesterday was, 'Mother, you've gotten smaller.' What made you say that?"

A mockingbird perched on the pitiful elm, trilling as if cued to fill the gap between the question and Elizabeth's answer. Eventually she said, "I'm not sure I know why I said it. Somehow you seemed, seem, different. I thought smaller was what it was. Now I'm not sure."

"You may be right. Maybe something is different about me." Now she'd put her foot in it. Dorothy Faye closed her mouth before she could expose anything else she didn't intend to.

"Is it anything you can talk about?"

"Oh, honey, you're so sweet. There you are taking me seriously. No, you don't need to be concerned. Whatever made me seem different is nothing bad, I'm sure. I'm not sick. And I don't think I'm going to have to take up my hems anytime soon."

Elizabeth fiddled with her bold red necklace, continuing to look at her mother.

"One thing I've been doing has made me feel good, though. You know I told you about parking at the hospital. Well, part of your daddy's idea about doing that was that we'd seem legitimate if I visited in the hospital. He hadn't worked it out in any more detail than that. Visit who? So I decided to visit in waiting rooms, so it wouldn't be obvious I wasn't attached to any patient. In one of the waiting rooms, I met a man who was there with his mother. She's in a coma."

"You met a man?"

"Don't look like that—he's a nice, sad, young man who needed someone to talk to. Anyway, I won't go into his problems, but before we left to come out here, he said talking to me really helped him. I felt good about that."

Elizabeth studied her mother a minute before responding. "I can see why you felt good about that. You're a very good listener, with years of practice. If anyone had eavesdropped at our house, they would have thought that three of us there led really interesting lives. You encouraged us to talk. You listened and never talked about yourself." She sat back in the recliner, flipped the footrest out. "Having someone listen to you is important. I wish you would talk to me. I would listen." She waited quietly until Dorothy Faye spoke again.

"Maybe it's my age. I'm nearly fifty-six. I've never been this age before. And I don't know what other fifty-six-year-old women think about, do with themselves, how they feel. That's been on my mind." Dorothy Faye inhaled deeply, staring at her hands. "Could it be that the reason I look a little different is because now I've started to wonder about that? About a lot of things." She stopped talking and nodded once, as if that said all there was to say. Then, looking away, she said softly, "Maybe you caught me thinking about myself."

"Do you have any pains or headaches or dizzy spells or anything like that?"

"I promise I'm not sick. Now I want you to quit worrying about me."

"If you say so, Mother. I believe you. But I'm still going to talk to Daddy because I want him to promise he'll let me know where this trip is going. Do you mind staying here while I get him to go to lunch with me?"

CHAPTER 9

You Have to Promise Me

H arold and O.D. hadn't talked much for the first several miles on the way to the lease. O.D. drove the back roads and hummed tunelessly. Harold thought about what he'd say to Elizabeth. He knew she'd demand an explanation.

O.D. turned in the gate to his lease. "How was everything at your house last night?" he asked.

"Fine. Elizabeth had been there and went shopping for a dictionary and cell phones. You can tell Janiece we're connected now. Maybe later on I'll tell her the number. No sense wearin' it out using it too much."

"Then don't tell me before you want her to know. You know I can't lie to her—if I did, I'd probably drop dead on the spot. Even bending the truth like we did the other night is risky for me. I swear your sister can scare me to death when she wants to. What made Elizabeth come out here from Dallas? She'd called the other day and we'd told her you were both fine."

"Well, you know Elizabeth. She expects to know what's going on all the time. She calls us or we call her once a week. Speaking of people who can scare a person, that sweet little girl grew up to be mighty tough." He spent a few seconds pressing some of his new phone's buttons while watching its screen. "Until she was about fourteen or so, she was just like her mother, real sweet and helpful. Then, soon as she, you know, started fillin' out, she started changing. At first it was just asking questions all the time. Then later, she'd just come up with these ideas. Mind you, I admire a person having lots of ideas, but it was a change from the little girl she was before. Like one time she decided she'd be a Catholic, maybe even a nun. I guess that would've been okay, but she'd never even been a Baptist—had no practice with having any religion, much less goin' to a convent."

Staring out the pickup windshield, he removed his toothpick from the right side of his mouth and held it, pausing a long time. Then, as if he had come to a conclusion, he put the toothpick back in and started talking again. "Anything much to do out here today?"

"This'll be it." O.D. stopped at the final well on the oil lease he tended. "I'm gonna check these gauges. I'll be right back and then we can get you back to the KOA. You stay in here where it's cool. You've had a hard couple of days."

O.D. came back and got a wrench and returned to the gauges. Harold got out and walked quickly to the tailgate. About five minutes later he walked back toward the pickup as O.D. tossed the wrench in the toolbox and wiped his hands on a shop rag. "You okay?" O.D. asked.

"Yeah, fine. It's good we're getting back soon. Elizabeth will be there. I need to get her settled down and back in Big D so we can get back to the hospital. She distracts her mother with all her questions. Say O.D., do you ever have any trouble gettin' started when you go to piss?"

"Can't recall it, if I have." He wrinkled his forehead, quiet as he drove slowly. "Nope. What made you ask?" Harold was staring through the windshield again.

"Oh, I heard an old man I know say something about that the other day. I wondered if it meant trouble. I'd hate it if anything was bad wrong with him." He shrugged like the topic wasn't important, then looked at O.D., smiling again. "Yep, I'll bet Elizabeth has plenty to talk to me about. Maybe you ought to stick around when we get there. I might need help."

"Wish I could. But Janiece will be looking for me if I'm not in by twelve thirty for dinner. By the way, you know that plumbing problem that old man had could be something simple—maybe just enlarged prostrate gland, you know."

"*Prostate* gland," Harold said.

"Yeah, like I said. I think maybe you ought to go talk to that old man and tell him to get it seen about instead of waitin' till it turns into something bad."

Harold nodded, continuing to concentrate on the landscape. Back at the KOA, as he got out of the pickup, he said, "You know, you might be right. About that old man, I mean."

———————◆———————

After she hugged him and took a good long look at him, Elizabeth said, "Daddy, Mother said she's not hungry for lunch. So why don't you and I go over to the airport so I can arrange to keep this rental car one more day? We can stop at the County Line for lunch."

He cocked an eyebrow and grinned. "Okay, I don't have any important appointments this afternoon. But I might get a phone call. Now that I have this cell phone, it just never stops ringing."

She poked him on the shoulder and put her arm around him. "Always joking. Let's go now. I'm ready if you are," she said.

They hadn't been gone from the KOA more than five minutes before she got down to business. "Now tell me what's really going on. What's this trip all about?"

"Well, we hadn't been on a trip in a long time and I thought it would be fun. The hospital parking lots and visiting were just a little bit to add to the excitement." He doubted she'd understand, but thought it would distract her. "I didn't have anywhere in mind, in particular, that I wanted to go. Wanted to decide as we go along. Just fun. And a good excuse to get a new pickup too."

"What's the point if you're not going anywhere? You've only been thirty-five miles so far."

"We're not in any rush."

"Why was it necessary to move and to get rid of all the furniture and to sell Mother's car? That makes it seem like a lot more than a vacation to me.

There's more to it." She was talking faster, driving with one hand and gesturing with the other to emphasize her points. "Is it fair to Mother to expect her to uproot and leave home like that, just because it seems like fun to you?"

"She didn't disagree when I told her about it. In fact, I think she was pretty happy to get rid of that ugly end table and some of her old clothes." He'd thought Elizabeth would appreciate that because she hated the table too. She didn't even laugh. He turned his head to check for traffic as they exited to the airport. "All clear. She's never complained about having fun before. Did she say she was upset about it?"

"No, Daddy, she didn't say anything about anything. She never does. But that doesn't mean she might not feel upset."

"Well, I'm pretty sure she's not in a rush to get back to Whaley."

"Do you intend to go back there?"

"Not right away. Maybe not ever." He felt his answers getting shorter. He concentrated on the view out his side window.

"All right. So this is just for fun. Fine. But promise you'll let me know where you are. Will you?" In a lighter tone, "I expect you to let me know where I can send mail. You might need a care package."

"That's a deal. We may run out of Slim Jims and pork rinds if we leave West Texas. For sure we'd need a care package if that happens."

"I'll only ask one more question for now. Are you feeling okay, taking your medicine and checking your blood sugar every day?"

He smiled a slow smile in her direction. "Don't you worry about my diabetes, honey. I'm doing fine." He paused a second. "In fact, I've started using a new test. The mirror test."

"Mirror test? I haven't heard about that. Is it like the A1c?"

"Better. See, every morning, first thing before I eat, I go and look in the mirror, real hard. If I recognize myself, and I'm standin' up straight, I passed. I know I'm good to go one more day." He pointed left to the final turn to the airport. He could see her shake her head.

Waiting for their lunch order, the rib special, she tried another line of questioning. "Since you won't talk about yourself, tell me about Mother.

You say she's not upset about this trip. But she seems different to me. What do you think?"

He poked at his potato salad for a minute, then stared at the peacock strutting around the rim of the little pond. That pond and the cluster of trees that had managed to stay alive in this tiny canyon where the restaurant was located attracted as many customers as the barbecue. "Here's what I think, Elizabeth. Your mother's fine. And the main thing I think is that you got worried because we made a move without telling you. That made you imagine the worst."

It was her turn to ignore her plate. "It's just that I like to know that you're okay and where you're located."

"I understand that. But location is something that can change. You'd probably be happier if you were the one moving around and we'd stay put. That'll happen soon enough."

She stared a while at the peacock. "You're right. I had this idea that you'd stay right where you were forever and I'd never have to worry about you. You'd be just the way you always were. Mother taking care of Mrs. Ottley and you working on the leases, doing kind things to help other people, and telling stories at the coffee shop." She turned back to him and there was something different in her face. She looked the way she had when she was thirteen and hadn't realized yet that he and Dorothy Faye weren't the whole world. "It's just that I love you both and want everything to be perfect."

CHAPTER 10

You Were Warned

Day 16 June 3 2:45 p.m. KOA outside of Lubbock

I intended to write about the second odd thing that I mentioned. That was yesterday; it's obvious I'm avoiding doing it. Maybe that's because I never did have any reason to think much about it, about sex, before now. Sex with Harold has always been nice, seemed like it had to do with love as much as it did with lust. I've never been the one to make the first move, never had to. Not to say that Harold's always after me or anything. But I can always tell by a particularly sweet look he gets. It's a look like I'm the only thing in the world that's of any interest to him. He seems to be studying me like he might not have ever seen me before. And then before long, he's moved close to me and touched me, just a tiny touch, maybe moves a curl off my forehead or straightens my collar. Next thing you know, no matter what time of day or night, we're making love, both of us enjoying it.

I don't recall anything being different the last time either. What's odd is that for these past five months, he seems to have not been interested. He doesn't get that look. He's perfectly nice to me, hasn't said a thing that would make me think he's upset with me. In the past, if a while went by between, I just thought he had been busy and then tired. To tell the truth, I didn't even think about it at all until the other night when I was brushing my teeth. Maybe that's odd too—that I didn't even notice for five months. Did I just not let myself notice?

I'm trying to think if there's something I've missed, something that changed while I wasn't paying attention, while I was busy assuming he'd never look at anyone else or assuming he'd always be interested in me whether he looked at anyone else or not.

I suppose I could just ask him. But that seems so… well, it seems so unlike me to even write about sex, much less talk about it. Maybe the best thing to do is to just *wait and see what happens. I can still decide later to bring up the subject if—*

She heard a car coming near, crunching on the gravel next to the trailer. Her right hand shook as she hurried to hide the notebook.

"This is a surprise, Janiece. Come on in." Technically, it was no surprise. Dorothy Faye had peeked out the window and seen Janiece's Cadillac pulling up near space twenty-six and chose to surrender rather than attempt to flee.

Janiece surveyed the living area and chose Harold's recliner to settle on. Instead of reclining, she perched on the front of the seat, leaning toward Dorothy Faye.

Dorothy Faye's gaze roamed the living area and lit on Harold's coffee cup. She asked, hostess-like, "Can I offer you something to drink—coffee?"

"No, thanks. There's something I need to tell you. I'm not sure how to say this. But…"

Dorothy Faye waited. Janiece didn't usually have any difficulty deciding how to say anything.

"Well, the thing is, I think maybe you should watch Harold. He's up to something."

Dorothy Faye laughed and felt her frown, the one that had formed when Janiece started talking, relax. "He's nearly always up to something. Always a new idea. Watching won't change that. In fact, I'd probably be disappointed if he wasn't up to something."

"No, I'm serious. I think he may be seeing a woman." She hesitated briefly. "There, I said it." Janiece leaned back into the recliner. Her mouth prim and small, her eyes narrowed, she was the picture of righteous indignation, or maybe it was satisfaction.

The minute that elapsed before Dorothy Faye could speak seemed like an hour. Finally, when she thought she could control her voice, she said, "Why would you say that about Harold? As far as I know, he's never done anything like that before." Dorothy Faye tried to smile. Her top lip stuck to her teeth.

"You recall the other night when they told you they were going fishing? Well, I know for a fact that wasn't true. O.D. admitted it to me. Of course, that was only after I confronted him with the evidence." Sounded like she was working for the FBI. "I believe him when he said that Harold left him at the bowling alley in Levelland and went off for about three hours. He said Harold told him something about seeing a man to find out about when or where our father died. That's about as weak a story as I ever heard. None of us ever cared what happened to him after he left us. Anyhow, I thought you ought to know."

"Thanks for being concerned and for making the trip out here to tell me."

"Well? Is that all? What are you going to do?"

"Do? I intend to think about what you told me, if that's what you mean."

"You amaze me. I'd be checking his clothes and searching the pickup before you could say Jack. But not you. You say you'll think about it! I swear, you'll probably pack his bags for him if he decides to leave you for a younger woman." She stared at Dorothy Faye, shaking her head. No response. In the silence, Janiece opened her purse, dug out the keys to her Cadillac, checked her reflection in her compact, and shut it with a loud snap. "Well, I've done what I can do. Don't say you haven't been warned."

CHAPTER 11

God's Own Hitchhiker

Outside in the parking lot of Consolidated Medical Center, a car door slammed. Inside the trailer, Harold lined up the cereal, milk, bananas, and sugar substitute on the countertop with quick, efficient motions. "Since Mr. Sam's cooking supper these days, I decided I'd take over at breakfast. Like I promised, you'll never have to cook again if you don't want to," he said.

In response to his big smile and jovial tone, Dorothy Faye smiled, a reflex she had never tried before to control. Nodding and gritting her teeth, she sat still as he finished his preparation. She focused on the cereal flakes as they dropped into his bowl.

"Orange juice?"

She shook her head. Pouring her own cereal and milk gave her time to compose a neutral expression. She'd practiced that expression last night all the time they were getting things together at the KOA to move over here to Consolidated.

He resorted to studying the milk carton's nutritional information. His table manners were impeccable this morning. The occasional slurps he usually made eating milk-soaked cereal never escaped past his spoon; coffee cup met saucer without a sound. He continued smiling between bites.

Dorothy Faye hadn't begun to eat. She replaced her spoon on the paper napkin. She put both hands in her lap, drew a deep breath, and raised her neutral expression to confront Harold's grin. "Harold, this is your chance to tell me where you went when you pretended to go fishing the other night." She stopped. She'd said all she'd rehearsed.

Dorothy Faye stayed absolutely still, hands clasped together in her lap. She looked at the living area as if it were hostile terrain.

"I just didn't want to tell you, didn't want you to worry. I thought—"

"You didn't think much or you'd have known Janiece would find out and come running to tell me. She could hardly wait to make a trip out to the KOA to say you were probably just like all men your age—out with some younger woman, going to leave and—"

"Oh, honey, you know I wouldn't."

"No, I don't know. I don't know anything. I never imagined you'd lie to me, so maybe there's a lot more I haven't imagined either." She managed to make the words come out slowly and calmly. She pushed her uneaten cereal away, stood, took three steps, and realized she'd end up in the bathroom if she took another one.

Harold could have touched her if he'd reached out. Instead, he hung his head. "I made a big mistake."

"I agree. You did and you're still making it. You haven't answered my question."

"I went to Levelland. There's a man over there who was a friend of my daddy's. I wanted to talk to him, to find out some things about what happened to my daddy."

"If that's true, why lie about it? As much as I hate to agree with Janiece, that can't be all you were doing in Levelland. You could have told me if that was all there was to it. Have you ever known me to disagree with anything you wanted to do?"

Head down, so quietly she could hardly hear, he said, "I didn't want you to worry about—"

"About what? About what you really were doing? I'll tell you this, if you plan on making a career of lying, you need to get better at it. I knew even before Janiece..." She stopped in mid-sentence to take another deep breath. She raised her head, but not her voice. "I didn't want to..."

"Didn't want to what?"

She looked at him, only for a second. She stared past him, seeing a dim snapshot, saying nothing for a long time.

"Never mind. I asked you and you told me. If what you say is the truth, then that's all I want to know. I don't want to argue. What you do is your business—find out about your daddy if you need to. Just don't lie to me."

He opened his mouth, then closed it and chewed on his lower lip for a few seconds. "I'm sorry you're upset. And I'm sorry you had to put up with Janiece sayin' whatever she said. I shouldn't have told you something that wasn't true."

Before he'd finished his last sentence, Dorothy Faye poured the contents of her bowl, milk and all, into the trash. She cleared the dishes away, then began wiping at the counter with a dishrag, never looking Harold's way. "I'm going in the hospital, and after that I'm going for a walk. So don't worry if I'm not here at noon," she said.

"O.D.'s comin' to get me. We're going over to Littlefield. He says there's a little air show over there today with ultralights and maybe some gliders. Do you want to come with us?"

She kept wiping the clean counter for a minute. "No, I don't think so. I'll see you this evening." She heard herself saying the words, but the voice wasn't hers. It sounded like an old woman's sounds after she's cleaned house all day—tired and flat.

High ceilings and marble borders around the large carpeted areas, couches, and floral fabric-upholstered chairs—the spacious lobby could have been in an expensive hotel instead of a hospital. The employees at the information desk wore blazers and tailored skirts and offered each visitor who approached a bright, businesslike, "How can I help you?"

Dorothy Faye stood just inside the revolving entry door and endured an assault by the fragrance of bouquets waiting at the desk labeled Guest Relations. *Guests?* The funereal combination of carnations, roses, and gladioli on their way to Consolidated's "guests" did nothing to lighten her mood.

Dorothy Faye made one full turn in the revolving door before she managed to exit onto the sidewalk. A valet asked, "Can I get your car for you, ma'am?" Shaking her head, she walked fast, then faster, away from the hospital and from the parking lot, not caring about a destination. After about thirty minutes, she arrived at one—a park. She sat at the nearest picnic table, intending to rest a while before heading back toward the trailer. The dim snapshot she'd seen earlier was back, clearer now. But it hadn't been a recollection of a photograph. It was a memory of the last argument she and Ronnie had—the one before he left.

He'd said he was going on the road to witness for Jesus, leaving the next day. She heard his words and hers from years ago as clearly as if the young couple speaking them were standing near the picnic table she'd chosen.

"You don't understand. The Lord has called me. It's what I have to do. I know you don't understand, but I know now that his will is why I can't get and keep a job. He wants me doing his work, not staying here and working day labor just to feed you and the baby. I'll send you some money when I can. Your mother will take care of you," Ronnie said.

Tears had dried on her face. She was past crying now, yelling at him. "God's will, my butt! You're just too lazy to work. You promised me when we got married that you'd settle down, quit going out and drinking with your friends. You said we were meant to be together, you'd die if I didn't marry you, you'd kill yourself if I didn't. What happened to all that love you talked about?" A steady ache had begun at the base of her skull.

He started to answer. Before he could, she continued. This time, her voice was low and controlled and her face grim. "If you're unhappy with what you got from all your romance and threats, don't blame it on God. If you can't grow up and be responsible, it's because you still want to run and play with your friends, sneak around with high school girls who tell you how handsome you are. You'd rather fool with those little girls instead of taking care of this little girl who's your own child." She pointed at Elizabeth, fussing in the playpen. As if on cue, the baby changed from fretting to pitiful wailing.

"Don't try to stop me on this. God will punish you." Ronnie's face reddened as he shouted.

"Why wouldn't God be happy if you took up witnessing right here in Lubbock instead of going on the road? Tell me that. If He's been speaking to you, did he answer that?" Her volume matched his now. She'd picked up the baby and rested her on her hip, her pregnant belly making her lean at an angle to keep her balance.

"I told you all this before. Jerry's going to take me up to Vega, where Route Sixty-Six goes through. My mission is to witness to every person heading west who picks me up. I'll be God's Own Hitchhiker."

She wanted to tell him how ridiculous he sounded. Instead, she tried to sound reasonable. "How do you plan to eat? Where will you sleep? Do you have any plan except to leave your responsibilities here and get up to Route Sixty-Six?"

"I have faith that God will provide for me as I do his work."

"Well, is God planning to pay the hospital and doctor bills when I have this new baby? Did you intend to be out witnessing to strangers when you should be witnessing the birth of this next baby?" She'd given up trying to be reasonable. She turned her back to him, searching for Elizabeth's pacifier, muttering, "Witnessing, hah!"

"I'll try to get back by next month around that time. By then I'll know more about exactly how the Lord intends for me to do his work."

Dorothy Faye faced him. Her mocking smirk backed him away a step. "That means you expect to be completely broke by then. You'll come back just long enough to get your clothes washed and mooch some more money. You have no idea what it's like to be a parent. It's a job. You signed up for it when you wouldn't let me consider taking the pill." She started crying again, hopeless sounds that kept her from telling him she couldn't imagine how she could manage alone.

"I'm not listening to any more of this. I'm going and that's that. You straighten yourself up and quit crying this minute and say a decent good-bye in the morning or I'll leave right now."

Elizabeth had gone to sleep on Dorothy Faye's shoulder, a thumb in her mouth and the other hand over her ear. Dorothy Faye put her down in the playpen. She stood up as erect as she could and went into the bedroom, not saying a word. She threw all of Ronnie's clothes out of the closet onto the bed. He came into the room as she emptied his dresser drawer out on top of the heap of jeans and shirts. "I don't think God's Own Hitchhiker should keep the sinners on Route Sixty-Six waiting. Get your clothes and go. And don't wake up the baby on your way out." She expected him to slap her. She stood still, daring him with her eyes.

Maybe his newfound religion stopped him. He jerked up some of the clothes and stuffed them in his duffle bag and pushed the rest onto the floor. He stomped out the back door without stopping to look at the sleeping baby in the living room.

He'd returned a month later for a single day, the day after the birth of his son. "We should call him Ronnie Jr.," he'd said. She had nodded, too tired from a thirty-six-hour labor to do anything else. She slept for the next two days except for when the nurses brought the baby to breast-feed.

When her mother picked her up from the hospital, she didn't bother to ask—he had already left again. There was a note from him that her mother pointed to when they got to her house. "You might as well plan on movin' in here," June Carson said. "That no good so-and-so's not ever comin' back to stay. You mark my words."

Dorothy Faye had cried, more from fatigue than from anything else. Three days later, she'd gotten her things from their fifty-dollar-a-month rent house and told her mother she'd pay rent to her as soon as she got a job.

"You don't have to pay me. You're my daughter and you've got enough to worry about taking care of these kids. I've made plenty of mistakes myself. And now you've made enough to last you for a long time. You can worry about a job in a few weeks. Just rest up a while."

Dorothy Faye had never known her mother to be so understanding. She didn't cry again, not even when she got the news a few weeks later that Ronnie's body had been found on Route 66 between Seligman and Valentine in Arizona. The police said he'd apparently been hit by a truck.

Dorothy Faye had kept herself busy with the kids and her new job at the truck stop. She was so busy that she didn't have much time for thinking—about the future or the past. When she finally did take a day off, she slept for fourteen hours. She woke up knowing for certain that when Ronnie left, she'd hoped he wouldn't ever come back.

She thought she should feel guilty about that. She waited until the next day to decide whether she did, and she thought about whether anything she had done, other than her fleeting wish, had caused his death. She thought about a lot of other things she had wished for in her life, none of which had happened. She thought about his determination to leave and to do—whatever he actually wanted to do. And she thought about her feelings—afraid, yes; empty, yes; sad at loss of her *Ladies Home Journal* dream, yes; guilty, no.

She didn't—feel guilty. And she felt a little pride in her rational consideration of the entire question. The only regret she admitted to was based on also realizing she had not been as rational in agreeing to marry him. She never mentioned any of this to her mother. Instead, she got up and got back to work.

She promised herself back then that she wouldn't ever think about him leaving or dying or anything else that made her feel sorry for herself again. Until now she hadn't, in all these years. Even now, she couldn't call the feeling she had right now sorry for herself; it was more a feeling of dismay that this was all coming up again.

Dorothy Faye slowly walked the park's perimeter. After twice around, her shoulder muscles relaxed and she breathed more deeply. A woman placed a bulging black plastic bag into a trash container on a curb. As Dorothy Faye passed, the woman said, "Beautiful morning."

"Yes, it is," Dorothy Faye said, continuing her walk back toward the trailer.

CHAPTER 12

Call the Concierge

Day 17 June 4 3:00 p.m. Consolidated Hospital, Lubbock

I had a good long nap and woke up feeling ready— but I don't know for what. I do know it's not the hospital, at least not yet.

Finishing what I began on this page may be what I'm ready for. We'll see.

The sentence on the last page that Janiece interrupted with her forecast of doom was going to say, "I can still decide later to bring up the subject if something else makes me suspicious." After Janiece left, my first impulse was to call Mrs. Ottley. She's the only person I could ever tell about how confused I was just then. I'm proud of myself for sitting still and thinking instead of feeling sorry for myself all afternoon. It took me all afternoon, part of last night, hearing Harold's explanation this morning and his apology, and a good long walk today. Now, I've decided. I'm not going to spend my time being suspicious.

If Harold had been interested in another woman, playing around would have been easier without taking this trip. I'd have never had a suspicion. He could have just left me doing what I was doing and he could have done anything he wanted to. I'd never have questioned his being gone all day or, if he'd manufactured a good excuse, like a new project, even gone overnight. Although Janiece suspects all men of being willing (or eager) to wander, that's not what's going on with Harold. What sense does that make? Even when he has a new idea cooking, his reasoning makes sense.

It didn't occur to me earlier because I was thinking about whether I was still attractive or whether I'd done something to upset him, but I probably don't even have much to do with what's wrong. And I don't think that going to Levelland the other night is necessarily related to why we haven't had sex in five months. I think it's more likely that his diabetes is causing impotence. Not that I'd mention that to Janiece as a possibility. It's not her business. I know from all I've read about diabetes that diabetic neuropathy or vascular changes or both can cause that. And another possibility is side effects of medications. The more I think about it, the more I think that's a good possibility. I don't mean it's good, but highly likely.

Now, the question is how to get him to talk about it, if impotence—no, the euphemism these days is "erectile dysfunction"—is a problem. I guess I could wait until there's an ad for Viagra on TV and bring up the subject then. Ha! I know he's going to have to see his doctor, regardless; it's been nearly a year. Getting him there may take some doing.

———•———

Still feeling ready, and still not knowing why, Dorothy Faye entered the hospital lobby. This time she went through the wheelchair-accessible door, avoiding the possibility of another do-si-do with the revolving one next to it. That hazard negotiated, she walked briskly to the "You are here" map on a pillar in the ornate lobby. No one watching would have guessed she hadn't any idea where she intended to go. The far side of the map showed the pediatrics area. The waiting rooms there should be busy, a perfect place for her to observe. The emergency department was nearer, but probably riskier. Someone might ask her for information about an unconscious patient.

She turned in the direction the map indicated would eventually lead to the children's hospital. The difference between Consolidated and the much smaller Lakeview seemed to be more than a matter of the number of beds. The halls here were full of people all moving quickly, on important missions, it appeared. A large portion of the first floor housed the administrative offices. Brass letters above a long series of doors in walls of dark wood paneling marked the territory "Executive Offices." *How it would it feel to be an executive? How would it feel to think your purpose was important? My only purpose is to find the children's hospital and to seem to visit someone.*

Dorothy Faye followed a nurse who passed her, accelerating to match the woman's brisk pace. Dorothy Faye reasoned that their speed would enhance the impression she knew where she was headed. She strode down a long hall, certain that she appeared to be attached to some unnamed guest. Stopping abruptly, she backtracked to look at the sign on a door she passed. Maybe she misread. Concierge. *Concierge?* It wasn't that she didn't understand the word. She just didn't believe it. Shaking her head, she continued down the hall, slowly, thinking about hospitals pretending to be hotels. Her worries about being an impostor almost disappeared. Surely any hospital official who confronted her would understand a charade.

Pediatrics' first-floor waiting room occupied the base of a three-story atrium. A large mobile of fairy-tale characters and toys hung from the ceiling. No one waited there. The area's hard benches did not invite resting. The mobile suggested that a toy store might be nearby. Dorothy Faye took the glass elevator to the third floor. As the door opened, she heard a child whining.

He appeared to be about two years old and was acting his age. Whining escalated to screaming. He tugged at the pants leg of the man sitting near him. That got no response from the man. He continued sitting, staring at the wall. The child rolled on the floor, kicking his feet. Two other children, a boy in pajamas and girl wearing mismatched socks with her taffeta dress, ignored the tantrum. Playing tag, they used the man as base. "You're it."

"No, you're it," the girl said.

The man, speaking softly, said, "Everybody please sit still and be quiet. As soon as your mother comes to talk to us a minute, we'll go get some lunch." The tantrum continued. Tag was abandoned. Both older children busied themselves pulling knobs on the nearby snack-vending machine.

The man raised his head, then gave a defeated-looking shrug. "I'm sorry about the uproar. They mind their mother better than they do me."

"They're just being kids," Dorothy Faye said. "Letting off nervous energy."

"You're probably right. I'm nervous too. Our baby is real sick. Only six months old. My wife's staying with her." He pointed to the children. "Besides these three, we have two more at school. There's no one but me to take the kids. My wife, Anna, she's the one who always sees they mind."

He shifted and looked down at the floor like an explanation was printed there. "All I know to do is send them to their room, or if they act real bad, threaten to give them a spanking. They probably see through me. They aren't bad kids. It's me. You ought to see the mess at the house. I don't know how my wife does it all." He picked up the two-year-old. The little boy snuffled and wiped snot on his sleeve and across his cheek. Now the man looked embarrassed. He said, "I'm sorry, you didn't need to have to listen to all that."

"This whole situation must be stressful," Dorothy Faye said.

He didn't respond for a long time. "I had to take off work without pay. I don't know when I can make up the hours. We just about had the bills paid from when the baby was born and now this." The little boy squirmed, trying to get to the floor. The other two had found magazines. The girl giggled as she tore out a picture of Tickle Me Elmo. The boy tore out a smiling Martha Stewart. "Stop that. Don't tear things up," their father said. To Dorothy Faye, he said, "See what I mean?"

Dorothy Faye made a decision. "Maybe I can help a little. Tell them I'm a friend of yours and that I'm going to play with them while you go see their baby sister. That way you can spend a little quiet time with your wife and the baby. After while, if you want, I'll help you figure out how to manage the kids and the house until things settle down."

"Are you sure?" The relief on his face would have convinced her if she'd had any doubts.

"I don't mind a bit. But just so you'll feel safe leaving them with me, I'm going to write my name and phone number down for you." She was pretty sure he'd have left the kids with Lizzie Borden if she'd stopped by, phone number or not. He smiled a little when she handed him the information on a page she'd torn from her notebook.

"Thank you so much." He told the children to mind her until he came back, then started toward the patient rooms. After a couple of steps, he turned back and handed the two-year-old to Dorothy Faye. "See how confused I am? This is Robbie." He started off again and turned back again. "I'm Daniel Martin."

As he walked away, Dorothy Faye jiggled the toddler on her right hip and wiped his nose so quickly he didn't have time to say no. "Let's find a book we can all read together," she said.

Daniel and Anna found Dorothy Faye with Robbie asleep in her lap and the other two listening quietly as she read to them.

"Let me take him off your lap. He's heavy for such a little guy," Anna said.

"He's fine. You look like you could use a nap too. Sit here beside me for a minute. Daniel, maybe you can take Rebecca and Danny to ride the elevator. Down on first floor you can look up at the hanging toys. You two try to memorize their names, and we'll talk about them when you come back."

Anna Martin, pale and plump, leaned back in the chair. She closed her puffy eyes. Without opening them, she said, "You're right. I could sleep for days. Every time I think the baby is settled, they draw blood or do a breathing treatment. That wakes her up and she won't stop crying until I rock her. When she does sleep, I stay awake because I can't help listening to be sure she's breathing." She choked back a sound, like a sob in reverse. A tear ran down one cheek. "Poor Daniel is so worried about her and about losing pay for being off work."

"You don't have family here to help?"

"The truth is he grew up in an orphanage, and I ran away from home to marry him. Since then my family won't have anything to do with us."

"Could anyone from your church help?"

"I don't know anyone. Since we moved here last year, we haven't even been to Mass. That's another thing I worry about." She stopped talking, drew a deep breath. "I guess we'll get it all figured out as soon as the baby gets well. They say she has pneumonia, but they can't seem to get it controlled. They're checking to see if there's something wrong with her immune system. I don't understand it all. They keep telling me it's all right for me to rest, that me just being in the room is what's important for her."

Robbie stirred against Dorothy Faye's chest. She rubbed his back in small circles until he relaxed again.

"He usually doesn't take to strangers," Anna said.

Rebecca and Danny ran to their mother when they got off the elevator. They competed for attention, telling her about the mobile's giant toys.

Anna gathered them both into her arms and told them to help their dad and be good while she stayed here to take care of the baby. She hugged her husband and offered her hand to Dorothy Faye. "Thank you for helping."

Shifting Robbie to free her right arm, Dorothy Faye took Anna's hand, held it. "You're welcome. Take care of yourself. You're very important to some important people."

Smiling a faint smile, Anna stood straight, nodded, and walked back down the hall.

Daniel sat beside Dorothy Faye. "I'll take him off your hands now."

"Not yet. I want you to get that pen out of my purse and write down a couple of things to help you manage until the situation gets better."

He smoothed the crumpled paper she'd written her phone number on and held the pen he'd dug out of her purse. "Ready."

She dictated a seven-item list that included brief instructions on laundry, meals for the children, basic housecleaning, naps, making a daily to-do list, and using distraction to manage the kids. She finished by adding, "Remember, you're smarter than they are."

He looked at the list and started to laugh. "Why didn't anyone ever tell me these things?"

She shrugged. "Maybe you didn't need to know before. Take Robbie and I'll make you a little shopping list. You'll be able to feed yourself and the kids without spending money on fast food. Kids don't have to eat a lot at one time, just a little of everything you make. Three meals, two snacks. That way you don't get into arguing with them about eating."

"You're right about the fast food. They want everything they see on the TV."

"Turn it off."

"Turn what off?"

"The television. Let them choose two favorite programs a day and fill the rest of the day with other activities. When they do get to watch those programs, they'll sit still and watch them. Kids have a short attention span. You need to be one step ahead of them with the next thing you'll have them do. You won't be watching television either. You have important work to do—being the adult in charge."

The grocery list began with disposable diapers. Robbie was a bit fragrant. "I put a few suggested meals on there. All you need to do to make them is slice things and read the directions on boxes. And always wash the day's dishes before you go to bed. Nothing's more depressing than a sink full of dirty dishes. Take a look at that and see if you have any questions."

He read. He looked up when he reached the bottom of the page. "You've helped me so much. Thank you. Will I see you again?"

"I'll make sure to be here tomorrow. About the same time. Now I need to go."

Robbie was still asleep on Daniel's shoulder as Dorothy Faye left them at the elevators. Rebecca and Danny waved and said, "Good-bye, Miss Dorothy."

She wondered if she should have told Daniel to call the concierge.

———◆———

Near the chapel, as Dorothy Faye made her way back to the main lobby, she passed a small woman wearing a navy-blue skirt and white blouse. Her name tag assured Dorothy Faye that the woman's white-edged, blue head covering was a version of a religious habit. Without a second's consideration, she said, "Sister, do you have a minute? I need some help."

CHAPTER 13

Date Night

The pickup was outside, but Harold wasn't in his recliner when she went in. "Harold?" She saw him lying on the bed. "Oh, there you are. Did you take a nap?" He was staring at the ceiling. "You feel all right?"

"Come sit here beside me," he said.

"What's wrong?" She took his hand, felt his forehead with her other hand.

"Nothing really. I've been layin' here thinking about this morning. I feel bad about it. We hardly ever have a cross word. And I just hate it when we do. Are you still mad at me?"

She kissed him on the forehead. "No, and I really wasn't mad." She turned to look out the tiny window at the parking lot. "I was hurt that you'd lied to me, and I couldn't understand why you did it. But I've said all I wanted to say about that." She looked back at Harold. "We won't bring it up again. Did you eat at noon?"

"Yes, I ate. I'm okay." Harold sat up, reached for his boots. He stopped after putting on the right one. He caught her hand, pulled her down to sit on his lap. He held her tight with both his arms. "I don't think I mentioned it lately, but I love you, Dorothy Faye."

She put a hand on either side of his face and looked into his eyes. "I believe that's the truth. And I don't mind you telling me that anytime at all. I love you too. Now, I'm getting up before your legs go to sleep."

——•——

Harold said they should go on a date—go to the 50 Yard Line for a steak. Dorothy Faye put on the only dress she had in the little closet, a soft royal-blue silk with white polka dots and a white portrait collar. She'd bought it a long time ago and never worn it. She added the only costume jewelry she'd bothered to keep, a string of simulated pearls and the little pearl stud earrings she wore every day. Her white sandals had a wedge heel that made her seem taller. Until she tried to put on the dress standing up, she didn't realize it was nearly impossible to put on clothes any other way than top half, then bottom half, in the low-ceilinged bedroom area. When she finally managed, what she could see of herself in the little mirror on the closet door looked pretty good—tall and graceful.

Harold whistled when she came into the living area. "You look real pretty, honey. Is that a new dress?" He'd put on starched Wranglers and another new shirt.

"No, I just haven't had any place to wear it until tonight. You look mighty nice yourself, Mr. Bell." She didn't ask about the new shirt.

——•——

A waiter brought an appetizer tray as soon as Harold placed their order. Dorothy Faye immediately chose a carrot stick and some olives. "I know I look like a vulture. I forgot to eat after breakfast."

"You must have gotten interested in what was going on at the big hospital. You didn't get in until nearly five thirty."

"I was," she said. Then she waited. She hadn't had time to think much about what she'd done, but she knew she felt good about it. If he asked, she'd tell him.

He grazed on the vegetable appetizers.

A large group at the long table next to them broke into a loud version of "Happy Birthday to You." Harold and Dorothy Faye applauded along with the other diners in the room. "I'm glad we heard that. It reminded me R.J.'s birthday is next week," she said.

"Well, that's right—June eleventh. It doesn't seem possible that little boy is thirty-four, does it? We need to be sure and call him. Do you think he'll ever move back to West Texas?"

"I doubt it. He seems happy where he is. I wish we could see both of the kids more often, but they have to lead their own lives. I suppose we could go and see them instead of waiting out here like a couple of old folks for them to come see us." She paused and selected another carrot stick. "Odd, isn't it, how people just get in the habit of doing certain things, even though nothing would keep them from doing something completely different?" She didn't expect an answer—(*rhetorical* again—puzzle #93).

Harold's puzzled look suggested he'd never thought of it either. Several bites of steak later, he said, "We should have a date every week."

"I'd like that. Now that we're footloose we can try lots of new places— in lots of towns. Maybe we could go down to the coast and have fresh shrimp," she said.

"Maybe we could," he said. He looked at her a long time without saying anything else. They both ate silently for a few minutes.

They both passed on dessert, although Dorothy Faye considered having the chocolate cake. Thinking of Harold's diet, she ordered a cup of decaf coffee. He had the same.

And then he came as close as he could without actually asking her. "You haven't told me what kept you busy all day."

She told him about the Martin family and their troubles—going clear through a second cup of coffee. He listened without interrupting or changing the subject. When she finished, he said, "Honey, that's a good thing you did today. That's visiting that made a difference." She inhaled deeply, catching the words and lodging them next to her heart—"made a difference."

On the way back to the hospital, she said, "Thanks, Harold."

"Why, sure, me and Mr. Sam are happy to do the cookin'. I'm glad you liked it."

"I did enjoy the meal," she said. "But I meant thanks for asking about what I did and thanks for listening."

He nodded and kept his eyes on the street as if it required considerable vigilance.

At the door to the trailer, he said, "I sure appreciate you going out with me this evening. Can we do it again real soon?"

"Yes, I'd like that." She cocked her head to one side, fluttered her eyelashes. "Would you think I was forward if I invited you in, Mr. Bell?"

"I was hoping you would."

They both laughed as they entered the living area. "Well, I guess I'll go on to bed," Harold said. "I know you'll be up reading a while. See you in the morning."

She sat in her chair in her polka dot dress and took a while removing her shoes and her simulated pearls.

Day 17 Sunday, June 4 11:00 p.m. Consolidated Medical Center, Lubbock

That edginess I've been having was gone this afternoon. I'm not sure exactly why. Maybe I felt like I had a reason to be here. And maybe, since I'd said to Harold just what I thought this morning, I had sort of aired out that irritability—the way you air out an old blanket. Once the dust is out, it's not such a bad blanket even if it is old. I don't much like that when I "hung it out," it made Harold feel bad, though. But I didn't light into him like Janiece would have. I'll bet when she's got a dusty old blanket bothering her, she enjoys setting fire to it and watching it burn.

It shouldn't have to come down to a situation where either I walk around feeling bad, smothered, or Harold does. To tell the truth, most of the time, even when he doesn't seem to be paying much attention to me one way or the other, he's never cranky. Tonight, after that airing out, he paid attention and even asked about my day. I don't like that I had to be cross with him to get the "better, improved" Harold to show up. Why can't people just keep being their best all the time? Silly question. Everybody has spells when they aren't at their best. I know I do.

I can truly say the only thing that bothered me about this evening was that it was over sooner than I hoped for. He went straight to bed and was out like a light. I need to think more about getting him to see the doctor.

She closed the notebook and stared at puzzle #172 for a long time. Midnight, and she wasn't sleepy. She looked at the walls of the trailer, her little cell. If she let herself, she could get irritated again. She stowed the notebook in her puzzle book and entered the bedroom, prepared to un-dress—top half, then bottom half.

CHAPTER 14

I Wonder

She woke in a better mood, ready to see Sister Mary Joseph. Harold had set out their cereal. He said, "Will this be enough breakfast for you or did you want some chocolate cake? I saw you looking at it last night at the 50 Yard Line."

"Caught me. No, I need to watch what I eat. I don't want to outgrow that dress you whistled at."

"In case you didn't know, it was you, not the dress, I was whistlin' at."

"Whatever it was that got your attention, I liked it." She seated herself across from him at the bar and winked at him, flirting over the Total. "What's on your schedule today?"

"O.D.'s taking me to some place he plays dominoes. Wouldn't tell me where it is. Said it's gonna be a surprise. I'll guarantee you Janiece's already approved it, or we wouldn't be going. What about you?"

"I'll be busy in the hospital. I told Daniel I'd see him and the kids again. I'll help while he sees Anna and the baby. I didn't tell you about the nun I talked to yesterday. She's going to come up and talk to them. She said Catholic Family Services could help with finding child care. I can't imagine how those young people can provide for six children on one wage. They've had all these expenses, and it makes me sad to see them without any family to help them—I told you that part, didn't I? I wish there was more that could be done."

"I bet you'll think of something." He cleared the counter.

She patted him on the arm and gathered her purse and puzzle book. "Be careful out there. Domino sharks are everywhere. See you this evening."

She couldn't think why she was in such a hurry to get to the hospital, except that was where she would find a way to make things better for the Martins. She wasn't certain what, but it was going to be more than babysitting. Although she did have a good time doing that.

She evaded the main lobby by entering through the emergency department waiting area. If anyone asked, she could say she was waiting to see Sister Mary Joseph. Which was true. The nun had agreed to meet her at two o'clock. Until then, she would observe or work a puzzle, and later she'd walk to the campus bookstore and get books for the children.

The people in charge of the makeover (hospital to hotel) hadn't missed an opportunity. Instead of calling the cafeteria what it was, this place where staff hid for a few minutes to consume a brief meal had been named "Choices." Staff and visitors scurried between refrigerated shelves and several short steam tables, making her think of roaches caught in the light. Signs indicated that the entrees were pizza by the slice, fried fish, baked pork chops, and roast beef. The meats looked a lot alike.

As she ate, Dorothy Faye thought about the Martins and about her own situation when she had two babies. Hers had been healthy, not ever hospitalized, and she'd only had two, not six. Even so, she'd worried she could never pay the bills on her wages from the café. And she'd had the advantage of having her mother's help with child care. As bad as she felt for Daniel and Anna, she ached for the children, for their prospects—never enough.

"Choices" did not encourage lingering over one's food. People exiting the lines stood holding their trays and eyeing tables that were fully occupied, silently urging those seated to move on to the cleanup conveyers. Dorothy Faye cleared out quickly.

———————

Sister Mary Joseph entered the chapel so quietly that Dorothy Faye didn't notice her until she saw her kneel and cross herself. "Hello, Mrs. Bell. Come, we can talk in my office."

Sister showed the way into a tiny room just behind the chapel. She pointed to one of the room's two chairs. "Please, be comfortable," she said. "Thank you so much for finding me yesterday. An opportunity to help a family in need gives me joy. I'm interested to know how you learned about the Martins. Apparently they hadn't mentioned to any of the staff that they had problems or I would have heard."

Dorothy Faye wished Sister would continue talking. Listening to her soft Spanish-accented words felt like holding a favorite pillow. "It seemed accidental, Sister, although I'm not sure I believe in accidents. I was in the third-floor lobby at the children's hospital, stopping to rest a minute before leaving. Daniel, Mr. Martin, had two youngsters plus a toddler, and all of them, including Daniel, seemed at a loss for what to do. It was obvious he could use some help. Before long he'd told me about the other two children at school, the baby who's hospitalized, their money trouble, the whole thing. Later, when his wife came out to see the kids, she explained about why they are without family. I felt so bad for them."

"Do you have a patient here in the hospital too?" The nun's face invited confidences.

"No, Sister, I was just visiting." Dorothy Faye took out the books she'd bought for the children. She hoped the nun wouldn't ask for details. "I believe I'll be able to keep all the children busy with these to give you time to talk with the Martins without interruptions."

Sister smiled. "Do you have grandchildren? You certainly seem to know a lot about what children need. I see you chose books for each age."

"No, neither of our children has any yet. I enjoy kids and I love reading. I think it's important for them to have books of their own." She stopped talking and made a neat stack of the five books. Her face was warm from embarrassment that she might have spoken as if she thought she were an authority on the subject of children. She bagged the books. After a deep breath, she said, "Sister, I have a question."

"Yes?"

"Is there a way that, if I bring you some money for the Martins, you could see that they get it? What I mean is, I don't want them to be embarrassed or think that I'm—someone's feeling sorry for them or—this is difficult to explain."

"Take your time."

"Well, a long time ago, I had a hard time—money was a problem. But I know that if someone had tried to give me money—someone I didn't know, I would have been too embarrassed to take it. Maybe that's false pride. But I wouldn't want them to feel like anyone pitied them. I'm not explaining this well."

"I think I understand. You'd want any gift you gave to be anonymous."

"Yes, definitely."

"The hospital has a foundation that can make individual grants to deserving people if they apply. Or Catholic Charities can provide food and other household needs," the nun said. "You could make an anonymous donation to either of those."

"But Sister, I want the money to go to the Martins. Isn't it true that money given to one of those places is meant to help lots of people and there's a process—not that there's a thing wrong with that—but I want to be able to get this only to them. I know they need it." She'd tied two knots in the handle of the plastic book bag as she tried to explain. Maybe Sister wasn't the right person to ask. She might be obligated to follow procedures.

"I think we can find a way. It's always possible to do good, even if we have to bend a few rules," Sister said. The dimple that showed when she smiled made Dorothy Faye think she probably enjoyed getting around rules now and then.

Danny spotted Dorothy Faye as the elevator opened. He started running toward her, then slowed when Sister Mary Joseph followed her. Daniel stood, holding Robbie. The other children sat very still, staring at the nun.

Dorothy Faye introduced Sister to Daniel and the children as a friend of hers. "Daniel, I hope you won't mind that I told Sister we need to find some help with child care so that you won't have to be off work. She works here. Since your family's Catholic, you probably know that nuns can get things done. I was concerned, so I asked her if she could help."

She couldn't see anything in Daniel's face but surprise. At least he didn't look upset. "Please tell me if you're upset that I asked for her help."

"No, I'm not. But I hadn't thought there would be anyone here at the hospital who could do anything about finding baby-sitters."

"Why don't you and Sister go somewhere quiet to talk?" She spoke louder, so that the children could hear. "I have surprises for these well-behaved children."

Like a five-part chorus, they all began talking at once, even Robbie. He came to her as she put her arms out for him. "Okay, you big boy, you walk and hold my hand. I have something here for you, and for Danny. and for Rebecca, and for—you must be Alicia—and for Joseph. First, let's everyone write your name in your very own book."

When Daniel and the nun returned a few minutes later, Daniel's shoulders were no longer drawn in; his head was up. He stood tall behind the tiny nun. Dorothy Faye felt lighter, just looking at him. She stood and took Sister Mary Joseph's hand. "I'll look for you tomorrow about the same time."

"I'll see you then." Sister Mary Joseph waved to the children as she left.

Dorothy Faye said, "Daniel, the kids and I have reading to do. You have at least thirty minutes off to visit with Anna and the baby. We'll be right here when you two come out."

Anna's weary face was not so pale and the puffy circles under her eyes were definitely less pronounced. "You look like you might have slept since I saw you."

"Yes, I finally slept because she's breathing better now. The doctor said they think they have a good idea about what's wrong with her immune system, but she'll have to stay a week longer, maybe two." Tears welled in her eyes. "Daniel told me…I don't know how to thank you." She hugged Dorothy Faye.

The four older children demonstrated their best manners—reading their books and sneaking frequent, concerned looks at their mother and Dorothy Faye. Only Robbie broke ranks and began tugging at Anna's pants leg. She sat among her children, a weary Madonna. "Let me see your new books. They are soooo nice! Did you say thank you?"

Nods all around. "See, Mama, here's my name. We're going to share, but it's mine to keep," said Joseph. Until now he'd been the quietest of them all, watching everything and saying little.

Dorothy Faye took Daniel aside as Anna sat with the kids to admire their new books.

"Do you know where Tech Terrace Park is?"

"Yes, ma'am."

"I could meet you over there tomorrow. The kids and I can play in the park for a long time—a couple of hours, anyway. That would give you more free time with Anna and the baby."

He hesitated. A wrinkle formed between his eyebrows.

"If you'd rather not, that's fine," she said. Maybe she'd been wrong. Maybe he was upset she'd interfered.

"No, it's a great idea. I was just thinking about getting the kids organized and over there."

"How about we plan for three o'clock? You'll have plenty of time. I'll bring an afternoon snack for the children. I need to say good-bye now, but I won't mention the park."

———◆———

Later, as she started toward the parking lot, a golf cart crossed from the front of the main hospital entrance toward the West Parking Garage. Dorothy Faye halted, turned quickly to face away from the street. She hoped the driver hadn't noticed her. He'd been busy avoiding traffic, but she had seen Alan's face clearly.

———— ◆ ————

Day 18 Monday, June 5 4:30 p.m. Consolidated Hospital, Lubbock

Wondering is different from <u>worrying</u>. For a while now I've been worrying. That means I didn't have any idea what to do about being irritable and feeling strange because I didn't know what could be causing me to be different. And I didn't (still don't) have much idea about what to do about how I felt. That's worrying, spinning around like a top, waiting to fall over when the momentum is gone.

Wondering is looking forward to seeing what's going to happen and thinking about the possibilities and how to deal with them. No spinning, just speculating.

I <u>wonder</u> what Harold's going to say when I tell him I want to give money to help the Martins. With so many children, buying food must cost several hundred a month. Plus there are other bills to pay. The amount I want to give sort of came to me without any calculating: two thousand. I'm going to trust my instincts. Combined with whatever Catholic Family Services can do about child care, it could give them a little breathing room. I wonder if we even have any extra money. I suppose I'll find out if we're without when I tell Harold.

The main reason I wonder about Harold's reaction is that I've never done anything like this before. The most money I ever spend is at Christmas. And then, it's never been two thousand at one time, even with all the turkeys we buy to give to the poor families in Whaley.

I wonder what they'll do with the money, what their priorities will be. That will be their choice. I wonder how Sister Mary Joseph can manage to make our gift anonymous. I hope it will be enough to make a difference. I know it's a good thing to do. I also know we should leave here as soon as it's done. I think that Alan, the security guard, saw me today. That worries me.

June 5 (continued) 9:15 p.m.

I don't have to wonder anymore. I said, "Harold, I need to know if we have any money left after buying this trailer and pickup." Just like that—a Janiece sort of question. He looked at me for a while and then he said, "Sure we do. We have plenty, like always." So I kept on talking. Harold listened and after I explained what I wanted to do, he said, "That's a real kind thing, to give them some money."

I wanted to cry, I was so happy. I didn't because I didn't want him worrying about me. It's hard to explain how being happy and proud of your husband can make you want to cry. Instead I said, "I'm so glad you agree." And then I cleaned up the supper scraps.

June 5 (continued again)10:30 p.m.

I'm writing again because this qualifies as odd. Me—I surprised myself today. First of all, instead of just listening and waiting for things to happen, there I was, hatching a plan. Second, once I had a plan, I took action. I talked to Sister; I explained to Harold. Something made him pay attention to me—no deafness. I shouldn't assume it was all me; could be there's more to Harold than I've given him credit for. Odd, anyway.

CHAPTER 15

Anonymous

She'd been sitting out here nearly an hour, since Harold parked and leveled the trailer. She pretended she could see New Mexico from this high spot near Post, Texas, as clouds began stacking up in the west. Half of the sun dipped behind the growing cumuli. Not much wind to speak of yet, but unless it emptied out over the plains, that front could bring a good shower in about three hours. From inside, the radio weatherman said that no severe weather warning had been issued. Then, probably to fill time, he had been explaining that these summer "rain events" usually carried from one-quarter to one-half inch of precip and occasionally a thunder and lightning display. He did slip in a caution about standing outside during lightning. As the weatherman's voice continued, Dorothy Faye studied the rapid changes in the clouds. The breeze picked up.

Harold called from inside, "Don't go gettin' struck, honey. The man on the radio said you should curl into a ball if you feel the hair on your neck stand up."

She wasn't worried. "I'll keep that in mind. Come sit with me and tell me about working on the oil rig during that storm, the one when lightning knocked the driller flat down on the derrick floor and you were watching from the doghouse. You can curl into a ball if you feel the hair on your neck stand up."

In a couple of minutes, he sat beside her on top of the picnic table. "That's a good story, isn't it, about that no-count driller. You know it didn't really happen to me. It was my daddy. He told me that story when I was a kid, more than once. I liked to picture him bein' brave, dragging the fella in and giving him artificial respiration. Now that I think about it, it might not even have been my daddy making the rescue. Could've just been a good story that everybody in the oil patch told when they wanted to make out they were heroes."

She stared at him as intently as she had studied the clouds. His smile was a little sad. "I'm not disappointed if it wasn't you. Did your daddy tell a lot of good stories?"

He laughed. "Oh yeah, he could tell some stories, all right. The more beer he had in him, the more he would tell. Mama and the girls always left the room as soon as he started—didn't matter what he was telling, whether it was what happened that day or one he remembered from some other oil field. They'd get up, like they were all put together in one piece, just stand up, roll their eyes, and leave the room. I can see him now. He'd sorta look surprised and then shrug and go on with his story. Sometimes he'd have brought in some roughneck for supper, someone who didn't have anyplace to go, or sometimes I'd be the only one there to listen. I'd stay right there till he ran out of beer and stories and went to sleep in the chair.

"Then Mama and the girls would come in, all together, and clean up. Just walkin' around him like he wasn't there. None of them said a word."

"Did that strike you as odd?"

"Not at the time. That was just the way things were when he was home. He was gone a lot, if a new field opened up. Truth is, I never did know him much except for those stories he told. He'd be there a while and then he'd come say to me he'd be gone for a while and I should take care of the women. Made me feel good, like I was in charge.

"Course, I wasn't. The girls and Mama ran things. Until the girls left. The three of them real close, talking about hairdos, movies, the girls' boyfriends. They didn't mistreat me, but I had the feeling they were a kind of club and I couldn't ever be a member. I figured that was what it meant to be a man. Supposed to be different.

"Then one day I came in for supper and they were all talkin', upset. 'He's left us, won't be coming back.' One of 'em, Janiece, I think, waved a letter at me, like I'd been the one that wrote it. The three of them were crying and cussing him and carrying on. I tried to get them to explain what had happened. 'As if you didn't know,' one of them said. To this day, I think they believe he'd told me he was leaving."

Dorothy Faye reached over and put her hand on his back. They stayed quiet for a while.

"I'm glad we decided to come on down here this evening," he said. "What do you suppose Mr. C.W. Post had in mind when he built that little town? Wonder if he expected it to be sitting on an oil field." He turned and looked down at Post, two miles east and about five hundred feet lower in elevation. The campground perched on the highest point above town, the edge of the Caprock.

"Some grand scheme, probably. But I'm glad it stayed small. It's a nice little place."

"I'm going in to finish the paper. You won't stay out here too long, will you?"

"Not if I see any lightning."

"It's what you don't see that'll get you. That's what I've heard." He chuckled and headed back inside. "I'm kinda tired. We had a busy day."

She looked at the mesquite trees down near town. Up on the Caprock, grasses, scrub oak, and juniper—not many mesquites—predominated as the natural vegetation. Observing this edge, the boundary between geologic regions, made her think of Harold's comment when he drove the big truck, often taking loads east—that he didn't feel like he could get a good breath until he got back up on the Cap, where he could see all the way down to the horizon in every direction.

***

She had heard him making coffee this morning when they were still at the hospital. "What time is it, Harold?"

"About six. You ready for coffee?"

Before she could answer, he was at the foot of the bed, a cup in his hand.

"Thanks. I haven't had coffee in bed in a while." She was pretty sure he had some sort of plan this morning that prompted the delivery.

"I've got a bunch of things I need to do. I'd better get moving. I need to go with O.D. first. He has a little work to do over on the lease. Said he should've done it yesterday, but he was winning, and it would have been bad manners to leave."

"Anybody at the senior citizens center threaten to shoot if he left the table?"

"No, but they're pretty serious about their dominoes over there."

"High stakes?"

"Nope, toothpicks and matchsticks. A matter of honor, I guess. Some of those guys play all day, every day. I know you have plans for the afternoon over at the park. Do you want to stay here after today?"

"Not really. In fact, I'd rather not." She hadn't mentioned seeing Alan. *Maybe Harold's becoming psychic these days.* "Do you have something in mind?"

"Well, yeah. O.D. told me an old boy, a driller we both knew a long time ago, died. His funeral's down at Post on Wednesday afternoon. We could move down there to that little park until we decide where we want to go next." He said he hoped there would be some oil field guys there about the age his daddy would have been.

"Is O.D. planning on going to the service?"

"He's not much on funerals. He might, though."

"I'll be finished with Daniel and the kids by around five o'clock. You could meet me at the park, and we could leave from there. The kids might get a kick out of seeing the trailer. And I know you'd like Daniel."

He nodded. She drank coffee and watched him gather his keys, pocket change, handkerchief, and reading glasses. As he packed up the final item, his billfold, she remembered. "About giving Sister Mary Joseph the money for the Martins. I don't know if we could get that much cash from the ATM on Sunday, but to be anonymous, cash would be better."

"I guess if you can't trust a nun with your money, you'd better not trust anyone. I have cash."

"That much?"

"And more."

She had to ask. "Why did you bring that much cash? That's quite a lot to be carrying around."

"I'm not carrying it. It's been right here in the freezer."

She stared at him, trying to think why he'd put money in the freezer. It could be that Janiece was right about him being stranger than usual, after all.

"Don't you remember last December when I was taking Y2K precautions?"

"I remember you bought a generator and a lot of dehydrated army surplus dinners."

"MREs."

"What?"

"That's what they call 'em—Meals Ready to Eat, MRE. Anyway, at the same time, I got ten thousand in cash, in case the banking computers went on the blink. Put it in a plastic bag in one of my dress boots, the left one, at the back of the closet."

"I don't recall you mentioning that."

"Probably forgot to, I was so busy layin' in supplies. After nothing happened, I've just been using it for spending money, as we needed it. Then when we cleared out over in Whaley, I moved it into the freezer in here since we aren't using it." He squatted and peered into the refrigerator.

"How much do you have?"

"There's fifty-nine hundred-dollar bills in this bag. Here's twenty. Would you like to have some more for walkin' around money?"

She took an extra hundred and decided she'd better take a good look later in all the cabinets and closets.

Day 19 Tuesday, June 6 9:30 p.m. Post

I could make a list, I suppose, to remind me of what happened today. It may help me clear things up. My mind is what needs clearing. At the same time that I felt good about parts of the day, I could hardly stand the sounds in my head. That seems like a symptom to me. I suppose I should be relieved there were no snapshots today. Instead, I heard a voice that sounded like mine or maybe my mother's commenting on everything that happened until we left Lubbock. Later, riding down here, I could still hear it asking questions, raising doubts. I wanted to keep my mouth shut tight so that voice wouldn't come out, or put my hands over my ears so I couldn't hear that woman criticizing me.

Here's the list and the things the voice said.

1. I met with Sister Mary Joseph. She looked like she could dance—smiling and having trouble sitting still. She even giggled, saying how it was breaking the rules, but that she'd decided she'd just give them the money without saying anything to anyone. She said she'd prayed about what to do. She finally chose not to mention it to anyone at the hospital. "After all, God knows," she said.

I handed her the money. She put it in a plain white envelope. She said she would give it to them tomorrow when they're together. She plans to keep in touch with them, said the Martins were a "special mission."

1a. The voice in my mind said, "Who are you to decide who needs charity? You should give that money to some agency, not to a nun you found in the hall."

2. Daniel met me at the park, right on time. All five kids piled out of their old car like pups that had been penned up for days. Every piece of play equipment got a workout—the slide, the swings, the seesaw. Daniel must have figured out how to do laundry—everyone had on clean clothes and socks that matched. Smiles appeared all around when I offered them oatmeal cookies after they finished the snack of fruit and cheese.

They weren't the only ones smiling. Harold said he noticed me having as much fun as the kids. When he drove up with the trailer, they all gathered around me and held my hands or my legs, depending on their height. I think they were a little afraid of him. But when I explained, they ran off to play some more. Harold said, "Looks like they'd take you home with them if they could. I'm glad you're having a good time."

Daniel told Harold he was a lucky man to have such a good person for a wife. That boy looked like he might cry when I told him Harold and I had to leave town and that I'd be keeping them in my thoughts. "You have no idea how you have helped me, all of us. We won't forget you," he said.

2a. A person who has an hallucination believes what he or she hears or sees is real. I know that voice was my own thoughts. It was no hallucination. But the voice seemed independent of me. I didn't want it there, but there it was, even when everything at the park worked out well. "You're taking yourself a little too seriously, aren't you? Maybe if you'd been a better mother, your own children wouldn't be afraid to get married and have kids."

Those words, those ideas didn't come all at once. They came in little snatches. I don't recall talking to Harold at all on the way down here; I was listening to that voice, even though I didn't want to. A couple of times when I looked in Harold's direction, I saw him watching me sort of solemnly. By the time we got to the campground, I felt like I'd been whittled on—little nicks taken out of me. Mother was able to make me feel that way when she thought I needed to be set straight.

3. When we got set up, Harold settled right away into his recliner.

3a. I don't know what I expected or wanted him to do, but him just sitting there irritated me. I took over where the voice had left off and told myself to go outside and keep my mouth shut. No sense spreading bad humor.

4. Harold knows me better than I realized. He left me alone a while and then came outside and suggested we call R.J. to tell him an early happy birthday.

4a. Nothing else could have been better to change my bad mood. R.J. sounded happy to hear from us. We both talked to him and before we hung up, he said he might come out on Saturday to see us, wherever we are.

After that I relaxed and watched the storm clouds.

More later.

P.S. Writing this didn't make anything clearer.

CHAPTER 16

Avoiding Disappointment

She couldn't locate the sound that had roused her. Definitely outside. Post, Texas. Harold must have left her asleep and gone to do something outside. She knew she'd better get dressed in case he was planning a change of location.

"Hi there, sleepy," he said when she opened the door. "Okay, we're set," he said, pointing to the air-conditioner on top. "You can put it on anytime you get hot."

She remembered the last thing on her mind before she went to sleep—his new shirts. They were still a puzzle. She'd thought of them as she made a mental list of things she would do today. Top item on the list was going through the cabinets to see if Harold had stowed any other surprises. She could ask, but...

"Good news," he said as he came in. "The other good news is that O.D.'s coming down to pick me up to go to the funeral. So you'll have the truck. You might want to go to Post and shop or something."

"When are you going?" She needed time to do a thorough search of the trailer.

"He'll get down early so we can go to lunch before the funeral at two."

The first place she checked was the tiny freezer compartment. The plastic bag of hundred dollar bills rested under the single, empty ice tray. Kitchen cabinets yielded no surprises. None of the soup cans rattled when she shook them. She'd seen an ad in a Lillian Vernon catalog for a soup can made to hide valuables in. She pulled the waxed paper liner and cereal out of its box. Nothing there. The light in the miniature oven shone on the walls of the never-used appliance. No surprises there either. A burglar must feel like this—jumpy, afraid she'll be caught in the act. For a minute Dorothy Faye thought of plausible explanations in case Harold decided to skip the funeral and spend the afternoon in his recliner—*change lost in the couch*—*pen missing, may have rolled under this chair.*

The toilet tank revealed only a float—no gun, drugs, or other contraband. The under-sink cabinet could be used to store shoes; no extra shampoo or cleanser filled the space. *Need to get some toilet paper.* So far, from her search she'd gained only a more intimate knowledge of the crannies in the trailer, the ones the brochure had labeled "storage."

After a brief rest in her chair and filling in L A R K, "a melodious songbird," in her current puzzle, she checked to be sure no one had arrived at the campground. Coast clear. She went back to the dictionary and looked for *larceny*; it came to her as she was searching the cabinets. It was too close for comfort—"the felonious taking and removing of another's personal property." She skipped down and found a new word, actually two words, just a few lines below. The words were *lares* and *penates*—"esteemed household possessions." She constructed a sentence to embed the new words in memory—"Bereft of lares and penates, the couple lived, with few possessions of any kind, in a metal box on wheels"—and laughed at her little joke. She doubted she'd have much opportunity to use those words in conversation anytime soon, unless Janiece brought up the question of the *real* purpose of their travel and housing. Continuing education completed for the moment, Dorothy Faye resumed her search.

The mattress and box springs rested on a platform (less vacuuming, as promised by the manufacturer and by Harold) that contained four drawers. On her knees, she confirmed that nothing new had been added among the towels, sheets, and foldable clothes she'd put in the drawers under her side of the bed before they left Whaley. Neither of the two compartments in the headboard hid anything suspicious—only another puzzle book, a novel by Robert Penn Warren, Harold's medicine bottles, his glucometer, and two sticks of sugarless gum. She stared at Harold's closet door. She had never searched through his things before. Why start now? She waited. No good answer came to mind. What did occur to her was that if she opened that door, she was guaranteed to be disappointed, either disappointed that she didn't find anything or disappointed in Harold. She never liked creating a reason to be disappointed.

Day 20 June 7 9:15 p.m. Post

There's no reason to ever be bored as long as I have that dictionary. Every time I look for a word, I see something besides what I started for. That's not particularly odd, but I'm writing it here because it's worth remembering. Finding and learning new words and their definitions can lead to ideas. An example is what occurred when I was browsing today.

The word I was originally searching for began with W A I N W. (I've begun using a new puzzle book, one that has many uncommon words.) The clue, "A builder or repairer of wagons," made me think that the end of the word would be W R I G H T. Means one who makes, constructs something. I started to put it in the puzzle but stopped because I'd never seen <u>wainwright</u>, except as a name. That made me question the W A I N part—I could have been wrong. I hate to look at the answers in the book. I learn more by checking the dictionary.

Wainwright fit. Below it a few words I saw <u>wait</u>. I suppose it attracted me because I was—waiting for Harold to come back from the funeral. There were both transitive and intransitive definitions. Wait (tr.)—"to remain or stay in expectation of" fit my activity. I always thought of waiting in that way—sitting around until someone or something else chose to act.

Then I read wait (intr.)—"to tarry until another catches up." Looking at wait that way describes part of how I've been for a while now. I'm somewhere different; others (Harold for instance) haven't caught up. The choice to act (tarry) becomes mine rather than someone else's. I don't enjoy either kind of waiting, but if I think of the choice as mine, it's far more tolerable.

Rereading that, I'm not sure I explained it as clearly as I felt the difference. Anyway, it seems worth remembering.

I called Elizabeth to tell her our new location. She didn't understand why we are still in the trailer, and said so. Then she said something like, "I've been thinking about you and Daddy. And I don't think I could ever love someone like you do him—enough to always do whatever he wants to, whether it makes sense to you or not."

I told her that she could be right; maybe that had always been true with us. Then she said, "Maybe that's what I'm waiting for, someone I could care that much about. But I want someone who will be concerned about what I want too, not just about their own plans. Is that expecting too much?"

All I could think to say was, "Maybe if you wait long enough, someone can catch up." I doubt if she understood. Maybe I should buy her a dictionary. After I hung up I wondered if waiting, transitive or intransitive, is just another way of taking the path of least resistance.

CHAPTER 17

What's a Fact Depends on Where You're Standing

Harold didn't have much to say about the funeral except that he had run into some old guys who knew his daddy. He explained that he was going to talk with all three of them and that it would probably take a couple of days. Although he didn't ask, Dorothy Faye didn't mind staying in Post. She had a book to read and plenty of puzzles.

She spent the next day reading and avoiding Harold's closet. The critical voice that had plagued her on the way to Post took a holiday. That afternoon, Harold came in around five. He usually came in with a smile and a story to tell. But he went directly to the bathroom, stayed for what seemed to her like a long time, then came out and told her he thought they ought to go eat. He was out the door as she got her purse.

"Dairy Queen all right with you?" he asked.

She knew it was the nearest source of food, which made her think he might be hypoglycemic. Although there had been things to eat at the trailer. Maybe it was something else. "Sure, that's fine with me." He seemed to be concentrating on driving.

Before Dorothy Faye could decide between a grilled chicken salad and tacos, Harold ordered his meal, a steak finger basket and iced tea. She ordered, paid, then joined him in the corner booth he'd chosen. He added three packets of sugar to his tea. She watched him, as she waited for the food and waited for him to say something. The food arrived first.

He ate two steak fingers, a slice of toast, and some gravy before pausing to wipe his mouth with his napkin. She inhaled deeply through her nose and began to eat her salad, determined to wait to hear whatever was on his mind. He finished all the French fries, the other two steak fingers, and the toast. The only leftover was the Styrofoam cup of gravy.

He wadded his napkin and pushed back his tray. "Well, that's better. I needed to eat in the worst way."

"I was worried about you. Do you feel better now?"

"I got so busy talking to George Speed that I forgot to eat lunch."

"Was a shaky spell all that was wrong? Was anything else making you feel bad?" She wasn't too sure he wasn't in pain; the vertical wrinkle between his eyes had deepened and his jaw muscles tightened.

"I'm fine now. My own fault for not eating. I need to pay better attention. One minute I'm fine, and the next I have to concentrate just to think and walk a straight line."

"You two must have found a lot to talk about. Did he know your daddy?"

"He did. They worked together in Iraan and in McCamey." He leaned back against the booth's thin cushion. Dorothy Faye felt her shoulder muscles loosen. Until then, she hadn't realized how tense watching him chew and swallow had made her.

"Course Speedy had lots of stories about lots of other people too. I think he got a big kick out of tellin' all those tales. He was moving slow when I got there. But he was smiling and kind of peppy when I left."

"Did he mention anything about a time he saved a no-count driller's life in a lightning storm?"

Harold laughed. "Nope, he didn't take credit for that one. He did tell me about how my daddy always helped out anyone who was down on his luck."

"That's a nice thing to hear, isn't it? Did he know anything else about him?"

"He recalled Daddy liked working midnights. Not many people did. He said the last he saw of him was about nineteen fifty-one up in Ochiltree County when a new field opened up. He'd helped someone haul pipe up there, and Daddy happened to be working the well he delivered to. I'm going to see those other two men tomorrow, one in the morning, the other in the afternoon. And I'll make sure to eat lunch."

"I was worried about you." She held his hand for a second.

As they left, he asked, "What did you do today? I wondered if you got bored sitting there with no television and no company."

"No, I was fine. I read and worked a few puzzles. Enjoyed it."

Back at the trailer, he took to his recliner to read *USA Today*. Soon he said, "Maybe I could use some cheese and a couple of crackers before I go to bed. And that's where I'm headed. I'm worn out from doing nothing much."

It may be more than his diabetes.

———◆———

The radio announcer reminded the listening audience that yesterday had been the anniversary of D-Day. Dorothy Faye sat down to her cereal. Harold was dressed and ready to go. *Amazing. He looks fine this morning, ate plenty of breakfast. His color is good.* "I'll be here when you get in this evening. Have a good time," she said as he went to the pickup.

Dorothy Faye read all morning. Some time after noon she made a tuna salad, sliced a tomato, and added a few saltines to the plate. She stopped her search for pepper when she heard a loud, low roar.

As soon as she saw them, she shut and locked the trailer door. It seemed puny, like a door on a dollhouse. She jerked the largest butcher knife from the silverware drawer. Too hard. The drawer landed upside down on the floor on top of the other nine pieces of flatware. *Why did I bring three place settings?* Her knife hand shook as she peeked through the window. Five motorcycles, two with an extra rider each, toured the small campground's circular road. Engine sounds echoed off the trailer's metal skin.

Dorothy Faye had never imagined that anything bad could happen to her in broad daylight in a campground just off a public highway. Now she imagined it. She dug in her purse with her left hand, searching for her cell phone. Not turning her back on the flimsy door, afraid she would miss something if she gave full attention to the purse, she dug for at least a minute before she finally found the phone. *Does 9-1-1 work from a cell phone?* She reminded herself to take a deep breath. In through her nose, out through her mouth. *Relax.*

She peeped out the window again. She opened the cell phone; it didn't light—*dead*. She'd left the charger in the console between the pickup seats. It had seemed a logical place to store it because the charger would plug into the cigarette lighter socket. The big man on the front cycle revved his engine even louder and roared back out onto the highway. The other four machines idled. Their drivers, in leather pants and jackets, used their legs to balance their machines upright. No one else seemed in a hurry to follow the leader. One of the extra riders, a slim female, swung off her perch, looking toward the trailer. She stood close to her driver, saying something. Dorothy Faye couldn't hear herself think, much less hear what the woman said. Maybe they had seen her cowering behind the doorway.

The clock showed 1:00 p.m. Dorothy Faye turned off the radio, hoping they would think no one was in the trailer. The air conditioner wasn't on. No lights. *Why are they just staying there running their motors?* She peeked out again. Big Hondas, not Harleys. That could be important if she needed to tell the police later. No helmets; pirate-style bandanas for headgear; straggly beards; long bleached hair on the woman. A scruffy-looking bunch. Three of the men were fat, as was the extra rider (beardless—male or female, Dorothy Faye couldn't be certain), who hadn't left the buddy seat. The fourth driver looked younger than the others. No guns showing; maybe they carried knives. *So do I. There could be guns in those saddlebags.*

She scanned the living area. No place to hide. She crouched and inched into the bedroom. No hiding place there. The trailer brochure had failed to mention that the "storage areas" were insufficient for closeting oneself in case of home invasion, no small print mentioning a panic room. Her pulse accelerated. *Settle down! Surprise is on my side. They don't know I have a knife.*

Another engine added volume to the throttling sounds outside the trailer. Back in the living area, she watched from aside the window as the leader rejoined the group, skidding and spraying gravel as he came to a stop. He reached to flip down the machine's kickstand with his right leg.

In a sequence that seemed to happen in slow motion, his motorcycle tipped to the right, then fell completely over on its side. The rider remained perfectly upright on the seat all the way to the ground, his hands tight on the handlebars. All engine sounds ceased, replaced by loud laughter from the members of his gang. The man on the ground, under the bike, yelled, "Okay, you assholes! It's a new bike and I'm not used to it yet. I'd have been fine if you hadn't sent me after Dr Peppers for your picnic."

What kind of outlaw gang drinks Dr Peppers? Dorothy Faye slowly opened the door. "Are you hurt?" she asked.

The big Honda was unharmed. The lead biker suffered the only injury, that to his pride. His embarrassed grin made his face pleasant, nonthreatening. He introduced himself. "I'm Bill Barnes, a Realtor from Lubbock. Guess I'll be riding last in line after this." He took off his gloves and offered his hand. It seemed clean. She shook it and introduced herself.

"I was making myself a little lunch." She intended that as a sort of explanation for the knife in her left hand. They invited her to their picnic. She brought her tuna salad and sat at one of the concrete tables, next to the bleached blonde, who, it turned out, was the receptionist for the Realtor. Everyone in the group worked in the same office.

"Yep, we've been planning this for quite a while. We closed the office for the rest of the week. It's easier than arranging vacation schedules and working short-staffed. We're heading south as far as we can go before we have to turn around and come back. Just seeing the sights. Until just a few minutes ago, that seemed like a good idea," the thin man said. He had introduced himself as Mike Reeves, the owner of the company. "Are you on vacation too?"

She said, "Yes, my husband and I are sort of doing the same thing you are—just traveling with no particular destination. He'd like to meet you, I'm sure. He'll be back from shopping pretty soon." Up close, they weren't as dirty as she'd thought. But she felt better knowing the knife lay on her lap, just in case. She'd added that mention of Harold for insurance.

"Where do you folks live—what town, I mean?" Mike asked.

"We lived over in Whaley for several years and we've decided to move. We may choose Lubbock." As soon as she'd said it, she wondered where the idea came from.

"If you do and you need any help with finding a place, we'd love to help you," said Mike. He handed her his business card. "If you call this number, one of us will be there. You might not recognize any of us in our 'civilian' clothes, and after a shave. This whole costume is part of the fun of riding the bikes. Lookin' a little rough. Women can't resist a rugged man."

"Yeah," Marcy said. "That, and we're married to the guys we ride with."

Bill, former front rider of the gang, cleaned up their trash. The others continued to rib him about his crash. "I'm never gonna hear the end of this. Mike, you're the boss. Can't you do something, you know, give an executive order?"

"Nope, I'm on vacation," Mike said. "You're the leader; you give the order. Let me help you get your machine started. I'll hold it up for you." He could hardly talk for laughing.

———————◆———————

Day 22 June 9 3:30 p.m. Post

It's funny now, but for a few minutes, I was scared. Five motorcycles with seven riders occupied my quiet little park this afternoon. I prepared to defend myself with a butcher knife. I can't recall the last time I was afraid. It could be good for me—make me more vigilant. I doubt it, though. I'm not going to spend my time being afraid. This trip's supposed to be an adventure. So now I've had my first solo adventure. I never would have guessed I had it in me.

It's a good thing they were a gang of real estate agents, not a bunch of toughs. Now I know I need to keep the cell phone charged and to get the number of the local police wherever we stay, unless it's in some nice, quiet, hospital parking lot.

Harold will get a kick out of this. And I know Mrs. Ottley would be tickled by the story. I miss talking to her. She's actually the only person I talk to much, besides Harold. It's different talking with her. She's taught me a lot.

I need to tell her that. That she's been my friend and I miss our times together. Someday she'll be gone and I want her to know before she goes.

More later

P.S. A good thing—no voices picking on me today.

She began puzzle #156. A knock on the door startled her. She'd heard a vehicle drive up, but thought it was Harold and had continued working on clue 48 Down. She reached for the butcher knife.

"Ma'am, I heard there was a pretty lady all alone in a trailer up here on the hill. I came to invite her out. Are you lonely?"

"No, sir, I'm not. Thanks for asking. But you can come in if you are. Lonely, I mean."

Harold stepped inside, grinning the reckless grin that meant he was having a good time. She put the knife away.

"It's true what they said. You are a pretty lady. You say you aren't lonely. But are you alone?"

"Not anymore."

"Well then, let me take you downtown. We'll take a walk on Main Street and find someplace to eat."

"I'll be ready in a second. By the way, what's your name? I should leave a note for my husband." She took his arm as they walked to the pickup. "I'm glad you're feeling good this evening."

"There's nothing like a good lunch to keep up a man's spirits."

Harold entertained her with a commentary during their walking tour of downtown Post. "You could get work with the chamber of commerce," she said. "Is any of that historical information true?"

"It's as true as most historical information, I reckon. Did you like the part about Mr. C.W. Post spending all that money rigging up the cannons along the edge of the Caprock to shoot into the clouds and make it rain?"

"I did. Did you make that up?"

"Not that one. It's supposed to be fact. Course we both know that what's fact all depends on where you're standing. I like the one where the cowboy rode his horse up the stairs at the Algerita Hotel, saying, 'My horse is my best friend. He sleeps where I sleep.'"

By the time they were back at the trailer, he still had not asked about her day. She had enjoyed seeing him have a good time and his being in such good spirits so much that she hadn't interrupted.

He was still talking. "I didn't tell you. That second man I talked to today told me about two other men who probably knew my dad. They live in a nursing home in Crane. If we leave here tomorrow, we could go to Odessa and park at the hospital. It's an easy drive down to Crane. You could visit at the hospital while I go down there," he said. He seemed to have it planned already, as usual. Until this minute, she'd not had a hint of her aggravation. But as she waited to see if he would ask her opinion, she felt it like a presence, the woman in a low-cut red dress who threatened to utter aloud the thoughts in Dorothy Faye's mind.

Harold's face was hidden behind the newspaper. She tightened her lips and searched for a thought that didn't involve the words "tired of you managing me." Without moving the news, he said, "We could either go from here to Big Spring and then get on Interstate Twenty down to Midland and across to Odessa, or we could go the country route and avoid the interstate by going west from here over to Tahoka. From there, it'd be Brownfield, Seagraves, Seminole, Andrews, and then Odessa. I think it might be better to avoid I-Twenty while we're pulling this trailer. Don't you?"

"Yes." *Simple question, simple answer.* A huge temptation urged her to wring out the dishrag and wipe the already spotless cabinet top. She made herself sit still. "Harold, there's something I'd like to do before we leave here." She was relieved that the words that came from her mouth were hers.

He lowered the paper just far enough to look over at her. "There is? What is it?" He sounded surprised.

"I want to go to Whaley to visit Mrs. Ottley. She'd be happy to see me, and she'd be especially happy to hear all about what happened to me today."

"She would? What happened? Would I be happy to hear it?"

"I don't know. You didn't ask about the day, so I haven't had an opportunity to tell you."

He didn't miss a beat. He said immediately, "Dorothy Faye, honey, I wish you'd tell me about your day. I know I'd enjoy hearing about it." He had that grin on again—teasing her. But he put the newspaper down. She relaxed a little. He'd gotten the point.

"I will. But first, let's decide about going to Whaley."

"It'll be fine with me. How long did you want to stay?"

"Long enough for me to take her out to lunch. We could leave there by two at the latest."

He nodded. "Now, tell me what happened today."

She told about the visit of the biker gang, elaborating on her brief, invigorating spell of fear and how she had planned to defend herself with the butcher knife. They laughed together about the slow motion rollover. Afterward Harold asked, "Were you really afraid?"

"Only for a few minutes."

"I shouldn't have left you out here by yourself in this trailer without any way to get help. I'm sorry. Talk about a no-count husband. I wouldn't ever have forgiven myself if something had happened to you."

"That could just as easily have happened right in the middle of town, with me in a house. I'm a grown woman and should have sense enough to take care of myself. Besides, why should you have all the adventures? The only reason I wanted to tell you at all was because now, looking back at it, it's funny. Don't you think so?"

"It is kinda funny, especially you in here looking for a place to hide, carrying a butcher knife in one hand and a dead cell phone in the other," he said. "Mrs. Ottley would get a kick out of that whole story. But still..."

"You quit worrying. I'm going on to bed. Thanks for the tour and the supper." He stayed in his chair. When she woke around midnight, she reached to his side of the bed. It was empty. She sat up and looked into the living area. He hadn't moved from his recliner.

CHAPTER 18

Necessary, But Not Necessarily Pretty

"Looks like a couple of good spaces here. We'll use this one," Harold said. In short order, he had the trailer backed into a space at Ector County Hospital, straight as could be. He popped out the stabilizer jacks, disconnected the trailer from the fifth-wheel apparatus, plugged in the electricity, and parked the pickup across the lot. Very efficient. All she had to do was watch.

She studied his movements, looking for signs suggesting a source of pain. The crease between his eyes had reappeared today. When he stood after squatting to connect the electricity, he moved slowly. She thought he might be favoring his lower back a little bit. That was odd. Since the course of physical therapy after the accident years ago, and retiring from driving the long hours in the big truck, his back hadn't caused him any trouble. But he moved like he was tired and as if he had pain or some deep ache. And it was only two o'clock.

He came inside, washed his hands, and then sat in his recliner. "In a few minutes I'm going to call one of those men in Crane and see if he's willing to have company tomorrow. I should be able to talk to both of them since they're in the same nursing home."

"Do you know if they're well enough to give you any information?"

"Not really. Rusty Burns up in Post said he talked to one of them, Elmer Goins, last month, and he was doin' fine, happy to talk. The way I see it, if they can't tell me anything, they'll probably appreciate a visit anyway. Seems to me that folks in nursing homes could get pretty lonely."

"I think you're right about that. I hope I never end up in one."

"You won't if I have anything to say about it. I'll take care of you as long as I'm able."

"One of my great-grandparents lived to be more than a hundred. You'd need to live to be at least one hundred five to take care of me. That's what you get for marrying a younger woman, Harold."

He raised his eyebrows, appeared to consider the prospect of living past one hundred. He scratched his neck and rubbed the whiskers emerging on his jaw. "I wish somebody had warned me. Guess you're right. I suppose it's no more French fries for me." He chuckled at his own joke. "Seriously, do you know anything about what people in your family have died of?"

Now he wants to talk. She put aside her irritation, thinking he might be ready to tell her what these visits were really about. She folded the dishrag carefully, then replaced it over the faucet, where it hung like a small flag at half staff. "Well, I know my parents were both healthy before they died in the accidents. And Mother's grandmother was the one who lived to be one hundred and two. I don't know anything about the others. They died before I remember. What about your grandparents?"

"I don't know anything about anyone, really, except for my mother. Maybe I'll hear something about my father from some of these fellows I talk to." He stared out the door. "Look over there. That trailer's hardly big enough for one person; it's a Scamp. I haven't seen one of them in years."

Don't think I didn't notice that change of subject. She waited to see if he had more to say. He began reading the paper.

"I'm going to see what the hospital looks like. I might as well get in some visiting right now so you won't have to start telling lies if the security man stops by."

She walked slowly toward the hospital entrance. *He's worried about himself. That's what this is about—the hospital, these old men, and wanting to know about his father. Maybe if I put my hands around his neck and shook him, he'd say what's on his mind. Maybe I'd feel better whether he talked or not.*

Nothing about the hospital's exterior suggested it was anything other than a county hospital, one that had been enlarged and remodeled more than once. Mismatched brick colors and uneven facades with a couple of doorways that had been converted to windows suggested that function was more important than form. They probably had patients here, not guests. The hospital's utilitarian appearance echoed the city's lack of pretense. Odessa did not apologize for being a town built to serve the oil field. Pipe and supply companies, heavy equipment dealers, and liquor stores lined the highway they'd come in on from Andrews. Downtown's highest building was only five or six stories tall. The town's appearance said necessary, not necessarily beautiful.

The information desk in the near-empty lobby employed one smiling volunteer. A large map near the elevator showed the location of the patient units and support departments. Dorothy Faye saw that the cafeteria occupied half of the basement. She took the elevator down, interested in comparing its approach to dining with the milling crowd scene at Consolidated in Lubbock.

She bought a soft drink, for cover, like a policewoman on a stakeout. Choosing a small table away from the serving area, she took out her puzzle book. It fell open to the spot that hid her little notebook. Staring at the "book of odd things," she considered writing something about this morning and about what she'd just realized—something's wrong with Harold and he's worried. Instead, she resolved to think more before writing. She also considered burning the little book. A No Smoking sign posted nearby advised her to avoid starting even a small fire. She smirked at the sign. *Maybe later.*

Pen in hand (cover in place), she eavesdropped on the woman sitting at the table a few feet away, talking on her cell phone. Apparently the connection wasn't good or the other party was hard of hearing. She spoke loudly enough for Dorothy Faye to hear every word.

"There she was, all propped up in bed, enjoying all the attention. At least that's what I thought. For a minute, when the kids came in to see her, she nearly smiled. I thought maybe being so sick had made her think about being nicer to people. The doctor said she nearly died from the pneumonia." The woman nodded, listening a few seconds. "She even thanked the preacher for coming and you know how bad she talks about him. She hasn't had so much company in forever, mainly because she's always so cranky, no one wants to stay around her."

Again she waited, then said, "I thought about that, but she's never been easy to be around. When I was a kid, no one wanted to come play at my house because she was so strict, or just plain mean. Yeah, I should go too. Sorry I was so pitiful. Bye."

She looked over at Dorothy Faye, then looked at the phone in her hand as if she'd been caught shoplifting. "I guess I was talking a little loud. Sorry if I disturbed you."

"You didn't." Dorothy Faye introduced herself, said she was from a small town near Lubbock. "You sounded like you were a bit upset."

"I'm Carolee. You're right, I was. Guess I still am, a little. I didn't tell my sister-in-law all that happened."

"I could listen if you'd like to talk a little more. I never pass along anything I'm told," Dorothy Faye said.

Carolee hesitated. "I'd hate to take up your time. It's not the first time my mother's upset me. Probably won't be the last," she said.

Dorothy Faye nodded. "My experience is that telling another person what's on your mind makes almost anything easier to tolerate." *Look who's talking, the woman who never opens her mouth.*

Carolee sat without saying anything for several seconds, then moved to Dorothy Faye's table. "I just keep hoping that someday she'll like me. I'm her only daughter, and I do my best to take good care of her. But nothing's ever right. My grades weren't good enough; my posture was bad; my boyfriends were thugs. She surprised me when she approved of Tommy, my husband. He's always ignored her crabbiness, been nice to her. He's so good-hearted, he tries to overlook how she treats me. I think he's extra nice to me to try to make up for how she talks to me. I won't be able to tell him about today." Carolee ran a hand through her hair, then stared at the floor, one hand covering her mouth.

After a long silence, Dorothy Faye said, "It's hard to tell other people about the things that hurt our feelings."

Carolee sat up straight and picked at a sticky spot on the table. She spoke without looking up. "It is. I feel like a whiner. The truth is, she didn't say anything awful. It was how I took it." She shook her head and spoke, not looking at Dorothy Faye. She studied the spoon she'd left on the table. "I don't know what's wrong with me. I tried so hard, but I couldn't get her to go to the doctor before she got so sick. She could have died right there at the house." She looked up and wiped away a tear that reached the corner of her lip.

"I doubt if you could have made her go until she was ready to admit to herself she was sick. Do you think she was afraid?"

"Maybe. But she's also stubborn. She wouldn't budge, swore she'd check herself out if we took her to the hospital. Wouldn't even see the doctor until she started coughing up blood." Carolee fidgeted with her nearly empty ice-cream container, scraping out the last bite with the plastic spoon. "I shouldn't have eaten that. I've gained weight in the past two weeks. I've been here all day every day and eaten nothing but junk, mostly sweet junk."

"I know what you mean. Stress makes me crave sweets and salty things."

"That's exactly what's happened to me. She's been sick with lung disease for a long time. She could die any time; she's eighty-five. I mean, it's not as if her getting pneumonia and being critically ill should be any surprise."

"She's been sick a lot?"

Carolee nodded. "She was fine living alone until about two years ago. That's when she got sick the first time, and that's when I convinced her to move in with me and Tommy. From the minute we got her to our house, she's complained about her bedroom—too small, never warm enough, the closet crowds her clothes. And the food never suits her because I don't cook like she did." She wadded the ice-cream cup into a sticky lump. "This is the first time she's been sick since the spell that caused her to agree to move in. When she got sick, she seemed to expect us to make it all better, to do something."

"Have you had any help taking care of her?"

"No, but my brothers and their wives help us with money for her and they come stay if we need to go somewhere."

"So your family doesn't blame you for this illness."

"No, but I blame myself. Now that she's getting better, I shouldn't be getting in such a state. But I was trying so hard and she got sick anyway."

Dorothy Faye watched as Carolee's eyes searched the room.

"And when she said—what she said a while ago, I just fell apart and stomped out like a teenager. I should go back up there."

"Is she expecting you to come back right away?"

"I doubt she's concerned now. A couple of cousins of hers are there. She won't miss me as long as someone's there."

"Do you think that if we take a walk, you might feel better?"

"It couldn't hurt. We won't get too hot if we go to the park over there a couple of blocks." She stood, then hesitated. "I hate to impose. Do you have anything you need to do right now?"

"No, not for a while."

As they walked, they kept to the shady spots cast by the buildings. Even though the temperature had risen above ninety degrees, the shade and lack of humidity made their stroll pleasant. Neither spoke until they arrived at the park.

"Being out of that hospital helps. I was being childish to get upset."

"Childish?"

"Reacting like a teenager when she criticized my hair. It's easy for me to forget I'm fifty-two years old when she talks to me like I'm sixteen."

"What did she say?"

"Well, you'd have to understand how it started. A few weeks back, I thought a new hairdo and color would sort of perk me up. I'd been wearing it shoulder length forever, and it was making me look like an old woman trying to be young. So I spent a lot of time looking at hairdo books every time I went to the beauty shop. I finally decided on a picture showing a woman about thirty with a cute short haircut and a real pretty face. I said to my beauty operator, 'I want you to make me look like that.' She said, 'Which part? I only do hair.' We always kid each other like that. As soon as I got home that day, I could tell Mother didn't like it. She just looked at me and didn't say a word. Tommy likes it, though, so I decided I'd keep it this way."

"It looks good on you."

"Thanks. Anyway, today with all those people in the room, Mother looked right at me when I came in. First thing she said was, 'When is your hair going to grow out? It looks like the rats sucked it.' She might as well have slapped me." Carolee stopped. She closed her eyes as if she were replaying the scene in her mind. "I said the first thing that came to mind. I said, 'Get used to it, Mother. I like it and I'm not going to change it.' I probably mouthed off like that because I felt like crying."

"Because of what she said or how you reacted?"

"Both, plus there were other people there. I realize now I could have laughed, like she was kidding. At least I wouldn't have felt bad about what I said. I don't expect her to quit saying hateful things. At her age I doubt she'll change. Unless maybe she gets scared of dying again."

Dorothy Faye laughed at that final comment. Carolee looked blank for a second. Then she laughed and said, "That's right. It's all kind of funny, now that I think of it."

Neither of them spoke again until they reached the hospital's front door.

"Thanks for getting me out of here and listening to me."

"You're welcome. I needed a walk myself. I have to meet my husband now. If I don't see you again, I hope things go well for you and for your mother."

"So do I. I plan to do my best to act like a grown-up, whatever happens. Thanks again."

After they ate soup for supper, Harold told her he planned to leave early in the morning to get to Crane. He went to bed before nine, saying that he wanted to get up and get ready in plenty of time. Dorothy Faye wondered what he meant by that—plenty of time—but didn't ask. He'd tell her if he wanted to, or he wouldn't. She thought about asking if he had any pain or another general question about how he felt. But she felt certain he'd deny any problem.

She didn't like going to bed before the sun set. She'd toss around a lot, trying to sleep, and probably disturb Harold in the process. Although, he seemed to be able to sleep any time he put himself to bed. She looked in on him. The wrinkle between his eyes had smoothed out. He looked peaceful. In fact, he looked sweet as a little boy.

Day 23 Saturday, June 10 8:45 p.m. Ector County
Hospital, Odessa

Being reasonable has its drawbacks. I've never
worked very hard at being unreasonable, or even a little
less than reasonable. It always seemed like it would be
a waste of energy. Taking a contrary point of view or
insisting on doing things my way with my mother,
for example, always turned out to be a losing proposi-
tion. It ended up feeling like I might have won a hand
in a poker game only to find out that she owned the
table and all of the stakes ended up in her pocket eventually. Why waste the effort? That's what I learned to
tell myself.

Apparently not everyone sees it that way. Take
Janiece, for example. Or Elizabeth. They both probably
think they are being reasonable and everyone who disagrees is just not smart enough or is too stubborn to see
that their way is best—whatever the subject. Elizabeth
approaches it all with a smile and persists until she gets
her way. Janiece throws fits.

Eventually the result is the same. Things go their
way. Which brings me to the point of all of this—
Harold. I don't even know if Harold expects everyone to
agree with whatever he wants to do or if it's only with
me. No, he doesn't throw fits like Janiece. He's basically

good-natured. His approach is different from either Elizabeth's or Janiece's. He either forgets (conveniently) that I might have a preference or he doesn't hear (also conveniently).

Here's the current example. When we went to bed last night, he had agreed to take me to see Mrs. Ottley today. We'd even talked about what time we'd leave Whaley in order to get to Odessa. This morning he gets busy unplugging and hooking up while I straighten up inside. Off we go. And we head straight to Odessa. "We're not going to Whaley?" I asked.

"I thought we'd stop there on the way back. It'll be better to get on to Odessa, in case we can't park at the hospital and have to look around for another place."

What did I do? I was reasonable. I saved my breath to blow my soup, as they say. I told myself I didn't want to waste the effort of saying anything more, trying to get him to turn around. I behaved reasonably, telling myself that Mrs. Ottley wasn't expecting us, so she couldn't be disappointed. Nothing I wanted to do or to say to her won't keep until later. Besides that, Harold's definitely on a mission that he's not ready yet to explain. I'm sure it has to do with illness. What kind, I don't know. I'll give him a little more time. But not much.

What is odd is that unlike my usual reaction, I'm as irritated (maybe more) with myself as I was with him. All the way down here I've been thinking (yes, the voice in my head) about (1) doing things Harold's way is not anything new. Nor is his not hearing or forgetting if we have agreed to a plan I suggest; and (2) since that's true, why am I getting upset?

I asked myself (that voice) do I want to not be timid, to not be reasonable, all the time, to not be that good wife I've always been? Then I ask, who says that's how a good wife acts? O.D. seems to think Janiece's just fine. Maybe I've been wrong all these years. Probably I'm irritable because I don't have anything to keep me busy. I can only wipe that counter so many times. Maybe I should dust! That also would be odd. I hate to dust.

Speaking of that voice, I think that even if Carolee's mother dies, she'll still be with her, just like mine is with me. Those critical voices find a permanent home. Selective deafness is the answer. I'll ask Harold how he turns it off and on. I just looked in on him and he looks so sweet, I can't understand how I could be upset with him. And the fact is, I'm not as upset with him as I'm bewildered by me. More later—unless I burn this book.

Nineteen Fifty-Eight Was a Long Time Ago

An odor of urine mingled with something meant to disguise it, faintly cherry scented, made Harold cough as he entered the nursing home. He recognized the smell as the same one that nauseated him at the nursing home where his mother had stayed years ago. He stopped, took a long breath, and thought about going back outside. It wasn't as bad as the smell surrounding him all day long every day when he drove a cattle truck; he'd get used to it in a few minutes. A woman in a pink scrub suit startled him. She said in a loud voice, "Can I help you find someone?" She didn't rise from her seat behind the large circular counter in the center of the building.

Harold got closer so he wouldn't have to shout his answer. "Yes, I came to see Elmer Goins and Bill Snider. They're expecting me. I'm Harold Bell."

She pointed to the nearest hall on the right, one of four that led, like spokes, from where she sat at the center desk. "They're in room one ten." Same loud voice. It must come with the job. With that, she went back to whatever she was doing when he walked in, giving it her full attention.

"Thank you, ma'am." He started toward the hall, then returned to the desk. "If they're allowed to go out, I'd like to take them to lunch after while, if that's okay."

That got her attention. She didn't get up, but she closed her magazine and looked at him a long time before answering. "Are you family?"

"No, ma'am, just a friend." He didn't try to explain he'd never seen them before, but that he was pretty sure they'd be pleased to get out for a while.

"They're both able to go out if they want to, but we'll need your identification. You have to sign out and sign them back in."

"If they decide to go, we'll come by here and do all that before we leave." He added, "If that's okay."

She nodded once, saving her energy, he guessed, and returned to her magazine. A large glass cage of small live wrens and lovebirds hung on the wall on the opposite side of the lobby. He wondered if they were too old to fly.

Television news, volume loud, reached him as he passed room 108. He had half-expected to hear distress cries as he passed the closed doors along the hall. But the broadcast coming from 108 was the first sound he'd heard. The rooms could be empty, or all the occupants might be asleep or unconscious or just waiting. The worst would be waiting—skeletal women and men in uncomfortable beds, eyes staring at nothing, lying on urine-absorbing pads, waiting for anything to interrupt the string of empty days. Being unconscious would be merciful. He'd do almost anything not to end up anyplace like this.

He knocked on the door to room 110. Quiet conversation in two different voices preceded a loud reply. "Come on in, whoever you are."

"Hi, I'm Harold Bell. Sonny Bell was my father. Are you Elmer and Bill?"

"What's left of 'em. I'm Bill. Come on in."

He didn't look like a man who belonged in a nursing home. Standing erect, he offered a hearty handshake. With his clean shave and creased

Wranglers, he seemed ready for the coffee shop. Then Harold saw that Bill was looking past him and off to the left a little. The unblinking right eye was glass. The iris in the other was clouded milky white. Bill did a good job of pretending he could see. But his lack of vision was evident when he waved his left hand toward the television set and said, "That's Elmer, my roommate." Elmer sat in a recliner on the side of the room opposite the television, wearing a sad smile and shaking his head as he watched Bill's effort to be hospitable.

Elmer said, "Hi, Harold, you'll pardon me if I don't get up. Haven't got my artificial leg strapped on yet." He lifted the short stump that had been his right leg to punctuate his statement. "Come on in and let's visit."

Harold steered Bill toward the other recliner, leading him by gently touching his elbow. Harold had the choice of an uncomfortable-looking straight-backed chair or either of the twin beds. He perched on the chair. "Y'all have family in town here?" he asked.

They spent a fair amount of time giving him the complete rundown. Both without family, they had become roommates here after their physical condition made living alone difficult. Bill said, "I got in touch with Elmer just before he decided to move in here. We thought it might be tolerable if we was roommates. Some days, the only thing that is tolerable is my roommate. This place can sure wear out a person's good humor."

Elmer looked up from adjusting his prosthesis. "I wouldn't have moved in this place, but I started having trouble keeping things up properly. So here we are." He'd gotten his leg on and now stood, taller than Harold had expected. "Bill, Harold here is interested in hearing about his dad, Sonny Bell. Do you recall workin' with him?"

Bill had Harold located now. He faced him directly and said, "I sure do remember old Sonny. We worked together in McCamey and then over at Iraan for sure, and I think maybe a couple of other places. He'd work a few months and then he'd quit and head back to where your mama and you kids lived. Where was that?"

"Levelland."

"Yeah, Levelland. I guess he worked some of those little fields up there, those times."

Harold nodded. Bill couldn't see him. He stopped nodding and said, "Yeah, sometimes he'd pick up some midnights. Other times he'd rest a while and then be gone again."

"That's the way it was with a lot of oil field guys. Specially if they had a family. I been tryin' to recall some things about him. One thing I remembered right away is that he'd always be the one that the tool pushers and the drillers would count on to teach the new guys what to do. See, Sonny was real smart and real patient. You ever do any oil field work?"

"No, sir, drove tank trucks a while. Then later I got on doing long haul and kept at it. You know, the oil field always looked like awful hard work to me."

Elmer had been pacing over by the window, getting his leg limbered up, Harold guessed. Elmer spoke up, "You're right about that. Hardest work I ever did was roughneckin', working midnights on them old rigs. Later on, I moved up to being a tool pusher and it got a little easier. Hardest part of that was bein' blamed for anything that went wrong."

Bill laughed. "Yeah, you got your share of blame. You remember that well over by Big Lake when we got to about four thousand feet and lost the bit down the hole? Couldn't fish it out for shit—took about six days. To hear that promoter tell it, the entire thing was your fault."

They traded stories for nearly an hour. Harold's tolerance for the straight-backed chair ran out at about thirty minutes into their recitation. Finally he said, "Say, what do y'all think about getting out of here?"

"Think about it every day—got no place to go," Elmer said with a grin.

"I was talking about lunch, maybe at that place I saw on the way over here—the Dairy Fluff," Harold said.

"Sure," Bill said. "Ready when you are."

"Aw, I hate to miss—let's see, it's Friday, that means we'll miss meatloaf and peas and tapioca. I don't know," Elmer said. "Maybe we ought to stay here."

"Well, I hadn't thought about the tapioca. You may be right," Bill said.

It took a minute before Harold joined their laughter.

They were on their third cup of coffee since finishing lunch. All three had eaten chicken-fried steak from the buffet. Elmer had gone back for seconds on the scalloped potatoes but had passed entirely on the salad. He said he only liked iceberg lettuce, not that stuff that looked like spring weeds. Harold saw Bill put an extra roll in his shirt pocket.

The conversation never lagged. They entertained him, and each other, with tales about wells blowing out, drillers who had been drunk on duty, and recollections of injuries sustained by men on the rigs. Harold thought about asking about the no-count driller struck by lightning. Instead, he asked the main question still on his mind.

"Did either of you know anything about how my daddy died? All I ever heard was that it was up in Wyoming about nineteen fifty-three. He'd have been about forty-one or two by then."

Elmer looked at Bill. Bill stared straight ahead. Neither answered for a while. Harold stirred his coffee and watched a waitress scoop her tip off the table next to theirs.

Bill cleared his throat. "Maybe I'm thinking about a different old boy. I could be wrong, but I seem to recall working on a job with him back in nineteen fifty-eight up at Kamay. They were water-flooding some of those old leases that were playing out."

"Nineteen fifty-eight?"

"I could be wrong. Could've been someone else."

"I believe you're right, Bill," Elmer said. "Remember, I saw you both there, lots of times. I was working at Holliday. We went over to Vernon that year to the rodeo."

Harold exhaled loudly. After a minute or two he said, "Doesn't that beat all? We'd heard he died in Wyoming in nineteen fifty-three."

Elmer said, "Maybe he went back to Wyoming; maybe you had the year wrong."

"Do you remember anything else about him being in Kamay?"

Bill cleared his throat again. "Maybe this is bringin' up bad news, but I remember some woman he was living with there. Elmer, do you recall her name?"

Elmer nodded. "I sure do. Martha Clay. Seemed like a real nice woman, kinda nice lookin' too. Worked at a bank in Wichita Falls, I'm pretty sure."

"Hmph," Harold said.

"Hope it doesn't make you feel bad to hear that, Harold," Bill said.

"It might have back in fifty-eight, but not anymore. But I would like to find out whatever happened to him—you know, what he died of and maybe where."

"Well, sure. That's understandable. Maybe we can help. There are a few of us left from back then. We've got telephone numbers for five or six. If you want us to, we could call them."

"Sure, making phone calls would beat making trash baskets out of egg cartons in activity period the next few days," Elmer said. "Course that would mean I'd miss spitting snuff juice in my coffee cup to upset old lady Branson. That's the only reason I even go to activity time."

"I'd be much obliged," Harold said. "Yeah, that'd be real helpful."

He stopped at a convenience store on the north side of Crane. The glass door of the refrigerated case reflected a face that looked familiar, but older and sad. He made himself look past to the rows and cans and bottles. The names blurred. He opened the door and grabbed the nearest silver can. At the checkout counter, the clerk said, "I can't sell you that on Sunday." It was Coors Light.

"Wrong can." He could feel her looking at him and saw her frowning when he returned with a Diet Coke. He paid and left before he could do anything else stupid.

He turned off of Highway 385 onto the first gravel road he came to. His next turn put him on a pumper's road. A man shouldn't drive if he can't keep his mind on the road. Right now, the only thought he had, the one he heard himself speaking, was, "Why didn't you take me with you?" He parked the pickup and stared at a cluster of storage tanks and a single large pump jack painted black and orange. The Diet Coke didn't cure the vacant feeling that occupied his chest, but after he finished it, he drove back the way he'd come and headed north again for Odessa.

Harold drove by instinct, not really seeing the flat dry scene he passed through. If he was correct, those two old roughnecks back there in Crane were living out their days in a place that was a cross between a storage facility and a prison. And the image he'd constructed years ago, of his father resting in a grave in some public cemetery in a small windy Wyoming town near an oil field, had been built on a lie. If Bill and Elmer were correct, his father was buried in some small, windy Texas town near an oil field.

Moving slowly, Harold stopped to aim his keys at the pickup. The lights blinked once as the doors locked. His shoulders slumped and he stared at the pavement as he walked. From the trailer door, Dorothy Faye said, "Hey, mister, are you lost or should I be suspicious?"

He looked up and gave her a smile, picking up his pace. "Lady, if this is Odessa, I'm not lost. What about you—what are you doing here in this parking lot with this trailer set up?"

"Planning to go into business." She winked at him. "I just haven't decided what my business is going to be." She opened the door for him and reached out to hug him.

He held her close for a long time. Then he kissed her for a long time. "That's the only business you need to be concerned about, ma'am. Just keep being here with me," he said. He hugged her again. He hesitated, looking around like he might have lost something. Then he sat in his recliner. Instead of picking up his paper, he stared out the screen door.

"Is something bothering you, Harold?"

He nodded. "Soon as I think about it a few more minutes, I'll try telling you." Getting that out took all the strength he had.

Dorothy Faye made it easy for him to get himself gathered back up. She said, "I'll take a little walk. We can talk when I get back."

———◆———

He began the story of his trip to Crane and then stopped. "Wait, I'll back up so this will make better sense. Two main things got me down today. First, that nursing home. The smell hit me when I walked in. I could have overlooked the smell, probably, but the entire situation gave me a bad feeling. It just seems so sad that these two old guys, both able to keep themselves clean and get around, have to live in that place, mainly because they don't have any family. They were happy to go out to eat, and they made good conversation. But there they are in that place that's like a warehouse for sick old people. Those two'd be fine if there was some good place to live where someone cooked and checked on them once in a while; someplace where there were things that old men like to do besides watch television. Dorothy Faye, it scared me. I don't want to ever end up like that.

And, I don't want those old roughnecks to have to stay there either. Okay, one of them's blind and the other one is missing a leg, but other than those things, they have their senses about them and—I'm not doing a good job of making this make sense, am I?"

"Did they mention anything that made you think they were being mistreated?"

"No, I doubt if they are mistreated. It's more like just being kept someplace till they die. I feel like something ought to be done, like I ought to do something."

He was quiet, pressing his temples and forehead with his fingertips. He stopped and sat up straight. He knew he could tell her. She wouldn't try to talk him out of how he felt. She'd listen and understand. He shifted and faced Dorothy Faye. "And then there was the second thing. They told me that my daddy was alive and working in Kamay, Texas, in nineteen fifty-eight. That's five years after we heard he died in Wyoming. Who knows, he may still be alive—may be living in some place like that nursing home. I just don't know what to think. Maybe Mama knew and didn't tell us, or maybe she was already—you know how she got. I need to find out, though. Kamay is the only place I know to start, where they said they saw him last."

She nodded and said nothing. He stared at his hands, not meeting her eyes.

"Hell, I don't know—nineteen fifty-eight was a long time ago. Maybe it doesn't make sense to even try to find out anything. What difference does it make? That's what my sisters would say. What do you think?"

"I think you're right, it was a long time ago. But you should do what will be best for you. Find out if you need to or let it be. It's up to you."

CHAPTER 20

I Thought I Saw a Superman Suit

T he sound of Harold opening and closing cabinets woke her. She didn't say anything. He always got a little put out if she had to help him find things. The sounds stopped.

He came to the foot of the bed. "I looked and looked for a sweet roll and a nice tray so I could bring your breakfast in bed. You were sleeping hard," he said. "Only thing I could find was some crackers. Doesn't do to eat those in bed, so I brought coffee—if you're ready for it."

"I am. Thank you." She stretched and put both of their pillows behind her. "Having room service makes me feel like a rich woman."

"Whether you're rich or not, you're a mighty good woman. Thanks for listening to all that rambling last night."

"Anytime," she said. She drank her coffee slowly. Last night, for the first time in a long time, Harold had held her close as he slept. Until the last few months, they had always slept that way—connected. Sometime in the night, she had woken and felt his left hand resting on her hip as he slept, breathing evenly and slowly. She didn't move away.

"You look happy this morning. What are you smiling about?" he asked. She didn't have to try to explain because a cell phone rang. She heard his side of a conversation from the living area. "You are? When? Sure, we're parked at the hospital in Odessa. It's a new red Chevy Silverado pickup with a fifth-wheel hookup in back. Trailer's right across from it. Where are you now? Okay, we'll look for you about four this evenin'. Be careful on the road."

He brought his coffee and sat on the foot of the bed. "That was R.J. He's on his way out here. That's a real nice surprise. We'll have to find a good place to go to supper tonight. You're smiling again. What are you thinking about?"

"I was remembering when he was four. That Superman suit. Special powers." She had made the suit from a pair of blue knit pajamas using red and yellow satin for the cape and the big letter *S*. He was so curious, she had to stitch it all together in secret so it would be a big surprise. One day he caught her working on the suit. He'd said, "What's that? I thought I saw a Superman suit." She barely managed to convince him she was making a skirt for Elizabeth.

"He's the only person I ever knew who could fly," Harold said. "He's a mighty good boy."

After reading the paper, around midmorning, Harold had sprung into action and left, saying he'd be back around three. He must have made some executive decision that didn't require discussion. She watched as he walked quickly toward the pickup, as if he had business to attend to. He seemed to be feeling better.

Her own good humor still intact, Dorothy Faye spent rest of the morning with her puzzles, working all the way through her lunch of tomato soup, crackers, cottage cheese, and peaches on #121. An acrostic embedded diagonally across the puzzle offered an interesting challenge. Fifteen letters—"easily persuadable." It could be more than one word, though; she knew Will Shortz's tricks. Her first tactic was to work on other clues. "One foot pound equals 13,560,000." She wrote in *E R G S*, remembering from some other puzzle a long time ago. "Do an impression of"—*I M I T A T E*. "Marilyn of the Met"; she didn't know the answer, but figured out *H O R N E* from two other connecting clues. Mrs. Ottley would have known. And she would have known "Dutch painter Jan" was *S T E E N*. They often discussed the words Dorothy Faye looked up. Soon the circles for the acrostic had *I _ _ _ _ _ E D T _ A G R _* filled in. Definitely more than one word. She wanted to be able to fill in the acrostic without using the other clues. "Calm endurance; tolerant understanding," 58 Down, would add the last letter. She knew that one—*P A T I E N C E*.

Dorothy Faye was tired of the confines of the trailer, but she didn't want to go in the hospital and chance running into Carolee. People who tell someone their problems often feel later as if they have been seen without their clothes. That sweet woman had enough on her mind without regretting their talk yesterday. A walk would be a better choice. Besides, the first word she filled in on #121 had been *P E R I P A T E T I C*—a message if she ever saw one.

Her route took her pretty far from the hospital, all the way east to Main Street and several blocks north. On the return trip she went in the county courthouse, mainly to cool off. On the first floor she found a historical exhibit. She studied the faces of the oil field workers featured in many of the large black and white photos of early Odessa, searching among the ranks of grease-smudged young men for someone resembling Harold.

Back on the sidewalk, her phone ringing startled her to a stop. "Hello. Wait just a minute until I can get where I can hear better." She stepped into an alleyway. "Now. Is something wrong, Harold?"

"Change of plans," he said. "We're gonna need to move the trailer. I see the security guard right now down at the space on the end of the lot. He's got a clipboard and he's checking on something, maybe who they're visiting. I'm going to pull out of here in about five minutes, before he can make it all the way down to our space. Where are you?"

She read him the street address from the sign at the intersection.

"Stay right there. I'll pick you up." He didn't wait for a reply.

R.J. said he wasn't a bit surprised he'd found them. He'd pulled into Holiday Rest RV Park about fifteen minutes after Harold had gotten them connected to water and sewer. In his hurried exit from the hospital, Harold had forgotten that R.J. would look for them there.

"When I didn't see your trailer or pickup at the hospital, I just pulled over at the next pay phone I saw and checked the phone book for RV parks," R.J. said. "This one was listed before KOA, alphabetically, so I came here first. I could have called, but it was more of an adventure to hunt for you." He waved the page he'd torn from the yellow pages. "See, we could have had a tour of Odessa in search of my parents. Too bad we found you on the first try." He laughed and hugged them both. "You both look good to me," he said.

"Why wouldn't we?" Harold asked. Dorothy Faye thought he sounded a little defensive.

"Elizabeth..."

"Oh yeah, well, she came out and looked us over too," Harold said. This time he smiled.

"Did she? I haven't talked to her since then, I guess," R.J. said. "Anyway, I wanted you to meet my friend, my partner. So this was a good time to come."

"Don't keep your friend waiting. Bring him in and let us meet him," Dorothy Faye said.

"Her," R.J. said.

Harold looked at Dorothy Faye and raised his eyebrows.

———◆———

Three of them ordered rib eyes for dinner. R.J.'s "friend" opted for broiled shrimp. She explained, "Dancers can't afford an extra ounce. If I eat seafood and no potatoes or bread, I can have what I love, dessert." She smiled a brilliant smile at R.J. He seemed to forget what he intended to say next.

Conversation before and during the meal was lively. They had only to ask a couple of questions to get Maia to open up. She told about her childhood as an Air Force brat, an only child, and about her parents—Vietnamese mother and American father, a helicopter pilot. The family settled in Austin when her father got out of the service in 1978. And about being a professional ballerina in New York City for five years from the age of eighteen. She said she realized she'd never make a complete life as a "member of the corps." "Everyone I knew was a dancer. I had no idea what was going on in real life. I came back to UT to get a degree and a teaching certificate." She had taught dance and PE at the arts magnet school there for the past six years. The whole time she was talking, R.J. watched her as if he'd never heard her story.

And she asked about them. What they were doing this summer? Were they having an adventure? Had they met any interesting people?

That last one got Harold started. "I guess R.J. told you about our little trip spendin' some time at hospitals. I'm sure Dorothy Faye could tell you lots more about interesting people, but I've met a few myself. In fact, I met one today I haven't even had time to tell her about." Maia nodded when he mentioned the hospitals. If she thought the parking lot plan was odd, it didn't show on her face. She gave Harold one of her smiles. He leaned forward, making it seem like what he was about to tell was a secret.

"This fella from Monahans said he was here to keep an eye on his daddy, who's eighty-six. Seems the old man lives by himself and had been doin' pretty well on his own until the accident."

"Car wreck?" R.J. had regained his ability to speak.

"No, nothing like that. He's supposed to use oxygen at night—heart trouble, his son said. Well, the old man still smokes, has for seventy years, not gonna quit now. Anyway, he knows that when the oxygen's on, he's not supposed to smoke. But he apparently forgot that one night. He was wearing his oxygen tube. You know, it goes in his nose." He demonstrated the oxygen cannulas by putting one finger in each nostril.

"So the old man fired up an unfiltered Camel and the oxygen ignited. His son said it blew the end of his nose off his face. Had to be reattached surgically. Lucky the whole tank didn't explode."

"Is he going to live?" R.J. asked. He had practice handing Harold straight lines.

Harold nodded. "His nose hairs got singed and he's got a cough, but he's doing okay now. His son said he wished he'd been there. I said, 'You mean so you could have stopped him from lighting up?' He said, 'Well, yeah, that too. But it would have been something to see when it happened, you know, his nose just lifting up clean off his face. He worked thirty years in the oil field without a scratch and then blew his nose up right there in his livin' room.'"

Dorothy Faye couldn't help laughing because R.J. cut his eyes at her and put two fingers in his nostrils, so briefly that only she saw it. Maia sat back with a dazed look, shaking her head. Harold said, "Anybody want dessert or coffee?"

R.J. and Maia left to stay the night with a college friend of hers, saying they would be back in the morning around ten. Dorothy Faye heard Harold tell R.J. quietly that he wanted a few minutes to talk to him before they headed back to Austin. She watched as the couple walked to his car, holding hands. She thought again about him in his Superman suit and about how much he still seemed like that sweet little boy.

CHAPTER 21

We Have Something Important to Tell You

R.J. had saved a big surprise. As soon as they got to the trailer the next morning and everyone was equipped with cups of coffee, he said, "Maia and I have something important we want to tell you."

Dorothy Faye waited, interested to see how he would announce that he was going to marry Maia. Even Harold waited without saying a word.

"Maia and I have been friends for nearly two years. Just seeing each other occasionally when we'd go out with a group, at first. Neither one of us is into the dating thing. After you're about thirty, it seems kind of silly to go out two or three times a week, auditioning different people, looking for someone you can really like." He looked at Maia. "I'm not doing a good job of explaining this. Maybe you should."

She put a hand on his arm. "You're doing fine. Explaining the context is important." She fired up another of her beautiful smiles and aimed it him.

He sat up straight, adoring eyes fixed on her. Dorothy Faye felt like an eavesdropper or a voyeur (puzzle #89)—again. R.J. said, "Little by little, we got to know each other. A few months ago we got together for dinner. We found out then how many of the same things we're interested in. Then we started talking about things we dream about. I don't mean dreams like when you sleep; I mean things we hope to do, to accomplish."

Dorothy Faye hadn't taken a breath for a while. She looked at Harold, who kept nodding. Maybe he was holding his breath too—helping Ronnie say what he had on his mind.

"As it turns out, we each had a similar sort of idea, so we decided to combine them. We decided to team up and go into business. Maia, you tell them about it." He looked relieved when she began, an intense, intelligent expression accompanying her earnest tone of voice. Graceful, gentle hand gestures emphasized her speech.

She explained their plan for a gymnastics and dance academy for young children, ages five to ten. Everything from their philosophy to their plans for operation.

She finished by saying, "The educational program is my area to develop. R.J. is in charge of creating the business plan. Of course, we both work on everything we do. It's a real collaboration. And besides that, it's a lot of fun—dreaming and planning with someone who is your good friend." She stopped, looked a little embarrassed. "R.J. should tell you where we are with the business plan."

He took the handoff smoothly, saying, "I imagine, since you've known me all my life, you might wonder what I know about developing a business plan. That was my first thought too. But over the past six months, I've spent a lot of time learning. One thing I did have going for me was all the projects you had me help with over the years, Daddy. I had learned about planning a project, in detail, and about not getting discouraged.

"Now, I also know how to put a financial plan together and the format for a business plan. The next part is the one we're ready for soon. We're developing a presentation to take to bankers or others with venture capital to get our start-up money." He stopped, like he'd run out of breath. Then he asked, "What do you think?"

Harold spoke first, after a look at Dorothy Faye. "I think if you're any good at all at teaching gymnastics, you could be onto something. Do you have an idea of how you'll get customers, I mean students?"

Maia responded quickly, with detail that showed much thought had gone into the plan. Dorothy Faye sat back, watching the two eager budding entrepreneurs respond to Harold's questions. Both Maia and R.J. asked Harold's opinion about each answer they gave.

She searched for a word to describe her feeling about the young couple. The only one that seemed to fit was pride. She felt pride for them both, for R.J. for being so interested in and so involved in a dream—for Maia for being so bright, articulate, and self-confident—for the two of them together for putting so much hard work into making their dream a reality. Another word came to mind, dismay. There had been no mention of any impending wedding.

Harold said, "I surely would be interested to hear your presentation before you go out to try to raise your money. When do you expect to have that ready?"

Dorothy Faye knew that Harold knew quite a bit more about business than he usually let on. Anytime he started a project, he laid out a budget, wrote his plan, and made notes of corrections and changes from plan to implementation. R.J. had worked with him many times, adding columns of figures on a yellow pad to come up with those budgets. Harold had taught both the kids the meaning of "break even" and "compound interest" and a lot of other useful things. Right now, he sounded for all the world like a businessman, one with investing on his mind.

"In a few weeks," R.J. said. "Would you like to hear it? Maybe we could come back or you two could come to Austin."

Harold stood. "We'll work it out. Before I forget, R.J., could you come out here for a minute? I want your opinion on something I'm thinking about doing to the pickup—custom mufflers and twin exhausts to improve the mileage."

After the men were out the door, Maia thanked Dorothy Faye for being so understanding of their dream. "Not like my parents," she said.

In a few minutes, R.J. appeared outside the screen door. "Maia, we'd better get started."

Dorothy Faye hugged them both. She whispered to R.J., "I love you, son."

"Y'all be careful on the road," Harold said as they waved good-bye.

Day 26 Tuesday, June 13 Holiday Rest RV Park, Odessa

Not odd—I've been wrong before. This time I was definitely wrong about one thing. I expected when R.J. produced his "friend," he had an engagement to announce. I would have bet money on it. Good thing no one was offering odds. Underneath, I probably hoped all along that he would find someone he could love enough to marry. Not that he hasn't seemed happy being on his own, but—I don't know what...just but.

Down deep I suppose I have the same attitude that lots of people do—that married is the best situation for adults to be in. But I'm not sure that's right. Married and miserable is definitely not the best situation, and lots of people are—married and miserable. What I hope for both R.J. and Elizabeth is that sometime in their lives they would have at least one person they could care enough about to join some of their dreams together, to work together toward something important to them both—to have someone they care enough about and trust enough to let them see who they really are, all the strong and weak parts. That's love, I think.

I also know it's easy to fool ourselves about love. We can convince ourselves that a person is trustworthy by refusing to acknowledge deceits; we can assure ourselves that they accept our less desirable parts (weaknesses or strengths) by never letting them see those parts. We can substitute hope for facts.

Now that I've reread those last three sentences, I wish I had an eraser. Not that I regret the first part about hopes for R.J. and Elizabeth. But I don't even know where those last sentences came from. Maybe I read them in a woman's magazine on a page between the latest guaranteed weight-loss scheme and a recipe for a fancy chocolate dessert! Enough of that.

Here's something that is odd. R.J. called about seven o'clock, on my phone. He said he wanted to let us know they made it back. Then he asked me if Harold is feeling okay. I said, "What makes you ask? Did he tell you he'd been feeling bad?"

"No, not that," he said. "It was something else he said that made me wonder. He said, 'Son, would you make me a promise you'll always take care of your mother if I'm not around?'"

I didn't know what to say. Then I realized I was holding the phone and not talking. I asked him if he tried to get an explanation from his daddy. He said, "No, I took it like you did—stunned. I just said, 'Of course I would, Daddy. You know you can both count on me.'"

Harold came in from outside about that time. I asked R.J. if he needed to talk to him. He said no, he'd call back when their presentation is ready. Then he said, "But you call me if anything comes up, will you?"

I tried to make my side of the conversation sound casual so Harold wouldn't ask a lot of questions. I didn't want to try to lie to him. I said, "I'm glad you called. We had a good time too. Tell Maia we look forward to seeing her again soon. We love you. Bye."

I told Harold that R.J. had called to say they were back safe in Austin.

His only response was, "Good. I'm glad they came." He looked like he was thinking hard about something. A few minutes later he spent some time in the bathroom and then went to bed without saying another word.

CHAPTER 22

But Not Sufficient

Harold decided they would stay at the Holiday Rest instead of going back to the hospital. "We need to stay here until I go back to Crane this Friday," he said.

"You're going back?"

"Yes, I told Elmer and Bill I'd be back on Friday."

She waited to see if he might ask her opinion.

He didn't. But he did say, "Maybe you'd like to go shopping or something. Just let me know if you want the keys or want me to take you out to the mall."

She said, "Maybe tomorrow or the next day. I have several things to read that'll keep me busy for quite a while. I'll stay here." As they talked, she observed Harold. He wasn't pale. His movements, as he assembled his breakfast, were steady and deliberate. As he crossed the small space from cabinets to refrigerator, his gait suggested no pain in his back or knees.

Short of checking his blood sugar, she saw nothing about him that offered a reason to ask about his health. She didn't inquire.

He must have caught her studying him. He surprised her by asking, "You feel all right?"

"Yes. Thanks for asking. How about you?"

He nodded, as if answering. "Seeing those two did me a world of good. R.J. sure picked a smart woman to team up with."

Now it was her turn to nod. She wasn't ready yet to try to explain whatever was making her both happy and a little sad. Even if she'd wanted to explain, the sentences she formed in her mind seemed inadequate. She thought she'd get over it.

"Well, I've got some things to do," Harold said. "I'll see you this evening. Don't wait on me for lunch." He kissed her cheek and gave her a quick hug.

Dorothy Faye stared at the acrostic, but couldn't concentrate. The dishrag that hung on the sink faucet silently encouraged her to useless sink-polishing. She exited the trailer, slamming the door on the way out. Walking beat wiping any day.

She walked the boundary of the RV park, hoping to distance herself from the worrying that threatened to replace wondering. It wasn't R.J. and Maia, it was Harold's cryptic request to R.J. that sent her out the door. When they were in Whaley, more often than not, they spent their days apart. Harold or Dorothy Faye, or both, were away from the house from after breakfast until evening. He frequently worked with or as a replacement for some of the pumpers whose leases covered the still-producing deep oil fields around the area. Other days he helped elderly people with household repairs or transportation, not for pay but because he liked helping people. If he had a project underway, he might work in his shop in the garage.

Over the past few years, his projects had focused largely on inventing and producing labor-saving devices. An automatic gate-opener that a driver could operate from inside a pickup resulted in more than a hundred orders. After he considered his design for the Stay-Put Gate Opener perfected, he gave it to Fred Gilstrap. Fred had hung around watching as Harold developed the device. He'd been laid off from a well service company and had lots of time on his hands, waiting for some kind of work to come along. Harold's interest lay in creating. Fred's new business resulted in employment for the new owner and two helpers. Economic development—Whaley, Texas, style.

She walked her second lap around the outer fence of Holiday Rest. If they were in Whaley, she'd spend the weekdays working, staying with Mrs. Ottley, learning from her. She wouldn't be questioning her own assumptions; she would attribute Harold's absences to his usual activities. She might not have even noticed that he was spending longer than usual in the bathroom or that he appeared at times to be in pain. She would be too busy maintaining the cycle of her own work, their meals, housecleaning, and grocery shopping to hear a critical voice in her head. She might not have paid any attention to unwelcome memories or to incomplete ones. Busy keeping things running smoothly, she probably wouldn't be picking at her emotions like new scabs on old sores.

For about half a lap, she wished they had never left Whaley. By the time she reached the trailer, that thought had been replaced. *Keeping everything running smoothly is useful but not sufficient.* She went inside and wrote it in her notebook.

———◆———

By Thursday, she was ready for something more than working puzzles and pacing the boundary of the RV park like an inmate. She used the campground's laundry to do a load of wash and returned to the trailer without seeing another person. Still solitary, she dumped the clothes on the bed and began folding them, thinking about R.J. and Maia as she coasted through the chore. She hung her slacks and two shirts in her tiny closet. On her knees, she pulled the drawer from under her side of the bed and lined up the underwear in a neat stack. She rolled the towels and washcloths and fit them into the small cabinet under the bathroom sink. Then she hesitated. Harold's closet. If she hung those shirts in there quickly, just open and shut, she wouldn't be tempted to prowl. Her pulse thumped in her neck. *Don't look for something you don't want to find.*

Getting caught wasn't her concern; Harold wouldn't be back until later. Putting off what she knew she was going to do eventually, she stooped to open his under-the-bed drawer instead of the closet. Whatever was hidden in that closet—a strong feeling told her there was something—she wasn't sure she wanted to know. Before adding the clean underwear, she began emptying the drawer and refolding its contents. On the bottom of the drawer, she touched something not underwear—paper. Her hand shook as she scooped out the last pair of briefs and three pairs of socks. An envelope rested on the bottom at the back. Across its face, in Harold's handwriting, she saw "Last Will and Testament of Harold Bell." Okay, she'd found something, without looking for it—not snooping. She could leave it and not open it. Staring ahead, thinking about what to do, she noticed another, separate piece of paper in the drawer.

The scrap, torn from an envelope, was stuck against one side of the drawer. It contained only a name, also written in Harold's script, Martha Clay. Leaving it in place, Dorothy Faye sat on the floor beside the drawer holding the last will envelope.

Her head jerked up as she heard a motorcycle engine rev outside. It couldn't be Harold, unless he'd bought a motorcycle too. The unsealed flap of the envelope invited her. He wouldn't know if she looked. *When did he write it? Why did he write it? Where has he been going every day? Who does he know in Odessa? Who is Martha Clay?*

Rising to her knees, she replaced the envelope and the scrap of paper and all the underwear and socks. Then she slowly pushed the drawer back under the bed. A tear dripped off the end of her nose. The voice in her head said something helpful, for once—*nobody's bleeding; settle down; this is not an emergency.*

Discarding the first three items on her standby list—those things she did when she was upset—she chose the third. She made the choice while wiping the countertop and polishing the sink. Those two activities weren't even on her list; they were automatic. Taking a walk (item one), she eliminated because she didn't want to change into her walking shoes. Number two—take a nap—was out of the question. If she were lying on the bed, she'd only think about the envelope underneath. The only alternate nap spot was the nubby-upholstered couch. Nope.

She opened the cabinet, aiming for number three—eat. Low-fat, no-salt crackers and rice cakes. She tried the refrigerator. Carrots, celery, and a diet soft drink. *Damn Harold and his diet!* She slammed the screen door as she headed to the park's convenience store, spoon in hand. In five minutes she was back, carrying a pint of chocolate ice cream, already a third eaten. She ate and sniffled her way to the bottom of the carton.

CHAPTER 23

If You Don't Know the Whole Story

A t the nursing home, Harold passed by the desk ungreeted and apparently unnoticed by the woman at the desk, the hefty one he'd seen before. He saw *Cosmo* on the desk. Elmer and Bill were ready, freshly shaven and dressed.

"Hey, Harold," Bill said.

"How did you know it was me? I could have been that fat gal from down at the desk."

"Nope, she never moves. We were expecting you. And I recalled the sound of your boots."

Elmer said, "We skipped breakfast, hoping you'd want to go to the Dairy Fluff again."

"Well, I don't want y'all to starve. Let's go."

Elmer and Bill ordered eggs, bacon, biscuits, and gravy, along with coffee. It was all served family style, large portions in big bowls. Harold had a small amount of scrambled egg.

"You're eatin' light, Harold," Elmer said.

"I already ate once, before I left Odessa. Y'all are gonna make up for me, it looks like."

"This is the first gravy I've had in six months," Bill said. He lifted a forkful of gravy-covered biscuit to illustrate. "You know gravy causes cancer."

"I don't guess I'd heard about that," Harold said. He wadded his paper napkin and then smoothed it out and refolded it.

Elmer and Bill both nodded. Elmer said, "It's a fact. See, they used to serve gravy over at the home. It was the only thing they had that made it seem anything like home. Then about six months ago it just disappeared. No more gravy. The only conclusion we could reach, and we discussed it quite a lot, was that it must cause cancer. They were doing it for our own good.

"Thing is, at our age, most of us would just as soon take our chances with cancer as give up gravy. But we didn't get a vote on that. Pass me a biscuit, would you? And the gravy."

Harold didn't ask about the phone calls. Waiting seemed like the polite thing to do, particularly since they were enjoying the food so much.

He didn't have to ask. "Thanks for the breakfast," Elmer said. "I sure enjoyed it. Real home cooking would be better, but this is pretty good." He wiped his mouth with his napkin and checked a gravy spot on the front of his shirt. Pointing to the spot, he said, "I did that on purpose. It'll make everybody jealous over at the home." He grinned at Harold and Bill. "I guess you want to hear about our phone calls this week."

"I'm glad we had a reason to call," Bill said. "Talking to those guys made me feel good. Nothing ever happens at the home that makes a day worth getting up for. But knowing we were goin' to be calling someone every day made the whole week pass a lot faster."

"It's kind of surprising, all of those guys on the list are still alive," Elmer said. "Trouble is, they all wanted to talk about their ailments. Hell, we've got enough of our own. We don't need to hear anyone else's bad news. We won't tell you all of those stories, but I will say three of them are in pretty bad shape."

Bill interrupted. "But that's neither here nor there. Fact is, out of the five, four of 'em remembered Sonny. They all said he was one of the best old boys they ever worked with."

Elmer nodded. He sat forward to pass along his next bit. "John Sagelin had a real useful piece of information. Course it took me a long time to get it out of him. He always was kind of closemouthed. Anyway, he still lives up in Wichita County, close to Holliday. He said Sonny quit working the rigs and started pumping. Said that was in the early nineteen sixties sometime."

Bill leaned toward Harold. "Now I hope this next part won't upset you. He told us that Sonny and Martha Clay lived together. Everyone thought they was married. But John knew different. He said she's still alive, living in Wichita Falls."

Elmer nodded, as if urging Bill along—not that Bill could see the cue. He interrupted again. "He didn't recall what year, but he said Sonny died when he was in his seventies. He thought it was nineteen eighty-six or eighty-seven. He went to the funeral, said it was real nice."

Harold sat back, slumped against his chair. Elmer didn't seem to notice. "If you want all the facts, the next step would be to see if you can get a hold of Martha Clay. If her mind is still working, she should be able to tell you the whole story."

Bill reached out a hand and found Harold's shoulder. He patted it. "I sure hope this didn't upset you, son. But you did say you wanted to know."

"I did. I'm not upset; I'm just surprised."

"You know, there's no explaining the things people do if you don't know their whole story. We shouldn't judge old Sonny. Not at this late date. Gotta remember too, everyone said he was the best they ever worked with—real smart and real patient."

"You're sure right about not judging people," Harold said. "I can think of three of four reasons at home why he might have wanted to disappear. I appreciate y'all for doing the detective work."

CHAPTER 24

Some Answers, More Questions

S he hadn't said a word yesterday evening when Harold came in, just went to bed early. This morning, he left early for Crane. Yesterday had left her restless and her mother had kept her from sleeping. She had dreamed, it seemed like the entire night, and her mother starred in almost every scene. But she didn't recall the details. This morning, she did remember something she hadn't thought of in years. She was fourteen and it was the day her father had been killed in a car wreck. Her mother said, "He was out chasing around with some woman. He'd never have been in that wreck if he'd been home where he belonged. Remember this, Dorothy Faye, no matter how long you know him, you should never trust a man completely."

The argument they'd had after that had been one of the few times she talked back to her mother. Dorothy Faye had loved her father and she hated her mother for trying to lessen her memory of him. As long as Dorothy Faye could remember, her mother had wielded criticism like a rusty knife. Neither her father nor Dorothy Faye escaped her slashing. Infractions of her mother's rules, from minor to major, all occasioned lacerations from the woman who, also just as quickly and with as much intensity, would shower them with tenderness. They each had their own ways of dealing with her. Dorothy Faye's way was to accept her criticism, usually to try to please her, and to ignore all the negative comments. After that one day when she shouted at her to quit talking about her father, Dorothy Faye reverted to trying to please her.

Later on, she had tried to understand her mother better, her bitterness at being widowed and how she transferred that bitterness to her husband, who could no longer defend himself. Maybe he did have another woman. There was no way for Dorothy Faye to know and she didn't want to know. But she resisted agreeing with her mother's generalization that all men were untrustworthy. Dorothy Faye thought she'd settled that in her own mind long ago. But here is was, like a virus infecting her thoughts.

She knew her mother had loved her, in her way, and had wanted the best for her. Until this minute, though, it never occurred to Dorothy Faye that her grandmother may have had a hand in teaching that wariness of men to her mother. Maybe it had come down through generations of unhappy women. She tried to recall if she had ever been guilty of teaching Elizabeth that same prejudice toward half of the human race.

She remembered another time her mother drove her lesson home. It was during the time after Ronnie left and while she and the kids lived with her. Near the end of a month, there had been no baby formula in the house. Her mother had turned her purse inside out to demonstrate that there was no money. She said, "See there. He left you and these kids and now me without a cent. He's off chasing women. If he ever comes back, he'll wish he hadn't. I still have a shotgun and some shells." Dorothy Faye took the twelve-gauge to a pawnshop that afternoon, solving at least one problem and maybe preventing another. But she knew the message stayed with her. Men are not to be trusted. They should be shot.

Pouring a second cup of coffee, she willed herself to wake up and focus on the present. She probably had a hangover from all that ice cream. She said aloud, "I'm on the wagon, taking the pledge this minute."

By the time she finished the coffee, she'd decided that if Harold didn't explain Martha Clay by the time they left Holiday Rest, she would ask. That settled, she moved to the topic of the will. That, she concluded, was his business. She shot a look toward the sink, then turned and started toward the trailer door. After three steps, she turned back, went inside, and stripped the bed.

———◆———

Today the laundry hummed with activity. Nine washers agitated. The crawler at the bottom of the television screen continuously updated items that passed for news. The audio competed with the chatter of two women and six children who occupied the chairs and part of the floor near the television. An old man sat across the room, near the bank of dryers, staring at one particular washer. Dorothy Faye emptied her duffel bag and some detergent into the large washer next to the one he continued monitoring.

Pointing to the chair next to his, she said, "Is this seat taken?"

He turned his gaze slowly from the washer, looking at her as if she'd just materialized there. "Why no, please sit down. I'm sorry, I didn't even notice you come up. I was thinking."

"I don't want to interrupt."

"You're not interrupting. Sometimes I get to thinking and tune everything out. Just now I was thinking about doctors, how disappointing they are these days. Nothing like it used to be."

"Have you had some bad experiences with your health care?"

"Seems like that's all I have. I'm eighty-one years old and I'll tell you, I think doctors ain't anywhere near as good as they was when I was younger." He paused every sentence or two to catch a breath, and each breath was shallow. The resulting slow pant, interspersed with his words, had a nearly hypnotic effect. He stopped talking and picked up a flyswatter, then took a swing at a fly. "Damn flies. Excuse my language. I hate flies."

"They seem to be fond of this laundry," she said.

"It's them trash bins out there," he said, pointing with the flyswatter to a row of large trash bins. "I'm going to move my RV to a space on the other side of the lot to see if I can get away from them. Gonna do it today."

They both stared at their washers.

"Like I was saying, doctors today don't know what they're doin'. Not a one of them can cure you of an ailment without sending you to a specialist.

Then the specialist will redo what the first one done. Eventually someone gives you some pills. They might do some good, but when you finish taking 'em, you're right back in the same condition."

"Sometimes it's necessary to keep taking the medicine to stay feeling all right. For instance, if a person has diabetes or high blood pressure, they'll take that medicine forever," she said.

"Yeah, I know about diabetes. My wife had it before she died. But take me, see, my feet will start swelling up, then my legs, then I feel tired all the time and the next thing you know, I have trouble breathin', specially at night. First time that happened, it went on quite a while and finally I went to the doctor. I'll admit, he did give me some pills that worked for a while. But he wanted to send me to a heart specialist too. Anyway, those water pills did the trick—the swelling went away, I could breathe, and I felt a lot better by the time I finished 'em. So I didn't go to the heart doctor. I figured the medicine had taken care of the problem. Then about six or eight weeks later, my feet started swelling up again. I decided maybe I was working too hard, so I cut my hours back and rested for an hour every day after dinner."

"What kind of work do you do?"

"I'm a machinist. Have my own shop in Sundown. There's always more work than I can get to. I hate to have to cut down my hours."

"Do you have any help?"

"I've tried hiring some young guys, but none of 'em ever stick long enough to learn how to do the work. They can't do much except sweep up and help me lift things. So, no, I don't have any regular help. Anyway, I got to thinking about doctors because of all that."

She waited a while before saying anything else, hoping to slow the pace of conversation and improve his breathing. "Are you on a vacation?"

"Yep, it's the only way I could get away from work. People keep bringing in jobs. And I like to work. I mean, that's what God put us here for, isn't it?"

Dorothy Faye nodded, noticing his breathing becoming more labored. "Do you ever use oxygen?"

"I have a tank, but I can't use it at work. It'd blow up. I don't know how that doctor thought I could use it. But he sent it over to the house, so I kept it. Easier than trying to get him to understand. They don't ever have time to try to understand anything you want to tell 'em." He stopped talking and stared at the washer again.

"Would you like me to check on your laundry? If it's finished, I'll put it in the dryer." If she was busy with laundry, he'd stop talking and rest a few minutes.

He nodded. "Okay, thanks." He leaned his head back and closed his eyes.

She moved slowly, stretching the task for longer than required. He didn't seem to take notice of her inserting quarters and starting the dryer. His load consisted of two pairs of boxer shorts; two undershirts; a plaid, long-sleeved Western shirt; two once-white towels; and two blue washcloths. She wondered where his socks were. Maybe he did a little hand laundry in the sink in his RV. Dawdling, she looked into her own washer—still agitating. He smiled at her when she returned to her seat—a sweet smile showing the perfectly uniform teeth of old-fashioned dentures.

"The last time I ran into a good doctor was nineteen sixty-five." Talking seemed more important to him than breathing. "They had a deal back then down at Scott and White in Temple. A man could go down there and go through the clinic. Get checked out from top to bottom.

"First thing, soon as you got there, you had a doctor assigned to you. I remember mine, his name was Dr. Smith, an American. Lots of 'em these days aren't. First off, he said, 'Mr. Childers, we're going to do the executive exam on you, that's the whole works.' I said, 'Well, have at it.' He asked a whole lot of questions and took a lot of time to understand my answers. Then he examined me. After that they did a chest x-ray and a heart tracing, had me exercise on some little stairs. They finished up by takin' a sample of blood. That doctor said he'd do forty-eight different tests on it. I went back the next day and he told me I was in as good a shape as a thirty-year-old. No heart problem, nothing. So, see, I don't need to see no heart doctor now."

"What year did you say that was?"

"Nineteen sixty-five."

"Lots of thing can change in thirty-five years, Mr. Childers."

"Yeah, I know everybody gets arthritis. I ignore that." He heaved his shoulders and tried to breathe deeply. "I intend to stay here for while and rest up. Then I'll get back to work. My feet are swoll' up a little today. I decided I'd take one or two of them water pills—started yesterday. Don't like to take 'em. The side effects."

"What side effects?"

"Have to go to the bathroom all night. Can't get no sleep."

"What time of day do you take the pills?"

"With supper."

"I know someone who takes those pills. He says that if he takes them first thing in the morning, he doesn't have to get up to go to the bathroom at night. I'll bet if you keep taking them every day like the doctor prescribed them, and take them in the morning, it would help." She didn't usually offer advice. That was as far as she intended to go.

"I'll think about it."

She put her load in the dryer, then walked to the vending machine and pretended to consider every item in it. She thought about taking her laundry back to the trailer wet. But that was no guarantee Mr. Childers would rest. He'd probably find someone else to talk to.

He beckoned her back to the chairs. "If I could go to a heart doctor that would try to understand me, I'd go. Course I'd want someone that speaks good English. You're probably right about it bein' a good idea to go."

She didn't recall saying that. The buzzer on his dryer sounded. He stood, more quickly than she expected he could.

"Well, that's me. I sure enjoyed talking to you. If you was a cardiologist, I'd make an appointment to see you right away. By the way, what's your name?"

"Dorothy Faye Bell." She shook his hand. "I hope you get some rest while you're here."

"Oh, I'll probably head on back tomorrow. There's work waitin' for me."

———◆———

Day 29 Friday, June 16 9:30 p.m. Holiday Rest RV Park, Odessa

I checked my back this afternoon. There's not a sign on there saying "Tell Me." But people do it anyway. I don't mind, really. And saying out loud what they're thinking probably does help them. Maybe I should try it.

There's a lesson to be learned from what happened when Harold came in from Crane this evening. He was late getting back. He said he'd driven around, just thinking, for quite a while before coming back. I hadn't worried about the time. I'd been too busy getting nervous about asking the Martha Clay question. I could have saved myself the trouble.

As soon as he finished eating—I intended to wait until the meal was over to ask my question—he said, "I need to tell you some things, Dorothy Faye."

"Okay, tell me," I said, thinking about that sign on my back.

Then he went into how those two men in Crane had gotten pretty definite information that his father had lived into his seventies and lived all those years near Wichita Falls.

Harold said, "That means he was alive another thirty or more years after I thought he was dead. I can't count how many times I passed right through Wichita on Two Eighty-Seven when I was driving trucks." Then he got quiet for a while.

When he finally started talking again, he said, "The other thing was that they said he lived with a woman named Martha Clay and that she's still there in Wichita Falls."

I felt bad for him and for thinking that Martha Clay might be some woman he was seeing. I asked him what he thought about the things he'd found out.

The odd thing, odd for Harold, who's usually certain, was that he said he wasn't sure what he thought or what to do about the information. I kept quiet a while longer. He sat there staring at his hands.

"I went to the library when I got back here and checked the Wichita Falls phone book. There's only one M. Clay listed. I called information, thinking they would have the latest listings. That was the only one and it's still connected," he said. "Then I just drove around and thought about it all."

I could see he was trying to decide on his next move. Telling little details to keep from getting to the point. So I waited some more.

Then he said, "I've got to decide if I want to try to talk to her. And I'd rather do it face to face if I do."

Finally, and I could see it was hard for him, he did another odd thing. He asked me, "What do you think I should do?"

I was tempted to tell him—to say, "Just get in that pickup and go to Wichita Falls and then call her and ask if you can come right over and talk to her. If you're already there, she's not likely to refuse." But I didn't. Harold, for sure, and most likely other people too, likes an answer he arrives at on his own better than one that's given to him. I said, "You're the only person who knows if it's important for you to have the truth about your father." Then I thought I'd better add that whatever he decided, he could rely on me not saying anything about it to anyone. He knew I meant Janiece and Rubyjo.

I don't know what he intends to do because after that, he just said, "You're right. I have to figure it out for myself." And then he went to bed.

Since then, I've been sitting here wondering what made him start thinking about his father in the first place. I guess I have to figure that out. Or I could ask him.

She looked at the acrostic in puzzle #121. <u>I</u> <u>N</u> <u>C</u> <u>L</u> <u>I</u> <u>N</u> <u>E</u> <u>D</u> <u>T</u> <u>O</u> <u>A</u> <u>G</u> <u>R</u> <u>E</u> <u>E</u> could have been in neon, it stood out so clearly when she looked at the letters that were filled in and the surrounding blank spaces—"easily persuadable." Yes, I am.

CHAPTER 25

Not Yet, But Soon

"Yes, we've been having some interesting times. You know there's seldom a dull day with Harold." Dorothy Faye smiled at Harold as she spoke into her new cell phone. She wondered if her face looked to him the way it felt to her, like a plastic mask. She resisted an urge to check the mirror. They were headed back to Lubbock. "I don't want to hold you now, but the reason I called is because I wondered if you would like it if I came down on Monday to visit and go out to lunch." She nodded. "Oh, good. I'll be there by nine thirty at the latest. Okay, you think about where you want to go for lunch. Slaton, Post, anywhere you'd like. I'll see you then. Bye, now."

She had checked with Harold before she called. He said he might just go with her on Monday, but either way, she would have the pickup to take Mrs. Ottley to lunch. That was after he had worn a pitiful look all morning—the kind that would have usually made her forget anything she wanted and concern herself with trying to make him happy. First, she had mentioned she would like to go to Whaley sometime next week. He had nodded, staring out the screen door. She knew better than to take that as a definite answer. Next, she had said, while he was pushing the cereal around in his bowl, not eating it, "If you and O.D. are going to be doing something on Monday, maybe I could go see Mrs. Ottley then." Another nod. Finally, just before they left Odessa, she had said, "I'll call Mrs. Ottley in a few minutes so that she can make plans. That will give her something to look forward to." By that time her jaw was tight with the effort of working so hard to get an answer. Asking to use the pickup also irritated her. It wasn't that she minded the days when she either stayed put or walked. She enjoyed walking. But still, without a word being spoken, this pickup had apparently become his pickup. Otherwise, why did she feel like she had to ask about using it?

This morning, again, he was walking carefully, as if avoiding impact that would start pain in his lower back, or maybe in his hip. He always relied on her to make appointments for his checkups. She considered making one without asking him. "Harold," she could say, "tomorrow's your appointment with Dr. Jenkins. Do you want me to go with you?" Nice idea, but she doubted it would work. Or she could try, "They called from Dr. Jenkins's office. They've scheduled you an appointment tomorrow." Implying that the office called without her prompting them would be lying. *Forget that.*

As they neared Lubbock, she stared out her window at a succession of cotton fields. Orderly rows of foot-high plants cast scant, short shadows in the eleven o'clock glare. Occasionally they passed irrigated acreage where the long arms of sprinklers created perfect arcs as they crept across the rows. Behind her sunglasses, her eyelids closed, lulled by the predictable geometry of the scene. She leaned against the headrest, waiting for Harold to tell her where in Lubbock he planned to park. No doubt he had a plan.

A speed bump in the parking lot of County General Hospital caused a little jolt that woke her. New scenery, at least.

"Did you have a nice little nap?" Harold's hands no longer gripped the steering wheel tightly. His smile seemed to come from inside, not just from the muscles of his face.

"It was easy because you're such a smooth driver. Before I went to sleep, I remembered that we need to get you an appointment with Dr. Jenkins. Your prescriptions need to be renewed. If I call Monday, it will take at least a couple of weeks to get in. Will that give you time to do what you need to do about, you know, Wichita Falls?"

"Gotta do it sooner or later, I guess." She wasn't certain what *it* referred to. "I'll call and get the appointment. No need for you to bother," he said. His smile disappeared. He concentrated on the parking lot, scouting for a space.

She patted his shoulder. That was easier than she had expected. He parked the trailer in a space at the end of an empty row. He got the rig straight in the space in one try. "You're getting pretty good at parking this trailer. You should enter a contest."

He shrugged. "Like ridin' a bicycle. Something you don't forget."

She counted three RVs and another fifth-wheel trailer on the opposite row as she went into the trailer. After he connected the electricity and unhooked the pickup, he said from the doorway, "Well, you're all set up. Do you need anything from a grocery store? I've got to go do a few things."

Before she thought, she asked, "What are you going to do?"

He frowned. "Get gas, check the tire pressure, check the oil. Stuff like that."

"No, we don't need any groceries. If I'm not here when you come back, I'll be inside." She moved to the screen door to try to see his face more clearly. But he had already started toward the pickup.

He had almost relaxed and she'd upset him again. She cocked her head, listening to a voice. It wasn't her mother this time. She heard herself. *Why didn't you wait for a better time?* Aloud, she said, "Why should I?" No response.

County General sat in the middle of a half-section of land that had once been part of a cotton farm on the north edge of Lubbock. In the twenty years since its construction, parking lots, medical office buildings, a rehabilitation facility, a nursing home, and other related structures had created a sprawling complex that covered at least fifty of the acres. The box-like main building and the entire set of connected buildings blended into the sandy fields nearby—all dirt-tan. At least from the exterior, there was no hint of an effort to mimic an upscale hotel.

The typical first-floor facilities greeted her—gift shop, vending area, information desk, smiling volunteer, and a few offices. The only surprise was the armed guard standing near the elevator. Dorothy Faye nodded and said, "Good afternoon," as she passed him. She checked the hospital map posted near the elevator. Emergency, surgery, laboratory, and radiology were clustered on the first floor. Unlike the arrangement in other hospitals she had visited, the cafeteria here occupied a space on the second floor.

As she entered the busy eating area, a gaggle of nursing students passed her, all wearing navy-blue scrubs and stethoscopes around their necks. Almost everyone wore scrubs of one color or another. No real uniforms. Few of the patrons appeared to be visitors. Instead, the majority wore name tags—doctors, medical students, residents, medical office staff, physical therapists, nurses. As if short on time and long on responsibility, all of them rushed, disturbing the air around her as they passed. For a second, she considered assembling a lunch of peanut butter crackers, diet cola, and a candy bar from a vending machine to avoid the crowd. But this place was more interesting than the trailer. So she plunged in by entering at a turnstile that separated the food from the eaters. Lasagna aroma led her to a counter of entrees. To her surprise, they looked fresh and appetizing. Trips to the salad bar and the beverage area completed her foray into the food service section.

She found an empty table for two. To prevent herself from eating at the rapid rate of those around her, she took paper and pen from her purse and began a new list.

1. Call Elizabeth.
2. Go to see Mrs. Ottley.

She ate some lasagna, slowly, as she considered #3. She should go to visit Rubyjo. But she never had gone to see Harold's sister that she didn't leave sad.

3. Visit Rubyjo.
4. Check on Dennis.

Returning to her salad and lasagna, she ate slowly, observing other diners. Alone or accompanied, each one she eyed consumed food quickly, some talking as they ate. She imagined the sound of a hundred vacuum cleaners. *No wonder so many of them are obese.*

She wondered if the atmosphere was contagious, if it contained bacteria that infected people with urgency. Was anyone immune; was she? Unease tightened her shoulders and an image of their trailer parked in an empty, dry, bare cotton field slid into her mind. She knew that she was inside that trailer, scurrying from one side to the other, mechanically wiping counters, straightening towels, urgently doing nothing worth doing.

———◆———

Maternal and child units filled the rest of second floor. As if she knew her purpose, Dorothy Faye followed the signs leading to the birthing rooms. Soft lighting, framed landscape prints on the walls, and muted music from speakers overhead distinguished the obstetric area from the busy connecting hall. She hesitated at the entrance, surprised at the almost tranquil tone the unit conveyed. "Could I help you with directions?" someone asked from behind her.

"Yes, thank you. I'm looking for the nursery."

The grey-haired woman who had offered help stepped closer. "I'm pretty familiar with this place. I'll show you. The newborn nursery is at the far end of the hall, just before you come to the elevator lobby. NICU, you know, for the prematures, is right in there." She pointed to double doors on the left. "That's where I'm headed."

"Are you on staff here?" Dorothy Faye asked.

"It might be easier if I was, as much as I'm here. But no, our baby's in NI. We take turns coming to feed and rock her. The nurses do it if we can't, of course. But we want her to know we love her." She paused and looked around as if she didn't want to be overheard. "I believe this is the hardest thing I've ever had to do. She's so small, not even two pounds. All those premature babies look like little tiny skeletons—just the remains of some life, not the beginning. I'm always afraid to hold her because I'm afraid I'll break something. And there are wires and tubes connected to her." Dorothy Faye watched the woman's eyes, listening. She knew there was no answer to the woman's words.

"I'm sorry. I didn't intend to start with my sad story." The woman made a weak attempt at a smile. "All you wanted was directions. Well, it's time for me to get inside."

Dorothy Faye thanked her and walked slowly in the direction she had pointed. The nursery windows were covered from the inside with curtains that had the appearance of old-fashioned quilts. The curtains slowly opened as she approached, like a play was about to begin—scene one, act one. Four babies in individual see-through bassinets on wheels lined the nursery window, each wrapped snugly in a receiving blanket and wearing a tiny knit cap. Nurses moved in pantomime behind them, tending to several more infants in identical containers positioned throughout the room. Dorothy Faye smiled as she watched a nurse conducting a one-sided conversation with a newborn.

A young man stopped near Dorothy Faye and glanced grimly at the babies before turning away. She got a brief look at his face, but couldn't read it—either anger or distress. He took a cell phone from a clip on his belt and punched in several numbers. He waited, then looked at the phone as if it had offended him and returned it to his belt. She watched his reflection in the glass of the nursery window. He looked directly toward her. Before she could even smile, he glared at her as if she had intruded on a private conversation. He turned abruptly and strode away, toward the elevators.

Dorothy Faye stayed, an audience of one for the nursery scene. Not a drama, more a vignette, a slice of life's beginnings, it suggested far greater orderliness than she knew to be true. Her first experience with childbirth had left her dismayed and the second had left her alone with two babies. She couldn't recall when she had last thought of her pain and tears during those first days after Elizabeth was born. Her mother would be surprised how clearly she could remember her leaking breasts and the smell, the sweetish, slightly fermented scent of a perpetually damp nursing bra mixed with postpartum blood. Her mother had told her it was all in her imagination. Dorothy Faye hadn't bothered to argue; it wasn't a bad odor, just different—new life's aroma.

She had been certain Ronnie would notice it, though. He didn't. He was fully occupied by his fascination with her breasts. "I hope they stay big and full like this forever." That was the only thing about the birth of their first child that seemed to interest him. That and when "things would be back to normal." She shook her head, putting the past back in its place.

Not eager to leave the hospital, she walked slowly to the elevator lobby. She chose one of the three chairs opposite the elevator doors and took out her puzzle book. She started on puzzle #52.

"I guess you found the nursery."

Dorothy Faye recognized the woman who had given her directions. "Yes, thanks. Is feeding and rocking time finished?"

"Yes, my next turn is six hours from now. My daughter's staying for the next two times."

"You're the baby's grandmother?"

"Great-grandmother."

"You look too young to be a grandmother, much less a great-grandmother."

"I'm forty-nine. But I feel a hundred today."

"Lack of sleep?"

"That's part of it." She moved toward the elevator, but hesitated and returned to the chairs. "Do you mind if I sit down?"

"Not at all. I'm resting a while myself."

The woman leaned back, closed her eyes, and breathed a sigh. "Have you ever felt like you might explode?" Her eyes still closed, she didn't wait for a response. She could have been talking to herself. "I'm holding it in pretty well, but I'm so mad at that irresponsible girl; and I'm mad at my daughter for letting her run wild and get pregnant. I'm mad at everyone. I'm afraid too—afraid the baby won't live—afraid it will—afraid my last chance for a life of my own has just disappeared. I know that in the end, I'll be the one to have to raise this baby. It's not the baby's fault. She's the only one I'm not mad at."

Neither one spoke for a couple of minutes. The great-grandmother's eyes remained closed. Just when Dorothy Faye began to think she might be sleeping, the woman sat up and shrugged her shoulders, but didn't move to leave.

"To top it off, her mother's gone. We don't know where. As soon as she was dismissed from the hospital nine days ago, she left with one of those tattooed freaks she's been living with. Not a word from her since. We didn't even know she was pregnant until about six weeks ago. She had been gone— who knows where—for about six months and then she turned up at my house late one night. I had just gotten home from the first date I'd had in five years. I'd gone out with a nice man from church and had a really good time.

"Just as I was getting ready for bed, there she was at the front door, looking like a refugee, crying, saying she was sick. I felt sorry for her and put her to bed. The next day I took her to the doctor. Her blood pressure was sky high and they said she was in danger of her kidneys shutting down. And oh, by the way, that's all related to her pregnancy. Pregnancy? She had not said word one about being pregnant and was so skinny, you couldn't tell by looking. Sixteen years old. I couldn't say too much because I was sixteen when I had her mother. But I was married and I had some sense. She has none, never has had."

"If you care for the baby, will you have anyone to help you?"

The woman leaned back in the chair again and rested her head against the high back. "I've been thinking about that. I'm the one to do it. I'm healthy and I don't have to go to work every day. My daughter has two other children of her own—divorced, working. She couldn't take on another child, especially one that might need extra care. It's only logical that I would do it. Even if I am older, I'd do a better job than my granddaughter would. But I'll tell you this. If I raise this baby, I'm going to adopt her so there can't be any interference later on."

Still resting against the chair, she turned toward Dorothy Faye. The worried frown had softened. "The truth is, no matter how mad I am at everybody, I know that baby already loves me. I can tell by the way she relaxes when I hold her. Her breathing settles down too."

"Babies are hard to resist. I always feel good, hopeful, when I hold a baby."

"That's exactly how I feel. But I still intend to pinch my granddaughter's head off if I get hold of her again." She was up now, at the elevator buttons. "I sound tough, don't I? I'd better go. Lots to do. Thanks for listening. I hope I didn't wear you out."

Dorothy Faye turned back to puzzle #52. Clue 1 Across—"false belief in spite of invalidating evidence." Eight letters. Nothing came to mind except "hallucination." Maybe the answer was two short words. She closed the book, stood, and pressed the Down button. Waiting, she wondered, could a premature baby love someone, or was that a "false belief" held by a wishful great-grandmother? She stepped in and watched the doors close. *Does the love humans offer to others make them ignore "invalidating evidence"?*

She stepped inside the trailer without making a sound. She held her breath and rapped three times on the inside of the flimsy door.

"Just a minute, I'm in here," Harold said from the bathroom.

"Sir, please step out now. We need to see some identification. We're checking for unauthorized parking." She tried to disguise her voice, but doubted she could fool him.

Harold slid the bathroom door open a crack and peeked out.

"Made you look," she said.

He laughed. "You sure did. Got me that time. I'll be out in just a second."

She heard water running. He came out wiping his hands on a small towel. "Yep, you had me thinking about bail money. Been out here long?"

"No, I just got here. Been visiting. Everything okay?"

"Sure, sure. We got real good gas mileage."

She had been asking about him, not the pickup. But she let it pass. He looked less worried than before.

"I drove by Janiece's. O.D. was out in the yard, so I stopped and talked a while. They're both fine."

That's debatable. "Did you see Janiece?"

"No, lucky for me, she was at the grocery store." He hesitated. "I still haven't decided for sure if I'm goin' to tell her what I heard. If I don't want her to know, I can't tell O.D. either. You know she can read his mind. He's like an open book."

———◆———

Day 30 June 17, Saturday 9:45 p.m. County General Hospital, Lubbock

Harold's got those two men at the nursing home on his mind. He talked about them at supper. He feels bad that they're in the nursing home and I think even worse about the fact that the home sits across the road from a prison. I'm not certain why that part disturbs him so much. He said, "They don't need much help. You should see how they help take care of each other. Bill takes in everything. Even blind, he can tell if Elmer's having trouble keeping up when they're walking, because of his artificial leg. He'll hesitate like he needs to hold onto Elmer's elbow to know where to step next. And when they eat, Elmer tells Bill, real quiet like, where each thing is on his plate. Bacon at two o'clock, biscuits at six, eggs at nine—like that. Bill eats without missing a bite. It's a damn shame those old boys have to be there. You know, I hope it's true that my daddy did have someone to live with if he was alive all those years. I'd hate to think that he ended up in a place like that. He was one of those men who needed to be out, be moving around." I wonder if he realized he was describing himself.

If I were a gambling woman, I'd bet he starts working on a plan to spring those two. He could think of it as another adventure, kind of like he was liberating Butch and Sundance.

I haven't seen anyone patrolling this parking lot so far. Maybe we're safe here for a few days. It's been a month since we started this "vacation." Every day I tell myself he'll be tired of it soon and ready for something different. I'm sure I'll be ready for something else *myself by then, but I don't know exactly what I'll be ready for.*

Looking at puzzle #52 again, she saw 6 Down—"erroneous perception or belief." Eight letters. She wrote in I L L U S I O N. That made the sixth letter in the word that had her stumped an I. "Rudimentary, basic," ten letters, was E L E M E N T A R Y—2 Down. She returned to 1 Across and placed O N after the I, guessing, because nouns often end in ION. _ E _ _ _ I O N—"false belief in spite of invalidating evidence."

CHAPTER 26

Step Four

D orothy Faye sat on the trailer step and watched the sun rise. Its first pale probes traveled on a faint breeze that whispered to her— confidences about babies and their mothers.

Harold's voice from behind the screen door startled her. "You got the jump on me this morning," he said. "How long have you been up?"

"Not too long. You missed a fine sunrise." She had heard him get up during the night and knew he had stayed up for quite a while. "You didn't sleep well last night, did you?"

"Probably ate too much. But I made up for lost time by sleeping late." He cocked his head, turning his left ear toward the door. "Is that my telephone ringing?" *Perfect hearing this morning.* She pointed out to the pickup, the sound's source.

She poured a cup of coffee and delivered it to him through the pickup window. He smiled and winked at her as he listened to the call. A few minutes later he looked in through the screen. "Has the carhop gone off duty?"

"No, sir. Just honk and she'll be right out. More coffee?"

"I'm coming inside. That was R.J. on the phone."

205

"Everything okay?"

"According to him, everything's great. He wanted to know if we'd be here around the Fourth of July. He and Maia want to come out and give us their presentation. I told him we'd make sure to be here." He looked past Dorothy Faye toward the door. "Morning, O.D. I didn't hear you drive up."

Harold and O.D. left without specifying a destination. She knew they could be happy without one. O.D. would need to talk. He probably hadn't been allowed to utter more than two sentences since they'd been gone. The pickup was available if she wanted to use it, but there was no place she needed or wanted to go.

She checked her "to do" list. Number 1—call Elizabeth.

"Hi, honey. Oh, I forgot this is your cell phone number. Can you talk or are you driving?"

Elizabeth was in the grocery store parking lot. She was happy to talk. She quizzed Dorothy Faye about the trip to Odessa. When Dorothy Faye told her about R.J. and Maia, she had a whole lot of questions, more about Maia than their new business.

"Does his girlfriend seem intelligent?"

Dorothy Faye corrected her. "He says she's his friend and business partner. He never said girlfriend."

"We can hope. What did you think of her? Does she understand how he is?"

"I liked her. And I don't know—what do you mean 'how he is?'"

"You know, kind of a daydreamer."

"He's not a daydreamer. He just thinks a lot about things. But yes, she looks at him like he's the only person in the room. I wish she was his girlfriend."

They discussed R.J. some more and then Dorothy Faye asked about Elizabeth's boyfriend. "Use the past tense when you speak of him, Mother. We broke up. Well, he broke up with me because I wouldn't make plans for a wedding."

"Honey, I'm sorry." *That again.* "I thought it was men who were supposed to be the ones who run from marriage."

"Don't be sorry. He wasn't the one."

"The one?"

"He wasn't someone I could ever treat the way you've treated Daddy all these years."

Dorothy Faye didn't say anything.

"Are you still there, Mother?"

"Yes. I noticed my phone is getting hot. I guess that means I need to hang up. But I wanted to ask you—do you think you could come out here around the Fourth of July? The reason R.J. called this morning was to say he and Maia will be here. It would be nice if we were all together."

Elizabeth laughed. "Will we have sparklers and homemade ice cream?"

"If that's what you want. I'll tell your daddy and you know he'll do it for you."

"I have some vacation days and no plans. I'll arrange it."

After they said their good-byes, Dorothy Faye thought about homemade ice cream. Harold would have a new excuse to go to Walmart. They'd given away their old wooden freezer when they left Whaley.

She worked on puzzle #52, fitting in several words without resorting to the solutions. But 1 Across—_ *E* _ _ _ *I* *O* *N* still waited for her. "False belief in spite of invalidating evidence."

Noon passed and Harold hadn't returned. Dorothy Faye ate a bowl of cereal and called it lunch. She swirled the spoon in the leftover milk and thought about Elizabeth's string of ex-boyfriends. Elizabeth could write a book about the men she had improved and then turned down. *Maybe I'll suggest that and see what she says.* She doubted she ever would mention the boyfriends to Elizabeth at all. And she wondered if there was something else the mother of a grown woman was supposed to do other than wait to be needed.

Just off the lobby in County General, Dorothy Faye noticed a door that appeared to open into a small courtyard. She could see three wrought-iron tables, each with four chairs. Trees and shrubs shaded the small enclosure on two sides, with exterior hospital walls on the other two. She was surprised such a pretty spot was unoccupied. She pushed the door open a crack, hoping an alarm wouldn't sound. Opening it farther, she saw a woman wearing maroon scrubs sitting alone at a fourth table, reading a small red book. The woman looked up a second, then returned to the book. Dorothy Faye took her diet cola to a table on the opposite side of the courtyard.

The puzzle book hung as she tried to get it from her big purse. She shook it and the contents clattered to the concrete. Dorothy Faye looked up from the spilled pile of billfold, comb, lipstick, ballpoint pens, chewing gum, notebook, grocery store receipts, and tissues and saw the nurse kneeling beside her. "I'll help," the woman said.

"That was bound to happen; I keep stuffing things in there," Dorothy Faye said. They gathered the items and she jammed them into her purse. "Hi, I'm Dorothy Faye Bell."

"Hi, I'm Lou Ann, and…" She stopped, laughed an embarrassed laugh.

"And…" Dorothy Faye said.

"I sometimes do it in the wrong places."

Dorothy Faye watched the nurse's eyes as they followed a tiny yellow butterfly from shrub to shrub.

"Do you have a few minutes?" the nurse asked. She grunted quietly and sighed softly as she got to her feet. Her weight didn't help, but Dorothy Faye suspected she'd had a leg injury of some sort.

"Sure."

The nurse retrieved her small book and sat at Dorothy Faye's table. "The rest of the phrase is, 'I'm Lou Ann, and I'm an alcoholic.' That's how we introduce ourselves at Alcoholics Anonymous. I've attended at least one AA meeting a day for the last ninety days. It's become almost automatic to introduce myself that way." She didn't meet Dorothy Faye's eyes.

"Recovery isn't easy work," Dorothy Faye said.

"You know something about recovery." The nurse stated it as a fact, not a question.

Dorothy Faye explained anyway. "Some, from a friend who now has several years of sobriety. She still attends meetings regularly. Calls it her lifeline."

The nurse turned the small red book over and over in her hands as she spoke. "They tell me it's the grace of God and the support of the group that can help me." She focused on the nearest concrete wall. "I'll tell you, if there's one day of the week that I need both of those, it's Sunday. That's one reason I'm here today. Working fills the time. I'd work every day if they'd let me. But during treatment they said one of the things that will get us in trouble is getting too tired. That and getting too hungry or too angry." She recited the words as if they were part of a litany. "I'm in the Recovering Nurses Program. It limits where I can work. No critical care or emergency—too stressful. Can't be in a charge position either. But when staffing is low, any unit can be stressful. Part of me resists following those rules." She stopped again, this time closing her eyes, seeming to turn inward.

"Being willful like that is something I have to work on. And I'm not supposed to skip meals or breaks either. I eat my lunch out here and read. If I eat with people from the unit, it's like not leaving work." Again, she took time before continuing, as if she was evaluating each statement before she uttered it. "The other nurses seem to be watching me, like they're afraid they'll say the wrong thing. Let me ask you something I've been wondering about. Does it scare you to think someone like me might be taking care of you if you were a patient?" She fixed her gaze on the red book.

Dorothy Faye waited until Lou Ann raised her eyes. She said, "No, I don't think so. My friend gained a lot of insight about herself and other people through AA. What about you? Would it bother you if you were your patient?"

"Not now." Lou Ann exhaled slowly, as if holding back the breath that wanted to escape. She told Dorothy Faye that, as a nurse, she'd felt guilty for believing that alcoholics were weak-willed, immoral people. And how she had convinced herself she would never lower herself to that level. Those beliefs had kept her from seeking help even when she ended up in the hospital after driving her car into a telephone pole, so drunk she tried to walk away on her badly fractured leg.

"When I sobered up, for the first two weeks, I resisted everything they tried to do to help me. I was sure that if I could just get back to work, I'd be able to get my life straightened out."

She said it took a visit from a nurse, one also in the program, to open her eyes. She was now working on step four in AA's twelve-step program. "That's where you must do a fearless and searching moral inventory, spiritual housecleaning. And you don't just do it once. Like housecleaning, it's a regular necessity."

No breeze reached the tiny patio. Lou Ann sat back and smiled, a tiny sad expression that seemed directed toward something only she could see. "Working on my inventory, I see I've had a lot of delusions about myself. The biggest one was the idea that as long as I didn't drink on duty, I was in control."

She shook her head, looked briefly at Dorothy Faye, then to the peeling paint she'd begun chipping from her chair. "Anyway, I'm making progress on step four. When you came out, I was rereading about how to do the inventory." She held up the little book. "You're the first person outside of AA I've told this much about myself. Something made me feel you would understand."

"I'll take that as a compliment. But I doubt if anyone can fully understand your experience. I admire what you're doing. I know it's difficult."

The nurse checked her watch. "I have to get back to the unit." She stopped at the door and said, "I hope I see you again. I promise I won't monopolize the conversation next time."

"Maybe we'll have another chance to visit. Keep up the good work," Dorothy Faye said.

———————

_D E L U S I O N_. She should have thanked that nurse for helping her. Now she had the word. She looked at it, tapping her pen on the page. _Do I occupy myself with puzzles to reinforce the delusion that I have something worthwhile to do? Ignoring invalidating evidence. Doesn't everyone do that, reject facts that don't fit with what we believe?_ She shook her head and closed the book.

She looked again at the "to do" list. Number 4—Check on Dennis.

She didn't explain where she was. He didn't ask. He said he was so happy to hear from her. His voice sounded relaxed. There had been no real change in his mother's condition, and he said he was satisfied with the care at the nursing home. He said, "Amazing as it may be, my brother also approves." They talked about his work and how he had "gotten his life reorganized," as he put it.

Dorothy Faye quickly filled the first lull in the conversation. "Dennis, I'm going to have to go now. But I'll call you again soon. I'm glad to know you're doing well." She didn't want him to ask about her patient.

"I am," he said. "And I'm so glad you called. Promise you'll call again. Remember, if there's ever anything I can do for you, let me know."

As she closed the phone, she congratulated herself on calling him. It qualified as one worthwhile thing she had done today. And she made a promise to herself. The next time they talked, she was going to tell him the truth. What did Lou Ann call it—spiritual housecleaning? She had the first item for a new list—her version of the moral inventory—*made intentional false impressions on unsuspecting strangers.*

CHAPTER 27

Juneteenth

G oing back to Whaley took a lot less time than leaving had. Dorothy Faye had to force herself to focus on driving. Harold had said, just before she left, "I'll take care of getting that doctor's appointment today. No need for you to bother."

The city limit sign, "Whaley, Texas, Population 2998," reminded her she had returned, and her watch told her she was early. Knowing Mrs. Ottley preferred punctuality, she drove the main streets to prevent arriving too soon. Some time back, the city council had decided to make each of the two-block segments of the business district one-way. Wall Street led south off the highway. Bank was the matching northbound segment. Back to back, they comprised a collection of vacant buildings and a few remaining essential establishments. Those necessities included a combination dry-cleaning drop-off and video rental; an excuse for a grocery store; a hardware/UPS pickup enterprise; and the post office. After the southbound tour assured her that nothing had changed on Wall Street, she took the single short block west on Bond to enter Bank.

City hall still seemed to be open, and the volunteer fire department's blue light shone, signaling that no fire was burning out of control in Whaley, Texas. Three vacant stores; an empty lot where the pool hall had been before it burned; the City Cafe; the Farm Bureau Insurance Agency; and the chamber of commerce all stood just as she had left them.

She tried to remember why she and Harold had stayed in this town for so many years. Maybe it was *inertia* (puzzle #96). Now it had been overcome and they were rolling! She'd heard other people explain their own reasons. Some came because of the schools and stayed after their kids were grown because it had become home. Others who farmed or ranched in the area or who pumped nearby leases said they had moved to Whaley because their wives were tired of living in the country. "This is as close to the ranch as we can get and still be in a town." Then they'd wink and say, "Well, sort of a town."

A one-doctor clinic and the nursing home attracted some older people who had grown up there to come back to Whaley. By now, quite a few of them were in the nursing home, their Whaley houses rented to younger people whose primary reason for coming to Whaley was the reputation of the schools. The school system served as the source of education, the center of entertainment, and the town's largest employer. A reputation for sound basic curriculum, an arts program, consistent discipline, and strong football teams had, in the past fifteen or twenty years, created the attraction. Teachers like Mrs. Ottley had helped build that school's reputation.

Mrs. Ottley's reputation had become something of legend in Whaley. The Ottleys' early days in Whaley were part of the town's lore by the time Dorothy Faye and Harold moved there in 1973. Carrie Ottley had arrived with her husband, the newly hired Whaley High School principal, in 1936. The school board was delighted they were both teachers. After about two years, the exemplary young English teacher shocked the town by leaving. She returned eighteen months later with something no other female teacher in the entire school possessed, a master's degree—and a year-old baby. And to the town's further amazement, she had traveled to New York City to acquire that degree at Teachers College Columbia University. No one knew exactly what to think. But many wondered if the couple would now move on to some larger city with better school facilities.

Contrary to speculation, the Ottleys didn't leave. They dedicated themselves to their daughter and to the young people of Whaley. Mr. Ottley never applied to be superintendent. He kept the job of principal from the day they arrived until he died in 1980.

Speaking of her husband, Mrs. Ottley had told Dorothy Faye, "He was my sweetheart, my only love. I shall miss him as long as I live. But he would have expected me to truly live, not to retire from life." And so she had. After his death, she continued for another five years teaching English and speech, directing the school's theater program, and traveling during vacations. For another eleven years after she stopped teaching full-time, Mrs. Ottley taught as a substitute. Her guiding principle, the one she allowed no student to graduate without reciting, was, "Never go to bed at night, any night, until you can truthfully say you have learned something that day." And she lived her own life by that same principle. She didn't simply read; she studied. She didn't simply observe; she sought to understand.

Mrs. Ottley greeted her when she tapped on the screen door. "Come in, Dorothy Faye. I'm so glad to see you. You've been on my mind a lot recently. Here, sit down so we can talk. I gave Priscilla the day off and Alma will come this evening. We have the place to ourselves."

After they hugged, Dorothy Faye asked, "Do you and Priscilla get along? Does she do a good job?"

Mrs. Ottley took that as a cue to regale her with a story about Priscilla, who she said was fine, if a bit too tidy for her taste. With her usual flair, she described how Priscilla had taken to singing along with the Broadway show tunes that Mrs. Ottley loved. She imitated Priscilla's half of a duet with Mary Martin doing "I'm Gonna Wash That Man Right Outa My Hair." She finished by saying, "I believe she likes my taste in music."

The older woman's taste in clothing was also worth imitating. Mrs. Ottley had once told her that life was a costume affair and that choosing one's costume was important in playing one's part well. Today she had chosen pale yellow silk slacks and blouse topped with a short silk jacket of several shades of purple with touches of yellow—a perfect echo of the arrangement of Dutch iris on the dining room table. Her shoes were low-heeled and also purple. Her long, white hair wound into a twist atop her head, emphasizing her still-elegant features. Dorothy Faye wondered what part Carrie Ottley had in mind as she dressed today.

All Dorothy Faye had to do to prompt another story was to say, "You look good. How are you feeling?" The former drama coach had her laughing again as she told of her latest interest—tai chi. She had ordered an instructional video after her daughter expressed concern about her mother's balance. "You know she stays concerned about something continuously. I'm too thin; I don't get enough rest, anything. 'Mother, at your age, a fall could be just dev-a-sta-ting' was what she said.'" Her imitation of her daughter was dramatic, and perfect. "When I showed her my tai chi routine, then she was concerned I might fall while practicing. I suppose if she had her way, I would be installed in a stationary position in a padded room until such time as I decide to make my final exit. I've told her again and again that I encourage her independence and that I expect the same consideration from her. We have that conversation at least once a month." She paused as if replaying the conversation with her adult child. "It's what we do, you see, because we love each other."

Dorothy Faye asked about recent local events. There were none to report. They discussed politics and Mrs. Ottley's concern about lack of funding for the school's debate teams. An hour and a half passed quickly. Then they agreed it was time to leave for the German café in Slaton Mrs. Ottley had chosen for lunch.

———◆———

Mrs. Ottley's silences pleased Dorothy Faye as much as her conversations. The older woman observed intently. She thought deeply. When she spoke, she spoke precisely, as if only after the silence had she determined what was worth saying. As the miles passed, Dorothy Faye did not interrupt her passenger's consideration of the countryside or perhaps of memories remaining there. "Do you know what day it is, Dorothy Faye?" Mrs. Ottley asked.

"Monday, June nineteenth." She waited—a lesson was about to begin—just one of the reasons she loved Carrie Ottley.

"Yes, that's correct. For many people, June nineteenth is an important day of celebration, Juneteenth, Emancipation Day. That was the day in 1865 when the slaves in Texas first received news of the Emancipation Proclamation issued by President Lincoln on January first, 1863. A Union Army general arrived by ship in Galveston and read the official order to the citizens there. It had taken two-and-a-half years for the news to reach them. That was only fifty years before I was born.

"As a child in East Texas, I knew some older black people who had lived as slaves. I think it was difficult for them to adjust to their freedom, at least partly because so many white people did not want to see things change. It's a stark example of how changing one part of a situation, whether in a small group like a family or in an entire nation, changes everything for everyone involved. And it demonstrates the pressure that is exerted toward maintaining the more stable or familiar situation that existed before the change."

They arrived in Slaton. Dorothy Faye attended to finding a parking space. She said, "I hope you will tell me while we eat what started you thinking about that subject."

Aromas of spicy German dishes and the sound of conversation greeted them as they entered the restaurant. Mrs. Ottley had chosen a lively, popular spot for their lunch. They both ordered the special, sauerbraten with dumplings and red cabbage. "Now," Dorothy Faye said, "tell me more about Emancipation Day."

Mrs. Ottley arranged her napkin and took a sip of water. Dorothy Faye had missed both the content of their conversations and Mrs. Ottley's elegant, precise speech. If she listened with her eyes closed, it seemed as if she were hearing a carefully reasoned composition being read aloud.

"Emancipation, the day, prompted my thoughts to the broader notion of emancipation, of one's suddenly being freed of constraints. Because I also have had you in my thoughts recently, it occurred to me that leaving Whaley could be an emancipation of sorts for you. I wondered how the changes—in location and in your daily responsibilities—might have affected both you and Harold, and perhaps others."

Their conversations often took this pattern. First Mrs. Ottley would outline key aspects of her thoughts on a subject. Next she would inquire about Dorothy Faye's perspective on the topic. Dorothy Faye would listen closely and wait to be asked. She waited partly out of respect for Mrs. Ottley's age and partly because she hoped to one day acquire the older woman's habits of speech. During their eight years together, Dorothy Faye's fascination with words had flowered as a result of their conversations.

She had been eating small bits of the day's special as she listened. Now she laid her fork on the rim of the plate. Mrs. Ottley would not interrupt as she assembled her response. "Truly thoughtful discourse is marked by its combination of precise thoughts and precise words expressing those thoughts." She had said that just after Dorothy Faye had begun staying with her. She had been explaining that she didn't want a housekeeper and did not need a nurse, but she did want a companion to converse with. *Emancipation, change, stability.* Mrs. Ottley sampled her sauerbraten and nodded her approval of the meal as Dorothy Faye considered how to respond.

"Change and disrupted stability I can address by describing some of what our trip has entailed." Dorothy Faye hardly recognized her own voice speaking the carefully chosen words. Her throat tightened as she felt the loss of daily contact with this woman's subtle mentoring. She took a breath and began telling about Harold's abrupt decision to buy the trailer, his secretive trip to Levelland, her hospital visiting, his ignoring her wish to visit Mrs. Ottley, his concern about the cause of his father's death, and of her own suspicion that none of these was precisely what it seemed to be, that something was yet to be revealed about his purposes for the move from Whaley and for the trip. She ignored her lunch as she described his distress about the two residents of the nursing home in Crane. "I actually thought of none of these things as real change other than our leaving here, because Harold has always acted on his ideas. He knows I support his choices even though he often doesn't consult me ahead of time."

"If your assessment is accurate, then Harold may be experiencing less change, less disruption of stability than you. How are the changes affecting you?" Mrs. Ottley asked.

Dorothy Faye said, "I'm surprised at myself. I don't know if leaving Whaley and following Harold's current idea are the source of it, but I've been alternately irritable and—I guess the word is excited. I won't bore you with all the details of my irritability, but I will say I've found myself wondering about things I haven't thought about in years, some of which leave me—irritable is the best word I can choose right now."

"Could you give an example?"

Dorothy Faye started to say the first thing that occurred to her, but stopped when Mrs. Ottley's eyes held her. *No wonder her students learned so much.* Very softly she said, "The main thing is wondering what I should be doing with the rest of my life."

"Change can encourage reevaluation. You also mentioned excitement."

"Yes, I'm not certain that expresses it as clearly as I would like. It's as if I know that I am about to discover a treasure of some sort. Maybe it's the same feeling Harold has when he starts one of his projects, acts on one of his big ideas." She filled her mouth with a dumpling. "He never said. I never asked. Did you and Mr. Ottley ever discuss those sorts of things—feelings, your dreams?"

"Yes," Mrs. Ottley said, "we did, on occasion. You see, we weren't only husband and wife. We were best friends. It was he who taught me the value of good conversation, beginning during our courtship." Her features took on the look of a woman recalling the best parts of love. "Had I not met him, I might have remained a pampered, East Texas, faux-Southern female, hiding my intelligence behind fluttery eyelashes and feigned helplessness."

Dorothy Faye smiled. "I'm trying to imagine your ever being helpless."

"Oh, I never was. But we were taught by example that pretending to be incapable of independent thought was the acceptable female role. Some were such good actresses that they even convinced themselves. Such a pity to waste intelligence that way."

———◆———

Mrs. Ottley wouldn't hear of Dorothy Faye's leaving when they returned to her house. "There's something important I want to tell you," she said.

"I shouldn't sit in the recliner. I'm so full, I might nod off," Dorothy Faye said. She chose the couch. Mrs. Ottley settled gently into her chair. Dorothy Faye hoped she could be as graceful if she lived to be eighty-five.

Mrs. Ottley said, "Knowing I won't live forever makes me realize that if there are things I want to say to people, I probably shouldn't wait." She looked across at the younger woman. "Now don't look so sad. I'm simply stating fact. I'm not planning on leaving anytime soon." She laughed at her own little joke. "The thing I want you to know, because I believe you are unaware of it, is that you have a gift, Dorothy Faye. When I use the word *gift*, I use it to mean a talent, much the same as the gift with which an artist—a painter or musician or writer—is endowed. Your gift is that you have a unique ability to listen to others and to help them feel hope."

"But—" It was all that Dorothy Faye could say.

"Don't disagree before you hear me out," Mrs. Ottley said. The serious voice of the teacher stopped Dorothy Faye from protesting further. "This is important. I know from my own experience with you, and I know from others who have told me of occasions when you helped them. The common thread in all the accounts is that you listen in a way that helps people unburden themselves. And without saying many words, you convey a feeling that there is a reason to hope.

"I chose to call your particular talent a gift. And I chose that word, gift, because of a book I read years ago." She explained that the book she mentioned focused on the concept that, in many cultures, anything received as a gift must be given away. The recipient must keep the gift in motion because in the act of giving, the gift increases in value and increases the value of the giver. Originally, the idea applied to tangible gifts, but the book's author applies the idea equally to talents that are gifts of ability, of creativity.

"Your talent is a gift. I want you to know that; to know that by giving it away, you are increasing its value and your own," she said. She spoke the words slowly and distinctly as if they were to be noted carefully.

Dorothy Faye stared at a piece of lint on the right knee of her slacks, resisted picking it off. After several moments, she raised her eyes to look at Mrs. Ottley. "I don't know what to say except thank you. I will think carefully about what you have said, not only about gifts, but also about change and emancipation. To tell the truth, it feels as if you have given *me* a gift."

CHAPTER 28

He's Going

T uesday morning, Harold said, "I've decided to go to Wichita Falls
tomorrow and see Martha Clay." He was talking from the bedroom;
Dorothy Faye was sitting in her chair in the living area. "I called
her yesterday. She sounded surprised, but I don't think she was upset. She
said to come on over and we'd talk. She lives in a retirement community.
Made sure to tell me it wasn't a nursing home."

She wondered why he hadn't mentioned this last night. Maybe it was
for the same reason she didn't tell him what Mrs. Ottley had told her. *Still
thinking about it.* They both had been pretty quiet at supper. Just talked
about the food and the weather, and went to bed early.

She waited to see if he was ready to say anything else and whether he intended to show his face when he talked. So far he had conducted his side of
the conversation out of sight, like a ventriloquist practicing a new routine.
When he finally did come into the kitchen area, he took a big breath and
fiddled with the pickup keys and checked his billfold. Finally he started
out the door, saying, "I'm going to go get O.D..." Then his voice kind of

trailed off. She thought he was gone. But a second later he was back inside. "Unless you just want to go, I'll go over there by myself."

"To Wichita Falls?"

"Yes, I want to get this taken care of, off my mind, before R.J. comes."

She didn't say what she was thinking—that he might have more on his mind after talking to Martha Clay. Instead, she said, "It'll be fine with me to stay here." She was thinking fast; no, wondering fast. *What is he not telling me? Settle down, keep smiling. This whole thing is probably hard on him. No sense making it harder.* She said, "I've been thinking I should visit Rubyjo. Maybe you could move the trailer over there in the morning, just in case." *At least I won't have to worry about County General's Security Services finding us out.*

He looked relieved and like he was trying to hide it. He said, "Yeah, good idea. But I think I'll move us this evening. That way I can get an early start in the morning." He drew another big breath, this time like it came more easily. She added to the list—*took a suggestion I made.*

He started out again and then reversed course once more. "I forgot to bring the mail in last night. Elizabeth sent part of the *Times*. You might want the puzzle."

She racked up another item—*thoughtful gesture.* Then she remembered. "I forgot to tell you, I talked to her Sunday afternoon. She said she'd come out for July Fourth if we would have homemade ice cream and sparklers."

That got a big grin out of him. "That's great. We'll all be together." He opened the door and Dorothy Faye followed, intending to get the paper. He said, "I really am going this time." Then he hugged her tight. She kissed him on the cheek and didn't say a word.

She tried to read the paper, but kept thinking about what Mrs. Ottley had told her. She pulled the notebook from its hiding place.

Day 32 Tuesday, June 20 County General Hospital, Lubbock

I tried to imagine what made Mrs. Ottley come to the conclusion that I have any special talent. Yes, I do listen and I think sometimes it helps people. I don't know about that "giving hope" part, though.

It's true that I have done a lot of listening, for as long as I can remember. People have told me stories of their childhood; I've heard tales about heroic acts. Children have spun fantastic epics starring themselves as heroes who fly and fight monsters. Many people have explained regrets for actions taken or for plans never completed. A few have exposed ignorance; many have named reasons for sorrows. Others showed me reasons for the gratefulness they feel, and a small number opened a crack in their armor and exposed their fears.

Have I listened only because their stories are more interesting to me than television? I could laugh it off and say, "At least there aren't any commercials." But I know I listened because I couldn't not listen. Although I didn't know it at first.

In a way, what she said about my being given a talent helps explain how I've felt about listening. Which is, if someone needs to talk, I must listen. I don't mean gossip, I recognize the difference between someone wanting to gossip about other people and someone needing to talk about themselves, their lives, their feelings, their actions, their hopes, and their sorrows. That's what I'm compelled to listen to.

If a test were given, with only one question on it— "What is the one most important thing you have learned to this point in your life and how did you learn it?"—I know the answer I would give. It's this—people tell stories about themselves in order to try to make sense of life. What they tell, they either believe to be true or wish to be true. I learned that from listening.

I've also been thinking about the idea that a talent is a gift and that gifts should be given away, kept in motion. That part makes perfect sense to me. But the idea of my being talented still seems pretty farfetched.

It seems like a good time to go visiting.

The first thing she did was take a tour. She had only seen parts of the hospital on Sunday. This time she covered every floor from the burn unit to the locked psychiatric ward, although she couldn't go into either one of those. From what she could tell, waiting rooms got little attention in that hospital's design. The general floors had only two or three chairs near each elevator lobby, uncomfortable chairs, so no one was likely to linger there very long. The surgery waiting room was so small that families milled around in the hall. Even the front lobby lacked comfortable seating.

The little patio she had found Sunday didn't seem to fit. Every place else pulsed with people, but that patio sat like a miniature island unconnected to the rest of the hospital. As she passed the patio door, she saw Lou Ann, who looked up and waved and then hurried to open the door.

"Do you have time to visit a few minutes?" the nurse asked. "I'm taking my lunch break early today."

"Sure," Dorothy Faye said. "I'm glad to see you. You look happy."

"I am. Come, sit over here in the shade." Today she wasn't clutching the little red book. "It did me a lot of good to talk to you on Sunday. I went to a meeting that evening, and afterward I talked with my sponsor about how I told you about myself and how calm I felt the rest of the afternoon. She said that what I had done was to try out a little bit of step five. That's the one that says…Well, here, I'll read it." She took the little red book from her pocket. "It says, '…we admitted to God, to ourselves, and to another human being the exact nature of our wrongs.' In the *Big Book*, the one that this little red one summarizes, it explains that you can do that even with a complete stranger as long as you are sure that what you say will be kept in confidence." She hesitated, tracing the book's title with an index finger. Then she looked at Dorothy Faye directly and steadily. "I knew I could trust you."

"You can. Your trust is an important compliment. Thank you, Lou Ann."

"When my sponsor told me I had tried out that fifth step, it made sense to me. Knowing I was going to have to get to that eventually was holding me back from finishing step four. Talking to you helped me feel like I can get through that inventory and work on step five when the time comes. You made it easy by accepting me and by being a good listener."

She stopped talking suddenly, like she had used all the words issued to her. She shook her head and said, "I'm sorry, I didn't even ask how you are today."

"Just fine. I'm glad you were here. We'll be leaving late this afternoon. I probably won't see you again. But I'm glad you feel you're making progress."

"I am. Well, guess I better get back to work." She collected the paper bag that had held her lunch.

"Wait," Dorothy Faye said, "Let me give you my phone number in case you ever want to talk again." Lou Ann wrote the number on a scrap she tore from a napkin. She looked at it, then carefully folded the scrap and put it in her little red book. "Take care," Dorothy Faye said.

------◆------

When she sat down back at the trailer, Dorothy Faye tried to give a name to the way she felt. She couldn't. But she fell asleep in the chair. Smiling.

Harold still wasn't back. Sounds of car motors starting, doors opening and closing, and bits of conversation rode the breeze in through the screen. Coasting on the edge of waking, she pretended she was speaking a description of the afternoon parking lot sounds. "Change of shift, the time when people turn away from the places they are in control, from the busy-ness of examining, testing, diagnosing, treating, medicating, cleaning, phoning, offering condolences, and sending new babies out to their uncertain possibilities. Leaving, these people face the paler parts of their lives, where chaos reigns." Articulate, precise, she would have made Mrs. Ottley proud. She roused herself and went to the bedroom to get her walking shoes. Then she put them back on the shelf. Harold was back.

As he walked in, he said, "I called Rubyjo. She's expecting us, invited us to sleep in the house if we want to. Said something like, 'Your trailer won't be in the way. I don't have much company.'" He shrugged and lifted his hands in a "what can you do?" gesture. Then he said, "Let's eat before we go over there. I can tolerate the gloom better on a full stomach."

He didn't say a word about an appointment with the doctor.

CHAPTER 29

Pay Attention

H arold was up by half past six, rummaging around. He talked all
the time he was putting socks and shirts in his small overnight
bag. "That's the biggest surprise, that computer. And she knows
how to use it too. That may be a good sign. I mean, she could be coming
out of it. She can send mail and she talks—chats, she calls it—with people
on it. Said she got it not long ago after seeing something on television.
Some computer service here in town came out and set it up and showed her
how to use it."

"Wonder why Janiece didn't mention it?"

"She doesn't know about it. Rubyjo said she was going to wait until
Janiece came over and then show it to her. 'Knowing Janiece, that may be
sometime next year, if ever,' was what she said. Some time or other, Janiece
got on her about her housekeeping, and Rubyjo told her she could stay
home if she didn't like the sight of cigarette butts." He shrugged, as if their
arguing didn't surprise him. "Maybe we should get a computer," he said.
"Do you know if they sell them at Walmart?"

"I don't know. I've never looked for one."

"We could send mail to Elizabeth and R.J. Rubyjo said you can get newspapers and do bookkeeping and…"

"I don't see any room in this trailer for a computer."

"That's something to think about." He drew a breath like he was about to say something else, but Dorothy Faye could tell he was talking for the sake of distraction, mainly to keep from thinking. Probably about what he might learn from Martha Clay. "Okay, I guess I'm ready." He turned toward the door, then came back and hugged her.

She was pretty certain he'd forgotten something, as jittery as he seemed. Sure enough, as he got in the pickup, she noticed his cell phone and reading glasses on the counter. He had started backing out when he stopped because she was waving both arms to get his attention. "Guess I'm a little distracted," he said.

"In that case, be extra careful. Call and let me know when you get there, please."

"Don't worry. I'll be okay." She wondered if he convinced himself.

Day 34 Wednesday, June 21 Rubyjo's house

Back in 1980 when Rubyjo and Eddie divorced, he had left her with this house. Even though he doesn't have to, he sends someone to make repairs and to paint every three or four years. I guess it's his way of making up for leaving. They married when they were just kids, fourteen and seventeen. When I first met her, when Harold and I married, the two of them traveled because Eddie worked, still does, for a highway construction company. They lived in lots of different places, moving around with a trailer house for years. After a few years, he learned to operate heavy equipment and eventually was made supervisor. He got another promotion that put him in management and made it possible for them to have a permanent home.

They bought this nice three-bedroom house just a little south of the university. It was built in the fifties and has a small, pretty yard with large trees. I've thought before that it's the kind of house I'd like to have. There are lots of windows, could be very light if she ever opened the blinds. And the hardwood floors are pretty. If I lived here, I'd be out in the yard every sunny day. But Rubyjo spends most of her time inside. I seldom quote Janiece, but I recall her saying that Rubyjo is a person who never did have any idea about how to be happy. Not that Janiece seems like much of a hand at it herself, but I have seen her laugh now and then. Rubyjo's never seemed to see the humor in things.

I'm behaving like Harold did this morning. Doing little useless things to delay going. All I have to do is step out of this trailer and walk to the front door. Maybe I can get her to come outside for a walk. I don't know though; she might evaporate if the sun strikes her.

Expecting to spend the afternoon trying to get Rubyjo out of the house or maybe just to smile, Dorothy Faye trudged across the lawn.

"Dorothy Faye, I'm glad you came over," Rubyjo said. Her smile was the first surprise. The blinds were open, the entire place was bright, and the smell of cigarette smoke had vanished.

She made some iced tea and brought it to the kitchen table. Instead of the television, music was playing somewhere in the house, Elvis Presley. Dorothy Faye reminded herself of the danger of assuming she could ever predict anyone.

"That's 'King Creole,'" Rubyjo said.

Dorothy Faye realized she was talking about the music. "We all loved Elvis. My mother threatened to throw my record player in the trash because I played 'Love Me Tender' so many times," she said.

"Eddie was working all day, and Elvis and I had the trailer to ourselves." Rubyjo smiled. It was an actual smile, not her usual unsuccessful attempt. "Back then was another life. Sometimes I like to remember parts of it." She stared off toward the other room, still smiling. Then she said, "Dorothy Faye, here's something I'll bet you never expected."

Dorothy Faye hoped she wouldn't ask her to guess what it was. She had decided never to anticipate anything again, not even as a guess. "What is it, Rubyjo?"

"You've heard that old saying 'starve a fever, feed a cold'? Well, I guess I thought it was 'starve a fever, feed a depression.' In the last twenty years, since Eddie left, I've gained at least forty pounds. But look at me now. I'm back to where I was in nineteen ninety. In another couple of months, I'll be the same size I was in nineteen eighty. And a lot smarter than I was then."

She stood up, turned sideways so Dorothy Faye could see her profile, and then turned her back and raised her shirt. Her rear end was definitely smaller. Dorothy Faye said, "I thought something was different. First I thought that your smile, which I haven't ever seen much of, was the difference. Now I see your shape has changed too. How did you do it?"

"I got up from this kitchen table where I'd been sitting all those years. Even when I worked, I would come in every afternoon and sit here and only get up to go to the refrigerator or the cabinet. I've started eating tuna fish and green salads and fruit instead of corn chips and ice cream. And I quit drinking coffee and I've almost quit cigarettes completely."

She wanted to ask what got her off the chair and away from the table. Instead, she said, "You should be proud of yourself." The she asked anyway. "What got you up from the table?"

"You might find this hard to imagine, but it was something I saw on television. I'd been watching this show one morning, sitting right where you are, with the TV up on the counter over there." She pointed to an empty, clean countertop. "I've made a den in one of the bedrooms and put the television and the computer in there. Anyway, I was sitting there smoking cigarettes and drinking coffee and half paying attention, like I did most of the time. They had these women on talking about how they had taken charge of their lives. The third one was the one that got my attention. She could have been me—married young, divorced after more than twenty years." Rubyjo paused and nodded, as if affirming what she'd said.

"She had sat around depressed for lots of years afterward. The main thing she did was feel sorry for herself and blame him. She'd gotten fat and hated herself and everything else. Then one day something made her realize that her ex-husband didn't make her that way. She was choosing to be miserable. She decided she could make a new choice, and she did. She called the whole process 'reinventing' herself."

Dorothy Faye's eyes never left her sister-in-law as Rubyjo's new life lit her face.

"To make a long story a little shorter, I decided I could do the same thing, if I wanted to. The only thing holding me back was me. I have a nice house and I have money. All these years Eddie has been depositing a check every month in my account. The only place I ever went was the grocery store, and the only clothes I bought were double-knit pants suits from a discount catalog. I had saved a lot. I had no excuse.

"I started by cleaning the house. Took me two weeks nonstop. The next thing I did was to buy that computer. I've used it to meet several women I'm in touch with several times a week. I've even started visiting the neighbor two houses down." An alarm clock jangled in the bedroom. "That's my signal to go for a walk. One of my online friends suggested that making a schedule would help me keep moving. And one of the things I put on the schedule is getting outside and walking. Will you go with me?"

Back in the trailer, changing into her walking shoes, Dorothy Faye had to stop and change socks. The first two she put on were mismatched. Her mind had been on the reinvented Rubyjo, not on socks. *I might not be able to keep up with her.*

They walked eight blocks from Rubyjo's house to Tech Terrace Park and the eight back, about a mile total, plus they walked twice around the outer edge of the park. And they talked almost the entire time. Rubyjo strung together more words in one afternoon than Dorothy Faye had heard from her in all the time she'd known her.

Rubyjo didn't do all the talking. Dorothy Faye told the story of the gang of motorcycle Realtors down at Post, dramatically, the way Mrs. Ottley would have, including her plan to defend herself with the butcher knife. And she tried to explain about the hospital parking lots. Rubyjo just shook her head and laughed. "No use trying to explain Harold. He's been that way all his life. He's lucky he married you. Most women wouldn't tolerate his projects and crazy plans."

Dorothy Faye told her that was part of what made him lovable. After she said it, she realized it was true, not a protective defense like her response to Janiece. She also found herself saying several things she had thought but not told anyone other than Mrs. Ottley. She didn't mention talents or gifts, but she did tell Rubyjo she wondered about her purpose.

"Besides loving Harold? I'd think that would be a full time job." Rubyjo walked a while without saying anything else. "Seriously, I think I know what you mean. For a lot of years, I took for granted that since I wasn't married anymore and didn't have children, I didn't have a purpose. The last thing I had accomplished was getting my high school diploma by correspondence—in nineteen sixty-six." She gave a wry little laugh. "I had the idea that the main thing I was doing was waiting to lose my mind like our mother did." She looked sad when she said that, but soon brightened up again. "Now that I have a plan and I can tolerate daylight again, I feel sure something will come to me. I just have to pay attention."

Dorothy Faye said, "Maybe a lot of people think about purpose at our age, fifty-five or six. Have any of your friends mentioned wondering about it? Or are they younger than we are?"

"They're all over forty. No one has mentioned wondering about her purpose in life, in particular. But it could be that it's what got them started reinventing themselves."

Dorothy Faye was glad that while they were out, Rubyjo didn't ask where Harold had gone. She might have had to faint to avoid answering. She wasn't going to lie. On the way back from the park, she told Rubyjo Mrs. Ottley's principle, the one about learning something each day. "Maybe when you say 'pay attention,' Rubyjo, you're saying the same thing as Mrs. Ottley. I'm going to think some more about that," she said.

Rubyjo stopped right in the middle of the block. She looked at Dorothy Faye and said, "All these years you've been my sister-in-law, I never paid enough attention to realize what a good friend you would be. Will you come in later for supper?"

"No," Dorothy Faye said, "we'll go out. My treat."

Harold finally called around six o'clock. She had considered calling him earlier, but didn't. He seemed worried enough without her adding to it. He said he'd be back late the next afternoon. He didn't sound upset, so she didn't ask for an account of the day's events. And she didn't complain about his not calling.

They had supper at a small family-owned Mexican food restaurant on the north side of town. Over taco salads, Rubyjo asked about Elizabeth and R.J. Dorothy Faye gave her details of Elizabeth's latest love-gone-wrong, R.J.'s business idea, and his partner-not-a-girlfriend. Rubyjo said, "I haven't seen those kids in I don't know how long. They've grown up while I wasn't watching. I'd like to see them."

"They'll be here for July Fourth. Maybe we could have a party. I've already had to promise Elizabeth homemade ice cream and sparklers to get her out here."

"That would be fun. We could have it at the park. I think I have an ice-cream freezer in the garage. Let's invite a bunch of people—even Janiece and O.D. I'll buy some new slacks for the occasion, and Janiece will be struck dumb by the sight of my improved figure."

"I doubt that," Dorothy Faye said. Rubyjo laughed and agreed.

They were ambling to the car when Rubyjo noticed the time. "Oh my gosh, I have to check in with my friends at eight. Those women are tough.

If I don't turn up, they'll be hunting me down, telling me to get off my butt and get with the program." She sounded proud when she said it.

———◆———

The first thing Harold said when he came in the next evening, after he hugged her, was, "I felt bad about leaving you here. I hope you were able to find something to entertain you."

"No need for you to have worried. Rubyjo and I have had a good time. You may be pleased to know she's reinventing herself."

"Reinventing? What's that?"

"Changing herself into a person who enjoys life. I'll tell you more after we eat and you tell me about your trip."

It took him quite a while to get around to talking about his trip. First, he studied the menu at Mitchell's Restaurant. He could have memorized it by the time he finally ordered catfish. She smiled and tried to look calm while he told her they needed rain out at Guthrie. "The Four Sixes Ranch looked mighty dry when I passed through there." She knew he was inching toward Wichita Falls because Guthrie is halfway there from Lubbock. Then he tore a roll into pieces and stared at the result.

He took a deep breath and said, "I'm not sure where to start to tell about Martha Clay and her story." He looked everywhere except directly at Dorothy Faye while he talked. Then the waiter brought their order. That delayed talking for a while longer. She had eaten half of her spinach salad before he quit fiddling with his food.

He looked up from the French fries and, as if he'd been in the middle of a sentence, said, "Okay, I could see why he liked her. She's a real nice lady— still sharp, and you can tell she was pretty when she was young. She doesn't look eighty. He was older than she was. She said they never married because he didn't want to get a divorce and upset my mother any more than he already had. She said not a week went by that he didn't talk about us kids, sometimes feeling bad about leaving us, other times just wondering how we turned out. She might have said that to make me feel better. I don't know.

"There were pictures in her apartment of him and of the two of them. He looked just like I remember him. She said I look a lot like him." He stopped talking and worked on getting bones out of his fish. When there was nothing else he could do to the fish, he looked up and said, "I felt sorry for her. They were planning to do a little traveling, looking forward to it. Then before they could get situated to leave, one morning she got up and found him dead in his recliner. He had had a mild heart attack a couple of years before. He'd had another one, a big one."

"What year was that?" She asked it to give him a break from trying to tell something that was so emotional for him; she could see he was close to crying.

"It was nineteen eighty-one. He would have been sixty-nine." He ate the last forkful of rice on his plate, slowly. "As sorry as I was to hear about him dying that way, I'm glad he didn't die in a nursing home, or even in a hospital. And I'm glad he was with Martha Clay. That woman said she still misses him every day. She loved him."

"Did she tell you how they met?"

His face relaxed. "Yeah, she did. You'll like this story. She said he came into the bank and she helped him open an account. Filling out the forms, he mentioned he was living at Holliday. She lived there too, and they started talking about one of the cafes in Holliday that made a good chicken-fried steak. She told him that even if she did say so, and shouldn't, she made the best chicken-fried steak in Archer County, maybe all of Texas.

"She told me he frowned and said, 'Ma'am, I'm the official judge in that contest.'

"She said, 'What contest is that, Mr. Bell?'

"'The contest that awards the title Best Chicken-Fried Steak in Texas. You can't make that claim unless I award the title. The official competition is next Friday night in Holliday, Texas. If you'd like to enter, just put your address and telephone number on this entry form.'

"She said, 'He handed me a blank piece of paper. I was so tickled, I did it. That was the best line anyone had ever used to get a date with me.'" Harold said, "I had to laugh at the way she told it."

He stared at the woman clearing dishes at the next table. "Nobody at our house, Mama or the girls, ever joked around with him. I don't know how it turned out that way. Mama was grim most of the time. Even with Janiece and Rubyjo, if she was laughing and talking with them, I'd get the feeling that underneath, she was unhappy. It doesn't surprise me that he left."

He added sweetener to his iced tea, stirred it for a long time. He looked up and said, "Martha Clay didn't steal him from us. He'd been alone for seven years working up in Wyoming before they ever met."

Dorothy Faye could tell when he was through talking on a particular subject. He might not be through thinking about it. He's always thinking about something. But when he's finished with letting you in on it, it's as if he's sealed a long letter in an envelope and is starting to look for a stamp. He's ready to send it away. He always brings up the weather. That's the signal. "It hasn't rained over in Wichita Falls since April," he said.

Someday he might be ready to bring up his daddy again. If I pay attention, I'll know when the time comes.

CHAPTER 30

BYOB

"She had me digging through all that stuff in the garage looking for the ice-cream freezer. Said y'all were planning a party on the Fourth." Harold was explaining why it had taken him three hours to get back out to the trailer after going in for a cup of coffee with Rubyjo that morning.

"I was concerned she might ask where I'd been and why. But she had something to do on the computer, so she didn't have time to talk. I swear, I'd think she was taking truck drivers' drugs if I didn't know better. She's got more energy than I ever saw her show in her whole life. And she smiles. That's the biggest improvement."

"We did talk about having a party, since the kids are coming." Dorothy Faye nearly asked if that was okay with him. Instead, she straightened her shoulders and said, "I know we'll all enjoy it."

She wondered why saying that surprised her. She could be *loquacious* (puzzle #21), chatty even. Just ask Rubyjo. *What's been keeping me quiet with Harold for so long, editing every sentence I utter?*

"Dorothy Faye, did you hear what I said?"

"No, Harold, I'm sorry, I was thinking. What did you say?"

He looked toward her with a sort of half-amused expression. "What I said was, 'I'm going to Walmart to get a new ice-cream freezer. I found Rubyjo's, but it's too small. Do you want to go?'"

"I'll stay here, but thanks for asking. I'm going to call Elizabeth and R.J. and let them know about the party."

———◆———

Day 35 Thursday, June 22 Rubyjo's driveway, Lubbock

Another reason I'd been distracted, and still was even after I talked to the kids, is that Rubyjo's change fascinates me. A word in one of the puzzles started it. Seven letters. I had <u>A</u> <u>C</u> _ _ _ _ _. A second C often follows when the first is preceded by a vowel, so I fitted in <u>A</u> <u>C</u> <u>C</u> _ _ _ _. The clue, "spiritual torpor, ennui," led me to the dictionary. Spiritual torpor, that's what led me to Rubyjo. Torpor's definition mentioned lifelessness. She had seemed lifeless for a long time. But she has decided to change and appears to be succeeding. Did that decision just swoop in one day and settle in her mind like a bird choosing a new place to nest? Or had she been worrying and thinking all the time she smoked and drank coffee in her kitchen? How long does it take for a person to change? I knew I wouldn't ever know the answer, but that didn't stop me from wondering. Not long ago, I thought people didn't change as they got older.

I turned to the ACC pages and worked my way down to "accident injuries." There it was, the next one, ACCIDIE. I constructed a sentence to help me recall my new word. "My sister-in-law, my new friend, suffered years of accidie before she stepped into the sunlight."

Now that she's changing, who will be affected? If Mrs. Ottley's correct, that's the natural consequence. Change in one prompts changes in all others connected.

She put away her notebook, got up, and wiped the counter; then cleaned the commode. That cinched it—time to stop wondering and take a walk.

Harold turned up back at the trailer in the middle of the afternoon. Dorothy Faye had been sitting in the recliner, reading, thinking she might take a nap. He said, "I got this at Walmart. You think six quarts will be enough? It was the biggest one they had."

She looked at the box and nodded. He apparently took that as a yes.

He got busy opening the box. "It's a hand-crank model. They make the best ice cream." He laid the pieces out on the floor. "When you called him, did R.J. say anything about their business plan or getting a loan?"

"No, he just said he and Maia are looking forward to coming and that things are going along well. He sounded happy."

He put the freezer can in the wooden tub and held the dasher in his hand. He said, "I think we ought to invest in their school if their plan sounds any good."

It took her a minute to recover when he asked, "What do you think?"

"I think that's one of the best things we could use our money for—investing in dreams and plans for the future, for those two," she said.

"Makes more sense for them to have money now when they need it than to get it after we die. I'll call that broker and tell him to sell some of the stock." He had the hand-crank mechanism fitted on top of the freezer, slightly off center. "I drove by Lakeview on my way back. There are three trailer spaces vacant. We should move or else Rubyjo's gonna get around to asking where I went. I don't want to try to explain to her."

He got the top situated and started cranking the handle, slowly. He spoke again, softer and slower, like his words resulted from turning the crank. "It won't do her or Janiece any good for me to bring up our daddy. All these years they had him buried in Wyoming and that fit with what they thought of him. Hearing about Martha Clay and all that would only make them think worse of him. It's enough that I know how he lived and died and that he thought about us. I saw where he's buried and I helped Miz Clay clean up the cemetery plot."

That part about the cemetery came as a surprise to Dorothy Faye. He hadn't mentioned it before. "Are those the things, all the information, you hoped to find when you started searching?" she asked.

He looked up and stopped cranking. "It's like a lot of things, you start out wanting to know one thing and you get a lot more than you expected. I thought all I wanted was to know what he died of. Now that I found out all these other things, I'm glad I did." He started taking the freezer apart, putting it in the box. He had trouble fitting it all back in.

"Here's the funny part. Looking for that information, I ran into those two old boys down at Crane. And now I feel like I should do something to help them. But I don't know exactly what it is. It's like I found them in place of him." He stopped trying to fit the freezer into the box, leaned back in the chair, and closed his eyes.

Rubyjo was in the backyard, where she had worked up a sweat pushing the old reel mower. "Let's sit on this porch and drink some iced tea. I'm finished here," she said when Dorothy Faye came outside.

"The yard looks nice," Dorothy Faye said. Two oak trees shaded the west side of the small area as the sun began its long afternoon arc. Only a few tufts of white dotted the faded blue sky—no rain would fall this afternoon. Grass had flourished during Rubyjo's years of inattention. "How did you keep that grass growing all those years while you stayed inside?"

"Automatic sprinkler and Eddie's yardman. I could have waited until next week and the yardman would have done this." She gestured toward the evenly trimmed grass. "But I wanted to see how much work it would be to do it myself. Now that I know I can do it, I'm going to tell Eddie I'll be responsible." She picked bits of grass off of her jeans, rubbed at a grass stain on her shoe. "In a way, knowing Eddie would take care of things made it easy for me to sit and do nothing. Now he'll have to find some other way to keep from feeling guilty, or just give it up."

———◆———

Late that evening, they returned to Lakeview's parking lot. "We're arriving under cover of darkness, like spies," Harold said as he parked the trailer. Dorothy Faye watched him connect the electricity and unhitch the pickup. He came to where she was standing, and pointed across toward the park. "Ma'am, would you like to take a stroll around that little lake over yonder? I think it would be right nice this evening." In an old cowboy movie, he would have been wearing a white hat.

He offered his arm. She took it and they crossed the street together. The perfectly still surface of the lake mirrored a nearly full moon. Its glow lit the park at ten o'clock brighter than daybreak. She said, "That's a sweetheart's moon."

"That's one of the things I was thinking."

"What else were you thinking, sir?"

"I was thinking this is the perfect spot and just the right time to kiss my sweetheart and tell her I love her." He stopped walking, pulled her close, and kissed her gently on the right cheek beside her ear. He whispered, "Dorothy Faye, I love you."

She didn't know what to think. The next kiss—the serious, full on the mouth, I mean it, I love you, kiss—made her stop thinking. And it made her start crying—not because she was sad, but because her heart had suddenly expanded—too large for her chest. And she didn't understand why, not really.

Without a word, he handed her his handkerchief and held her close to his side.

———◆———

Daylight changes everything. The night had been beautiful and quiet. They had stayed over at the park for a while and then had slept with the windows open to catch the breeze. No ambulance sirens interrupted the moon's bright, silent watch over West Texas. And if Harold got up during the night, Dorothy Faye didn't hear him. But around six o'clock this morning, traffic sounds and pedestrians' chatter woke her. She dressed and ate before Harold got out of bed. Today there would be a purpose for her visiting other than deflecting suspicion.

He said, "You're moving around early this morning. Where are you off to?"

"Visiting. Will you see O.D. today?"

"I haven't talked to him. I was pretty vague about what I was going to be doing, so he wouldn't want to know about my little side trip. But he'll expect to hear from me today. Maybe we'll go play dominoes again if he doesn't have work to do out on the lease."

"When you see him, will you tell him that he and Janiece should plan to come for ice cream and cake at Tech Terrace Park on the Fourth of July? Tell him that everything is taken care of. All they have to do is to be there about five o'clock, and it's BYOB."

"BYOB?"

"Rubyjo called it that—bring your own bowl.

"What else have you two planned?"

"Well, we planned that you and O.D. and R.J. will be in charge of doing the cranking. And don't forget, you'll have to go to a fireworks stand to get sparklers for Elizabeth. Is there anyone you want to invite? We decided it would be fun to invite everyone we can think of. You remember Dennis, the first man I visited with here at Lakeview? I'm going to invite him, and I'll see if Sister Mary Joseph can come and maybe the Martins too."

"I wonder if Rubyjo's new energy is contagious. I can't remember when I've seen you so talkative." He glanced at her and then hurried to say, "I'm glad to see you enjoying yourself."

He drank some coffee. "I'd like to invite Bill and Elmer from down at Crane. But getting them back to the nursing home would be the problem."

"I'd like to meet them. Maybe you'll come up with an idea of how to manage it." She kissed him on the cheek. "I'm going on inside now. See you later."

CHAPTER 31

Making Arrangements

"There's no telling. He said he'd be back to pick me up this afternoon and waved good-bye," Dorothy Faye told Rubyjo when she asked where Harold went after he dropped her off. But she didn't go on to tell her that all night last night, at least it seemed like all night, he had changed positions, mumbled—nothing she could understand—and at least once he had gotten up and stayed up for a while, part of that time in the bathroom. He sometimes thrashed around like that if his blood sugar fell too low during the early morning hours. But this morning the reading was okay at 108. The last few days he'd spent time helping O.D. on the lease. At the trailer he had been quiet, reading papers from the broker and staring off into space—thinking about the money, she guessed. He may also have been thinking about his daddy and maybe about those two men down at Crane in prison, as he called it. She'd told herself not to worry. He'd said he would see the doctor; she had done all she could.

She had visited at the hospital a little each day and often found herself thinking about what Mrs. Ottley said. Alan hadn't turned up at Lakeview. So far they were safe on that score. Dorothy Faye intended to tell him the truth about what she'd been doing, if he came back. If they had to, they could move the trailer back to Rubyjo's until Harold set his sights on the next stop. She was clearing her mind. She didn't intend to let herself worry about what they would do next. She had a purpose; the kids were coming, and they were going to have a party.

"Rubyjo, if you have anything planned for today, I can entertain myself just fine," she said. "I could just sit here and enjoy your house and yard and be happy for hours."

"No special plans, just the usual things I'm working on—checking in with my online friends, taking a walk, doing some laundry. I'll be glad to have your company."

Dorothy Faye took her coffee to the back porch where she watched a squirrel and a grackle try to push each other off the tree limb they both occupied. It wasn't true that she could sit for hours doing nothing at all. Lately, her tolerance for doing nothing had shrunk to even less than before. When her coffee cup was empty and the territorial dispute ended, she went inside to find Rubyjo.

"I was thinking, since today is the twenty-eighth, it wouldn't be too far ahead to bake the cupcakes, if you have room in your freezer," Dorothy Faye said. "I can bake while you're busy with other things."

They agreed that three cupcakes per person would be plenty. Leftovers, if there were any, could be sent home with the Martins. They came up with twenty people to invite and giggled about the odd assortment. Rubyjo made her laugh, describing how Janiece would wonder who all those people were and how they ended up at the party.

"Maia should be startling to her," Dorothy Faye said. "She's exotic looking because one of her parents is Asian and the other is Anglo. And if Sister Mary Joseph comes, Janiece will be worried there's going to be a prayer meeting and a collection plate passed. I doubt if she knows any nuns personally."

Rubyjo got a dreamy look on her face, like she could see something visible only to her, over near the windows. "I imagine this whole thing sort of like a little movie—people laughing, eating, having a good time visiting. It's in Technicolor. Until recently my life has seemed like it was all in black and white. I'm so glad we're going to celebrate." She stopped studying the sun's path through the open blinds and turned to Dorothy Faye. "I don't think I told you that my online friends and I have never asked one another where we live. Anyway, I invited all of them. Two of them sent e-mails saying they'll be here. One lives here in Lubbock and the other in Brownfield. I can't wait to meet them in person. Please don't say anything about me mentioning how I know them when I introduce you."

"They're your friends. That's enough of an introduction," Dorothy Faye said. She switched to a spy movie accent to add, "I know noth-ing."

By eleven o'clock, five-dozen cupcakes occupied all the countertops in Rubyjo's kitchen. After another thirty minutes on the phone, Dennis and Sister Mary Joseph had both said they would be there. Sister agreed to contact the Martins.

Dorothy Faye tried to imagine the party the way Rubyjo described it—a little color film full of happy people. She bagged the cupcakes to freeze and ate the one that threatened to overfill the last bag. She cleared crumbs from the countertop and wondered if Rubyjo's movie was as out of focus as hers.

Harold came in around six, carrying supper, take out from Furr's cafeteria. As they were eating, it dawned on Dorothy Faye, after he had asked about Rubyjo, talked at some length about the new ice-cream freezer, and began talking about the Fourth of July, that so much conversation was out of the ordinary for him. She barely had time to respond to a comment on any topic before he was on to another subject. She had no opportunity, without being rude, to insert any questions about his day, or anything else, for that matter. He ranged from one topic to another in no particular order. She thought he would eventually get to the real point, the thing he was avoiding. Eventually he did.

He said he had talked to the broker about selling stock. He pulled a folded sheet of paper from his right shirt pocket, smoothed it on the chair arm, and read from it. "He said he should warn me that our goals should be to assure our retirement, that's the phrase he used—like it was possible to assure anything—and to avoid high taxes. He recommended we reinvest the proceeds of the sale of stock in some other things he sells. But I think we should sell enough of that stock to do whatever we do for the kids and put some money in CDs. Not as risky. Even if it is Walmart, something could happen. That's what he meant about assuring our retirement. He didn't explain much about the taxes. But if you sell stock, you have to pay capital gain tax on what you make."

He looked up from his notes. "Nothing's simple, is it?" he said. "Anyway, about the stock, we can leave some of it or sell it and put the money wherever we want to. But we need to think about our old age." He looked at her, frowning. "That broker talked like we should expect to live to be ninety-five. Hell, I'll be happy if I see sixty-five." The grin that usually told her he was joking was missing. He folded the paper and rubbed his index finger along the crease he'd made in it. "I should have thought about all this a long time ago. I haven't been taking care of business like I should."

"When did you talk with the broker?"

"Yesterday afternoon. I told him I'd call him back. I should have made a plan a long time ago. The other thing is that you need to know about what we do, you know, just in case."

She didn't know why, but the way he said "just in case" made the next breath she took stop at her throat. She coughed and went to the refrigerator to get a drink. "I'm interested in learning," she said.

He sat back in his chair and extended the footrest. "I'll get this all taken care of real soon. Like I said, I should have done this a long time ago, all of it." He was speaking from behind his newspaper. "Don't you worry."

"I'm not going to worry. We have plenty," she said. She was talking to the back page of the newspaper. Again.

CHAPTER 32

It'll Be Nothing

S he'd started a puzzle, considering 6 Down, "putting off or delaying needlessly," when she heard the newspaper crumple. Harold said, "There's something else I need to tell you."

He sat forward, and the footrest on the recliner slapped down. He turned to face her.

Her ballpoint trailed off of puzzle #210. Something in his voice made her want to say, "Wait, not now." But she said, "What is it, Harold?" calmly, like she was asking the name of some new tool he had invented.

"I didn't tell you before because I didn't want you to worry. But now I have to."

She glanced back at the puzzle, thirteen letters. "What? Tell me."

"Let me finish. Then you can ask me questions if you need to." His voice sounded far away, faint, like a bad phone connection. "I'm gonna have to go in the hospital. Just for one day."

She looked at him as if his features had changed, but didn't ask anything. He'd said he would explain.

"I wasn't feeling right—couldn't pass urine easy as I should. And back pain, down low." His face showed there was pain in telling her. "I went to the doctor. She examined me and took some blood for a prostate test, PSA. It was high, so she sent me to the urologist. That was before we went to Odessa. Down there I got another opinion. Both urologists said I should have a biopsy. Could be prostate cancer. I told the doctor here to go ahead. It's day after tomorrow." He stared at his boots. "Doin' it right here at Lakeview. It'll be nothing." He touched her knee, held on. "Dorothy Faye, please don't be upset. It'll be nothing. They can clear out the urine problem, easy." Still holding onto her knee, he stopped talking.

She tried to see his face clearly. Blinking didn't help. He was underwater. She wouldn't allow herself to ask why he couldn't tell her before.

He leaned back into his chair, let his shoulders sag, like staying upright had been an effort he could no longer maintain. "I'd rather not tell anybody else until after the tests are done. No one needs to know. Wouldn't do any good."

She nodded. That didn't surprise her. After a long silence, she asked, "Is there any special preparation for the biopsy?"

He pulled another folded paper from his other shirt pocket, and handed it to her. She held the instructions without reading. "You've been worrying about this for quite a while," she said. "I wish you'd told me."

"It's something I've got to handle. I didn't want you to worry."

"I did. Don't you think I know when something's wrong? I've imagined all kinds of things."

"Well, you know now. Look here, Dorothy Faye, I'm supposed to take care of you, not the other way around."

"We're supposed to take care of each other." She closed her puzzle book and knelt in front of him. "Harold, I love you. I'll be right here with you, no matter what. I'm glad you've seen the doctors and you're doing what needs to be done." She leaned her head on his knees.

He stroked her hair and said, "Dorothy Faye, I'm sorry." He changed position. Maybe he was ready to tell her more. "Honey, like I said, it'll be nothin'. Those instructions are the only thing concernin' me."

She focused her attention on the paper. She looked back at him. He had his grin on now. "That part about a self-administered enema doesn't sound like fun to me," he said.

She smiled at him, the way she had a thousand times, the same smile she smiled at her kids when they'd tell an elephant joke—not a smile at the joke, but at them trying to please her. "I suppose there's a first time for everything," she said, raising an eyebrow. "You better get some rest. You'll want to be fresh for your adventure."

That night, as he slept, she lay close to him with her hand on his chest, over his heart, and pretended not to worry.

———◆———

Thursday morning Harold got up at sunrise and followed the pre-procedure instructions. "Well," he said when he came out of the bathroom, "I've had two enemas today."

"I thought the instructions said one." Dorothy Faye played along, knowing he was headed for a joke again.

"That's what it said, but it turned out to be two—my first and last. I'm not ever doing that again."

She couldn't help smiling. "Let's get on over to the hospital before I have to strangle you."

———◆———

"Dr. Higgins administered some medication to relax Mr. Bell, in addition to the local anesthetic. He'll be able to leave in an hour or so. Dr. Higgins wants to see him in his office at three p.m. tomorrow for the results." The nurse handed her an appointment card.

Waiting for Harold's release, Dorothy Faye practiced the kind of detached observing she had learned as a child. The detachment had stretched a distance between her and the noise of her parents' frequent protracted arguments. Later, she used it to put miles between herself and her anger at Ronnie's infidelities. Now, she needed it to push back the fear that Harold's "it'll be nothing" assurances were wrong. She watched nurses, visitors, and housekeepers, and she even let her eyes stray to the wall-mounted television set. The mismatch between the faces on the screen and what sounded like words in an alien language confirmed that she had succeeded in putting herself into some other time zone. She would return tomorrow at three o'clock.

The medication, the procedure and, Dorothy Faye suspected, the strain of trying not to show his anxiety combined to make Harold sleep all afternoon. After having soup for supper, he went back to bed. The next morning they both slept late.

Neither of them said much, other than to comment on Lakeview Hospital cafeteria's good food, during lunch. As they left, Harold said, "Let's take a little walk over at the park. We can stay in the shade. I think stretching my legs will help me get over this soreness."

He ventured out of the shade to the water's edge, where he tossed in a little rock. "See that ripple, honey? That's all this is. Just a little disturbance. In no time, everything will be back to normal." He tossed in another rock. "Dorothy Faye, I was wrong not to talk to you. I know you don't expect me to handle everything alone. The only one expectin' that is me."

Dr. Higgins studied the biopsy report. Harold and Dorothy Faye watched. The doctor finally looked up and didn't waste words as he spoke directly to Harold, telling him he had prostate cancer. After saying that most frightening word, *cancer*, the doctor took a deep breath, like he was relieved to have that part over with. "Now for the good news."

"I could use some," Harold said.

"The tumor we found is low grade, small, slow growing, and only in one site. Experience tells us it will respond well to treatment with implanted radiation seeds. We should be able to clear this up and then just keep an eye on you to be sure there is no recurrence."

He explained two other treatment options—surgery and external beam radiation—and also mentioned the side effects of each of the three types of treatment. He handed Harold a booklet that explained each treatment. Harold handed it to Dorothy Faye.

Dr. Higgins suggested the seed radiation because it had the least side effects and was not as invasive as surgery. "Of course, it's up to you to decide which of those you want. We won't rush into treatment. You think about it and we'll begin treatment, whichever method, in one month."

No one spoke for several seconds. The doctor straightened the papers in Harold's chart. Dorothy Faye asked, "Between now and then, is there any medication my husband is to take or any change in his activity?"

Dr. Higgins shook his head. "If you need some Tylenol for discomfort, Mr. Bell, take that. Otherwise, do whatever you feel like doing."

Harold thanked him. They left his office and were standing outside by twenty after three. "Well, one good thing about that, it didn't take long," he said.

CHAPTER 33

Lost and Found

S aturday morning, Harold announced in a strong voice that he was fit to travel, at least as far as O.D.'s lease. He had concocted some story that made it easy for O.D. to accept his not going out for the past few days. But he said O.D. was sure to be asking if he didn't turn up today. "I don't intend to let on about this whole business until I've decided what to do. Then I'll tell him. Or maybe I'll tell the kids while they're here and tell O.D. then. I won't spoil the party by mentioning it before." That sounded like a decision, so Dorothy Faye didn't comment. Then he asked, "Do you think that's okay?"

She told him that whatever he decided, she'd go along with, as long as the kids knew before he started treatment. "You know they will want to know, Harold."

After he left, she went to the hospital, thinking that helping someone else, if anyone wanted a talented listener, would be a good way to take her mind off Harold's diagnosis. She went only as far as the front lobby before stopping to watch the people coming from the parking lot. She noticed a very old-looking woman manage her way through the door. Her walker banged against the doorframe, knocking off one of the split tennis balls someone had put on the walker's legs to make it slide more easily. She had first seen the elderly woman as she parked in one of the handicapped spaces in the front row of the lot after making three attempts to get an old Buick straight in the space. Although she walked fairly steadily, the woman moved slowly, looking around after each step as if the terrain was unfamiliar. It took her fully five minutes to cross the street from the lot to the front door.

She angled herself over the seat of the first chair she came to, let go of the walker, and sort of collapsed onto the chair. Although she did let out a sound, "uh," when her body met the chair, she didn't grimace or frown. Apparently she wasn't in severe pain. After a few seconds, she straightened herself up and tipped the walker to one side, looking at the leg missing its homemade skid. Then she looked directly at Dorothy Faye. "Honey, do you see that tennis ball over there?" She pointed a knobby finger toward the tennis ball lying just inside the door. "Would you mind gettin' it for me? I need it to make this damned walker work."

Dorothy Faye delivered the tennis ball and sat in the chair next to the woman. The older woman jammed the ball back onto the walker and said, "Well, I'll never get there if I don't start. Would you mind doing one more thing for me?"

"Not at all. Tell me what to do."

"Stand in front of me so I can hold your arms to pull myself up. This walker's not steady when I try to get up out of a chair."

"Is someone expecting you right away?"

"My sister. She had a bad fall and broke her left hip. She's a year younger than I am, makes her eighty-six. She's expecting me, but not this early. She said to come this afternoon when I could ride with one of the neighbors. My sister thinks I shouldn't drive. I didn't want to ride with that neighbor because she talks too much and she smells like snuff. So I decided to bring myself over here early and get back to the house before the traffic picks up."

"How far do you live from the hospital?" Dorothy Faye asked. If she could keep her talking, the woman could get a little rest before the trek to her sister's room.

"Just six blocks over that way." She waved vaguely toward the east. "Or maybe it's sixteen. I don't recall exactly. My sister hasn't let me drive since last year. It took me a little while to find this place today because they've changed the streets a lot."

"What happened last year?"

"Nothing really. She got that idea about me not driving after I had some trouble getting home from the grocery store. She was just mad because the oleo melted on the way back."

"Did the car break down?"

"No, not that. See, I got turned around the wrong direction coming out of the parking lot and went out of my way getting back. She said that it wasn't safe for me to drive anymore. But I know it was the margarine." She gazed toward the parking lot. "Is that my car over there?"

"Yes, ma'am," Dorothy Faye said. "It's the third one from your left. I saw you get out of it." *This lady shouldn't be driving.* She stood in front of her and offered her arms. "I'll go with you. What number is your sister's room?"

"Well, honey, I'm not exactly sure. Is this the Lakeview hospital?"

"Yes, it is. Tell me her name and we'll ask at the desk where to find her." The strength in the woman's arms surprised Dorothy Faye. She might look frail, but she was wiry. "My friend would do better if I push her in a wheelchair instead of her using her walker," Dorothy Faye explained to the volunteer at the desk. Her "friend" laid her walker atop the arms of the wheelchair the volunteer offered and smiled up at Dorothy Faye.

Room 512 held a surprise. Her sister could have been her twin. "Alvina, have you hurt yourself? Why are you in that wheelchair?" Without waiting for her sister to answer, the woman in the bed asked Dorothy Faye, "Are you a nurse?"

Dorothy Faye introduced herself and explained she was visiting and had offered to help her sister.

"Wynell, I'm fine. This lady helped me so I wouldn't have to walk so far."

"Did you walk all the way here from the house? It's way too hot for you to be out walking," Wynell, the sister in the bed, said. She looked at Dorothy Faye again and said, "She shouldn't be out walking in the summer heat."

"No, I didn't walk," Alvina said. Her eyes scanned the room, never meeting her sister's.

"Don't tell me you drove the car."

Alvina smiled a tiny smile and said, "I'm not saying that."

"You think you're being so crafty. I know you, Alvina. You found those keys and drove over here." Wynell's voice rose and she shook her finger at her sister.

Alvina tried for an innocent expression, but the smile threatened again, twitching the left side of her mouth. She had her walker in front of her now and was doing her best to stand. The wheelchair scooted backward each time she pushed herself forward.

Dorothy Faye locked the chair's wheels and stepped in front of her to help. Alvina went directly to her sister's bed, leaned down, and kissed her on the cheek. "Wynell, I miss you being at home. I look for you all night. When will they let you out?"

"I don't know. But I do know you have to accept the fact that you have memory problems. You have to accept it and adjust. You can't drive anymore. You get lost every time you get out of sight of our house. What if something bad happened to you? I'd never forgive myself."

Dorothy Faye wished she could magically make them both young and able again. She moved to the door, intending to leave them alone. Wynell called to her from the bed. "Mrs. Bell, can I ask one more favor?" Alvina sat on the bed, patting Wynell's hand.

"How can I help?"

"Can you see that she gets home? I'll write the address here, and I'll call the neighbor to check on her later in the day."

Dorothy Faye looked at the address—3501 Twenty-Seventh Street. "That's just a few blocks south of here. I can drive her home and walk back to my place from there. It won't be out of the way. Your car won't be left on the parking lot." She turned to Alvina, who either hadn't been listening or had pretended not to. "I'm going to leave you two to visit. I'll come back in about forty-five minutes to see if you're ready to go. Is that okay?"

She agreed. Dorothy Faye sorted through possible ways to get and keep Alvina's car keys when the time came. Imagining having to wrestle the wiry little woman for the keys made her hesitate as she entered the elevator.

She looked up—Alan. He looked directly at her. She couldn't avoid him. The only choice was to talk fast. "Alan, I'm so glad to see you again. How are you?"

She left the elevator on first floor, intending to wait there until she went back for Alvina, and hoping that Alan had duties elsewhere. No such luck. He followed her into the lobby. "I'm glad to see you too, Mrs. Bell."

"I was upstairs on fifth helping a friend. I have to wait here a while and then help her get home. Tell me how you are. And did you decide about school? As I recall, you were trying to decide about law school."

"I'm doing fine. Through with classes, so I've been working lots of hours, saving money—most of the time over at Consolidated. Today is my first day here in a couple of weeks." He had remained standing when she sat on one of the lobby chairs.

She pointed to the chair across from her. "Can you sit and talk a few minutes?"

"I'll check in for a break." After a short phone call, he was back. "First of all, my parents were so pleased. I was glad, for their sake, that I finally decided to apply. I've heard from them I should be an attorney ever since we took aptitude tests in junior high. I was happy I was able to make them happy and still be doing what I think is right for me. I'll begin applying this August for admission the following August."

"How did you finally decide?"

He leaned back, studying her. "Now, that's odd. You are the first person to ask about how I made the decision. My parents were so happy I had a direction that the only question they asked was when I would be going. That's how they put it, having a direction. I think that made them feel like they had done what good parents should. Thank you for asking. It's important to me that someone is interested in what I hope for, not just what I plan to do."

He told, in such sad detail that it made her bite her lip to keep away tears, about how he had felt when he found a homeless man sleeping in the parking garage at Consolidated. He talked about how weary the man must have been to think that he was in a bedroom, how he had nothing except the clothes he wore, how the man couldn't figure out where to go for help, and worst of all, how he had to help send the man to jail. What a good soul this boy must be to have been so concerned about that man's situation. She wanted to hug him.

"An attorney could be a powerful force in helping homeless people. This might sound strange, but I want to be able to do a combination of social work and legal work that will help communities, not just individuals. And to do that, I need to go to law school."

He told her about his current job search to find work in social services for the homeless. He said, "Working at the basic level in some social service agency will help me learn more about the homeless. And it will also either kill my idealism or encourage me that I made the right choice." He checked his watch. "I have to get back on duty now. I hope I'll see you again, Mrs. Bell."

She was so relieved he hadn't asked why they were at the hospital that she almost forgot to go back to get Alvina.

Alvina peered at Dorothy Faye as if she didn't recognize her when she opened the door to 512. Dorothy Faye said, "When we get downstairs, I can save you a walk by pulling the car right up to the door. So I'll need the keys."

Alvina said with a wide-eyed innocent look, "You'll have to get them from my sister. I'm not allowed to drive."

"You won't mind having a chauffeur, will you? Let's take a look to see if those keys might be in that bag over there." Dorothy Faye pointed to the zippered pouch attached to the walker. She kept talking and eased to the walker—asked if they had had a good visit, were the nurses taking good care of Wynell, anything that came to her mind. The keys rested on top of a nest of wadded tissues. There wasn't any evidence of a billfold or anything that would have identified Alvina if she had gotten lost. Apparently she also lacked a driver's license.

The next-door neighbor was waiting when she and Alvina arrived at the sisters' house. The neighbor identified herself and said, "Alvina, I just made a fresh pie. Would you like to come with me now to have a piece?"

Alvina had been silent during the drive, except for pointing out her house when they turned onto her street. As Dorothy Faye parked the car, Alvina sighed and began to smile. Now she sat up straight in the seat and said, "What kind of pie is it?" Even before she received an answer, she got out of the car. Suddenly she was more nimble. She left the walker in the car and took the neighbor's arm.

Dorothy Faye said to the neighbor, as quietly as she could, "I'll leave these keys with Wynell."

"A good idea," she said. "I'll call Wynell to let her know Alvina's home. Alvina, Wynell was concerned about you driving. She was afraid something bad might happen."

Dorothy Faye heard Alvina's reply and had to laugh. "Well, nothing bad happened. Everything worked out just fine. What kind of pie did you say it is?"

———————◆———————

Dorothy Faye left Alvina's and walked toward the hospital. She didn't notice the street signs, only went west, knowing she would eventually arrive at or near the hospital. A few blocks from Alvina's, she turned onto a street lined with well-kept houses and tree-shaded lawns. A For Sale By Owner sign had fallen crooked in front of 3904 whatever-street. A man stepped out of the house, straightened the sign, and tapped the top with a hammer to drive it into the ground. He waved and said, "Hi, would you like to buy a house today?"

"Are you the owner?"

"I am. Trouble is, we bought a new, larger house to fit our family and have already moved. If this doesn't sell soon, we'll have two house payments. If you know anyone who's in the market for a house..." He stared at his sign. "I thought we could get closer to breaking even on it if we sold it without an agent." He invited her in.

Stories of female Realtors being mugged, or worse, in open houses came to mind. She moved toward the door, chattering about how she couldn't stay but a minute because her husband was expecting her back at the hospital. Maybe that would discourage any evil thought the man might harbor. She knew better, really. If he were a serial killer, he had just chosen a new victim. She wanted to see the inside of that house. Alvina would have gone in.

Hardwood floors in excellent condition, long windows with wooden blinds, new kitchen appliances, updated bathroom fixtures, and a small patio in the back all made it a showplace. Dorothy Faye imagined living there, having friends over, tending to it all. She felt her pulse accelerate, told herself to settle down. In no time, this would belong to someone else.

After he led her through the rooms, he said, "There's one other thing I want to show you out back." He pointed toward the garage. A detached extra-large one-car garage, as clean as O.D.'s, sported a back wall covered with pegboard, meant to store tools, and a workbench spanning the width of the building.

"This is a nice garage. Did you do all this work yourself?" she asked.

"Yes, I'm sorry to leave the workbench behind. But it doesn't fit in the new place. This isn't the best part, though. Step around to the side, and I'll show you." A narrow sidewalk led from the front of the garage to the side. A door opened to a one-bedroom apartment that contained a galley kitchen, a small living area, a bedroom, and a three-quarter bath. Sitting in the little living area, a person would be able to see the entire backyard, a yard worth seeing.

Neatly trimmed boxwoods lined the back fence. Colorful cosmos and daisies massed in several locations in front of the hedge, and the two far corners each were filled by giant pampas grass clumps. Planters full of petunias, lobelia, and impatiens surrounded three large trees. She could see the pride in his face. "You must have had to think long and hard about leaving such a nice house," she said.

"Yes, I hated to leave." He shrugged again, looking dejected. "But we're already gone and that's that. Now it's my job to sell it."

"If you don't mind my asking, what's your price?"

"I'd like to get ninety-nine thousand, five hundred for it. That's below appraisal. Comparable houses in the area are all priced above one hundred and ten thousand. I hope to sell it before the fifteenth."

She hadn't noticed until then that he still had the hammer in his hand. "Do you have any written information about the house?" she asked. "I know someone who might be interested."

"I do. Had it printed up this morning for an open house tomorrow afternoon."

Day 44 Saturday, July 2 Lakeview Hospital parking lot, Lubbock

A lot has happened since the last time I wrote about odd things. There's no need to write about finally knowing the truth about Harold's illness. I'll not forget that. But two things today were odd. And I don't want to forget them either.

The first one has to do with being afraid and being lost. After I left Alvina safely back at home, I pretended that I was, like Alvina, a person without a mental map of my surroundings. She did recognize her own house and her neighbor as soon as we were on her block, but everything else was either unclear or a mystery to her. Her manageable world had shrunk to one block on one street. Imagining myself in a world with only one block I could call my own safe territory, I could only think of being constantly afraid. Why hadn't she seemed fearful? In that situation, a person— me, for example—would have to choose among settling for being restricted to one block and being safe; leaving, full of fear; or venturing forth courageously. Would I choose the unknown, without dread? That eighty-seven-year-old woman did.

Then I tried something; I stopped right in the middle of a block. I hadn't driven that particular street coming from the hospital. I didn't know my exact location, but I didn't feel lost. Being lost may be mostly a state of mind. Mrs. Ottley will enjoy hearing what I've learned today.

The second odd thing was my reaction to seeing that house. I hadn't thought, maybe hadn't allowed myself to, how much I would love for us to live in a house of our own. Why hope for something you're not likely to get? I had a feeling it was no accident that I found that house. Sounds foolish, I know.

Now is probably the worst possible time to even mention it to Harold. It would only complicate things for him; he has enough on his mind. Waiting would be the simplest, probably the best thing to do. OR, I could tell him, say what's on <u>my</u> mind, and see what happens. That's something new to wonder about.

She opened the puzzle book to replace her notebook. It opened to puzzle #210, where she'd trailed off. Clue 6 Down, thirteen letters, looked different today— "delaying or putting off needlessly." <u>P R O C R A S T I N A T E</u>, she wrote. She closed the book and returned it to her purse.

CHAPTER 34

Independence Day

S unday morning, Dorothy Faye had breakfast, dressed, and because Harold was still sleeping, tried to sit quietly without disturbing him. That last part was difficult because she felt, even though the circumstances wouldn't necessarily have predicted it, that good things were on the way. Rather than see Harold's cancer diagnosis as a dire prediction, she felt glad a diagnosis had been made, without further delay. She didn't have to worry whether he was seeing other women; she didn't have to doubt herself, thinking she might no longer be desirable; and worrying about him "getting strange like Momma," as Janiece suggested, was unnecessary. She reminded herself of the doctor's description of the tumor—low grade, slow growing, treatable in three different ways.

Soft snores continued from the bedroom. Dorothy Faye retrieved her notebook.

Day 45 Sunday, July 2 7:30 a.m. Lakeview Hospital parking lot

What happened when I woke up this morning was out of the ordinary. Usually I'm slow to start, need coffee to begin thinking clearly. But today an answer, a big decision, presented itself, fully formed, as clearly as if I'd labored over it all night. All the pros and cons were identified, and the answer was clear—Do This.

I had gone to bed thinking about the house. I even pictured us living there, furniture in place, a couple of nice area rugs, new dishes—everything. I could see it clearly.

But that wasn't the big decision. In fact, the house didn't even come back to my mind until afterward. Instead, I woke knowing what I should be doing. It's this—I will do exactly what I have been doing, listening. But now, because I know that listening in a particular way—intently, openly, with concern—is a gift I can give, I won't be an impostor. I will be a visitor, a real one. My visits will be with people affected by the crisis of having a loved one or a friend hospitalized. There may be a few others, like Lou Ann, whom I meet and listen to because they find me in the hospital.

Now that I explain my big decision, it may not sound as important as it seems to me. It's important because knowing that I'm not drifting from day to day, that I have a purpose, doing something useful, is important to me. Having a purpose is different from having a job. Accomplishing a purpose requires work, but the reward won't be in the form of a paycheck. I'll know it in my heart.

Now I can make a plan. I'll decide on a schedule for my visits—some time every week, maybe every day. And I'll think about which places. I like Lakeview best. But I could go to other hospitals, maybe even nursing homes. I hope I won't have to explain myself to any hospital officials, at least not soon. They'd probably want me to sign up as a volunteer. Or they might suspect I have other motives. How would I explain that I don't want to be put in a pink smock, and I don't want a job, and I don't plan to commit burglaries in homes vacated during hospitalizations? I'll have to think about how to explain my reason for being who and where I am.

Now that I know my purpose, planning and explaining should be easy. Actually, it'll be easier when Harold decides if this current adventure is over. With the news about his needing cancer treatment and having settled his mind about his dad, he may be ready to park a bit more permanently. Regardless, we'll have to be here for a while when he has whichever treatment he decides on. We could be on the last leg of this trip right this minute, for all I know.

She heard Harold stir. She replaced her notebook in the puzzle book. She delivered coffee to him and told him she had a few more things to do for the party. He said not to rush. O.D. was going to pick him up later.

Lou Ann was reading her little red book when Dorothy Faye found her on the patio at County General. She looked uncertain when Dorothy Faye told her about the party and asked her to come. Dorothy Faye said, "Lou Ann, remember I promised to keep in confidence the things you told me. As far as anyone will know, you are a nurse I met at the hospital—that's all. Besides, you'll like Harold, my husband. There will be people there I don't know either. Some friends of my sister-in-law. You might meet some people you would like."

"I do like homemade ice cream. I could still make a meeting afterward."

"Okay then. I'll hope to see you there."

Leaving County General, Dorothy Faye managed to ignore the brief thought that her decision about being a listener could be a foolish dream. The voice that said *"foolish dream"* was her mother's, not hers. She nearly ignored a stop sign too. Getting back to the trailer at Lakeview settled her down, but that didn't last too long. Harold was still there.

"I decided I'd better stay here and do some more thinking about money," he said. "I've already decided about the other. I'm going to have the radiation seeds like the doctor suggested."

She nodded. "It sounded as if he thought that was overall the best choice. I'm glad you were able to decide so soon. That's one less worry for you." She checked the kitchen area to see if anything needed straightening, then made herself stop. "Harold, if you're not going to be too busy with financial thoughts this afternoon, there's someplace I'd like you to go with me," she said. No turning back now.

"Sure, where are we going?" he asked.

She smiled, hoping to look mysterious. "Let's let it be a surprise."

One time a long time ago, Harold said he thought they ought to buy a house. Dorothy Faye had wanted one back then, but hadn't said much about it. First he tried to buy the one they were renting. The owner wasn't interested in selling. The house had belonged to her family and she wouldn't sell until her mother died. Her mother was seventy-five at the time and going strong.

The next possibility, building a new house, would have been a big undertaking. With no contractors in Whaley, one electrician, and only two people who called themselves carpenters, assembling a crew to put up a house would have meant hiring people from out of town. Harold said it wasn't worth the trouble. She thought at the time he meant building wasn't worth the trouble. Could be he meant more than that. Maybe he didn't want to own a house at all. Since then, and that was at least fifteen years ago, the subject hadn't come up again.

He raised an eyebrow at Dorothy Faye when she told him to park in front of the house at 3904 Twenty-Eighth Street. "Right there, the one with the For Sale By Owner sign. This is what I want you to see," she said. She tried to sound matter-of-fact instead of as excited as she felt—excited and a little worried. She didn't want him to get upset or to dismiss the idea because it came from her. She didn't want him to disappoint her.

He didn't say much—asked the owner about the age of the heating and air-conditioning unit, mentioned the floors were in good condition. But he didn't hurry. He really did look carefully at every room. Dorothy Faye couldn't, or was afraid to, guess what he thought. In the garage he stopped and said, "That's a nice workbench." He and the owner talked a few minutes about how the tool board and bench were constructed and about the extra electrical outlets and the painted and sealed floor. He stood on the back porch looking at the yard for a long time.

The owner said, "I almost forgot to show you the apartment."

As soon as they went into the apartment, Harold got that look he got when an idea struck him. If there were a sound to go with the look, it would be the hum of a motor, gears meshing, wheels turning. He asked the dimensions of the rooms, about any city restrictions on rentals (there were none), and about the apartment's heating and cooling.

Dorothy Faye checked to see that the faucets in the little kitchen and the bathroom worked. Harold and the owner continued talking. They discussed a lot of things, from neighborhood property values to average price of utility bills and several topics in between. Harold kept glancing around the apartment, smiling and nodding as the owner did his best to make a sale. Next thing she knew, Harold shook hands with the owner and headed back toward the pickup. "My wife and I will talk about the house and be back in touch if we want to discuss it more," Harold said.

On the way to the pickup, she started consoling herself. He didn't want to buy a house, or they would still be inside discussing price. She was so intent on reminding herself this was a bad time that she didn't hear Harold talking. "What do you think?" was the only part she heard.

She barely had the presence of mind to answer, saying that the reason she had wanted him to see it was because she liked it so much. Harold said, "Well, we should probably think about it for a little while before we decide if we want to try to buy it." She didn't say a word, just nodded. She hoped he couldn't tell she was holding onto the armrest with her right hand. Otherwise, she might have floated up off the seat.

He drove slowly around the neighborhood, looking at the houses on the nearby streets. She thought she heard that humming sound again. "There aren't any other houses around here for sale. Mr. Owens said that was the case. His house looks well built and in good condition. The garage would be a good place for all those tools of mine we left in storage. Actually, that garage is better than any place I've ever had for working on my projects." He might as well have written it down and handed it to her—a list of good reasons to buy the house. She didn't let go of the armrest until he parked at the trailer. "Course, I'll need to bargain with that man, if we decide we want it," he said. "You should never pay the asking price."

"Harold, while you think about the house, I'm going to go in to visit. If anyone has been watching, they might have noticed that no one from this trailer has spent much time in the hospital today." She started out the door and then turned back. "Do you think there's any chance that someone else might try to buy the house today?"

"Could be. I told Mr. Owens that we would be back in touch soon to let him know if we're interested. I think if he does get an offer, he'd let us know, to try to get the best deal he could. You go visit. When you get back, we can talk about it some more. And we need to decide when to move the trailer over to Rubyjo's before the kids get here."

Things don't always work out according to plan. But maybe they work out the way they're supposed to. Dorothy Faye intended to go to 512 to see Wynell and ask about Alvina. She would make a bona fide patient visit. She hoped Wynell wouldn't give her the news that Alvina had hot-wired the old Buick and driven to Amarillo. But as she waited for the elevator, she heard someone say, "Mrs. Bell." Alan.

She wanted to tell him whom she was on the way to visit, to keep him from realizing that until she met Wynell, she had been an impostor. She didn't. She said, "Let's sit over there."

It was his turn to hesitate. She could tell he didn't want to say whatever was on his mind. "Mrs. Bell, my supervisor assigned me a job I don't want to do." He avoided looking at her.

"Alan, let me help you. I think I know what you're going to say. I'll save you the trouble. The first thing I need to say is that we'll be leaving this evening or in the morning." His shoulders relaxed and he sat back in the chair.

"The second thing I want to tell you is why I've been here and what I've been doing." She took her time, surprised by how calmly she spoke. Until today she would have wanted to run away rather than explain. That was before.

She explained the hardest part first—about Harold's idea for this trip, and the visiting, and that he had thought it would be fun. "I know that all probably sounds strange to you. But if you knew Harold, it wouldn't seem out of the ordinary at all. The truth is, I've always gone along with whatever he comes up with. It's never dull. I love him and I want him to be happy. I think the part about hospital parking lots and my visiting in the hospitals was his way of making the trip interesting for me more than anything else."

He leaned forward, taking it all in and not saying anything.

"There's one more thing I want to tell you. I think you'll understand. I intend to keep on doing what I've been doing. Not parking out front, but visiting. Not long ago, someone I respect told me something I didn't know about myself. She told me I have an ability to listen and to help those I listen to feel hope. Until this morning, I didn't know whether I believed what she said or what it would mean if I did believe it. Today I woke up knowing that's what I'm supposed to do."

Alan said, "I do understand. That's exactly how I felt when I knew I was supposed to help homeless people." He spoke just above a whisper.

"You can tell your supervisor we're leaving. If there's any charge, we'll be happy to pay it. I hope we haven't caused you any trouble with your job."

"I was pretty sure you didn't have a patient in the hospital from the first time you were here. I didn't mention it to anyone. I'm not sure why. The reason I needed to talk to you was because my supervisor assigned me to talk to everyone parked outside about the new corporate policy. Charging ten dollars a day for the spaces. I didn't want to tell you because I hated for you to leave if you might not have anyplace else to go." He had his head down as he said the last words.

"You are a genuinely kind person. Don't worry, we're fine." She stared toward the statue of St. Francis outside the entry. "That worked out for both of us, didn't it? I've come clean and told someone who understands about what I'm doing. And you did your job. We both ought to feel better. Do you?"

"Yes, I do, but I'm sorry you're leaving. I enjoy talking to you. I think the person who told you about your gift is right. I know you helped me."

"You'll be seeing me again. This hospital is my favorite. You'll need to help me figure out how to do my work here without being nabbed."

He winked and said, "I don't think listening is against any corporate hospital policy. But I'll check to be certain." They both sat quietly for a minute, pleased for different reasons.

"What are you doing on the Fourth around five o'clock?" she asked.

Dorothy Faye didn't notice Harold standing in the doorway until she neared the trailer. She was still occupied, thinking about her conversation with Alan. She'd barely gotten inside before Harold said, "If you like that house, I think I could make a good deal on it. Mr. Owens is in a hurry to sell; I think he'll bargain."

"What made you decide so fast?" Even for Harold, this was quick.

He sat on one of the barstools and picked up the pepper shaker, held it up to the light. He looked at the refrigerator, as if a suitable answer might be cooling inside. "I guess it's several things. The biggest one is that I've been selfish."

"What do you mean, selfish?"

"Thinking about what I want without considering what would be good for you. If anything happens to me, you couldn't live in this trailer. I might die before you do."

"That's true, but either one of us could be run over by a truck any day of the week, for that matter. I'm not saying I don't want the house. I'm not sure the remote possibility of your dying is a good reason to buy it, though." She swiped her hand across a speck on the counter. She took a breath and added, "You're going to have the treatment and you'll be fine."

Harold didn't say anything for a while, the silence a paragraph of its own. "The garage was probably what clinched it for me." His smile, the one he used to use to convince the kids that spinach tasted good, told her to forget talking more about his health. "I can fit all my tools on that pegboard. I've got an idea about building a piece to put on pumpers' pickups to save them a lot of steps getting in and out to read gauges. When I get a prototype built, O.D. can be my test pilot." She gave him time to come up with other reasons. "What do you think? Should I go try to make a deal?" he asked.

"What about our trip? Don't cut it short if there are other places you want to go."

"If we get the house, this will be as good a time as any to end this tour. I've found out what I needed to know. We'll keep the trailer for a while, at least, in case we want to go exploring again." He nodded, as if to assure himself. "Another thing about that house—we could get a computer and set it up in one of the back rooms. No telling what a man could learn to do with a computer."

She nodded. "If you're going to talk to Mr. Owens, you'd better get going. I'll tell Rubyjo we'll be moving to her place in the morning." Her stool didn't have an armrest to hold onto. She completely ignored the voice that tried to tell her not to expect too much.

——◆——

Dorothy Faye sat atop a concrete picnic table, pleased with all she could see from her perch. Sister Mary Joseph was talking to R.J. and Maia, he in an

Uncle Sam costume and she dressed as Miss Liberty. The Martin kids were giggling and squealing over on the swings. Feeling the late evening sun on her back, she knew she wouldn't forget this July Fourth, that it wouldn't turn into a faded snapshot.

She could see people talking and laughing, just the way Rubyjo had imagined, in Technicolor—Lou Ann in red scrubs, talking with Rubyjo and her neighbor and the two women from her computer group, like five longtime friends, smiles all around, gesturing with cupcakes in their hands—Alan, in a purple tee shirt, talking to Harold, who was whittling on a twig and looking up every so often to nod—Daniel and Anna, her face no longer pale, holding hands near where they set up the baby's playpen—Janiece, smiling as she filled a large blue trash bag.

Everyone ate their fill of ice cream and cupcakes. The baby went to sleep wearing a white frosting mustache. Rubyjo, wearing trim-fitting white slacks and a red, white, and blue knit top, blushed when Harold whistled at her. Dorothy Faye watched Dennis and Elizabeth walking on the trail at the edge of the park. Elizabeth was talking and he was listening closely, as if he wanted to remember every word.

O.D. sat at the same table as Dorothy Faye, down on the bench, not close enough to upset Janiece, but close enough for Dorothy Faye to hear him. A minute ago he'd said, "Dorothy Faye, this is the best time I've had in a long, long time."

Harold made the deal with Mr. Owens yesterday. He wrote a check to put up earnest money. By tomorrow afternoon, the papers would all be signed. They agreed not to tell anyone, just to surprise them tomorrow after they got the keys.

Uncle Sam and Miss Liberty were set up to entertain in fifteen minutes. They came from Austin prepared with recorded backup music and song sheets for everyone. And then they would all light the sparklers.

CHAPTER 35

A Long Way To Go

Harold was already up, making a list when Dorothy Faye came into the kitchen area. "Hey, sleepy. Did you have all the fun you could stand yesterday?" he asked. He caught hold of her hand and pulled her over beside him. "Take a look at this and see if I've forgotten anything I need to take care of today." He held her in a one-armed hug.

"Yesterday was a lot of fun. And then I had trouble getting to sleep because of looking forward to today's excitement," she said. The last thought she recalled before she fell asleep was that allowing herself to feel so much emotion could wear her completely out.

She read over his shoulder. His list included calling the broker to sell 15 percent of the Walmart stock and wire transfer the money to the bank, meeting Mr. Owens at three o'clock at the lawyer's office, hearing R.J. and Maia's business plan at five, and going out to dinner.

He pointed to the top item on the list. "That'll be enough to take care of paying for the house, whatever we do for R.J. and Maia, and setting aside some for the medical expenses. We'll figure out later what to do about the rest of the stock. Have I missed anything?" he asked.

She hugged him tight. "Not as far as I can see. Oh yeah, there's one thing. Duct tape."

"What needs taping?"

"My mouth. I'm going to have a hard time keeping it shut until this afternoon when we get the keys. Rubyjo and Elizabeth will both be so thrilled for us. I'm glad Elizabeth's staying until Friday. She'll want to help shop for furniture."

"Honey, I can't remember ever seeing you so excited."

"I've been excited before, but I just never let it show as much."

He looked at her with that wrinkle between his eyebrows for a second before he spoke. "Well, I'm glad to see it now. It makes me feel good, like I did something to make you happy."

"You do a lot that makes me happy, Harold. Don't ever doubt that." She kissed him on the cheek. "I'm going inside to see Rubyjo. Talking about the party should keep me busy for a while. Probably take a walk too. By the way, did Janiece say anything to you about the party?"

"Yeah. She asked me where we met those people with all the kids and wanted to know if Sister Mary Joseph is really a nun and if she is, why she doesn't wear a uniform."

⬥

She managed to keep quiet about the house all morning while she and Rubyjo dissected the party, worked in the yard, and took a walk. By noon she knew if she didn't leave, she'd end up spoiling the surprise. She wanted Harold to get to be the one to tell everyone.

Now that waiting wasn't her only occupation, she felt impatient when she did have to wait. But she hadn't abandoned waiting entirely. Harold still had to tell the kids about the cancer and treatment. She wouldn't prod. And she would wait for him to tell her what he had in mind for the apartment behind the house. She promised herself she would wait, without prying or pushing, for him to get around to both of those subjects.

Eating peaches and cottage cheese for lunch kept her busy, but not for long. Her puzzle book finally settled her down. Puzzle #207 held little challenge. She finished it in twenty-nine minutes. The one on the next page, #208, slowed her, though, and kept her attention until Harold rushed in at two thirty.

By exactly 3:32 p.m., the keys to the house hid in Harold's pocket, and they were first-time homeowners. And ten minutes later they walked in at Rubyjo's. She and Elizabeth were on the back porch drinking iced tea.

"Where have y'all been?" Rubyjo asked.

"We've been buying a house," Harold said. Dorothy Faye nodded so they'd believe him.

Elizabeth stood up, sloshing her iced tea. "I cannot believe it. Where?"

Harold grinned a sly grin and said, "Well, the lawyer's office is over on Broadway. And—"

"Daddy! You know I mean where is the house?"

"Oh, is that what you were asking, sweetie? It's a few blocks from here, just south of Lakeview Hospital—3904 Twenty-Eighth Street."

"I'm so happy for you, Dorothy Faye," Rubyjo said. "You too, Harold."

"When do we get to see it?" Elizabeth asked.

"We have time now if we don't stay too long," Harold said. "R.J. and Maia are coming over at five to tell us about their business."

"Later we're all going out to dinner," Dorothy Faye said. "You two are invited." Harold looked pleased, as if he'd had the idea all along.

"I'm sorry, but I won't be able to go," Elizabeth said. "I have dinner plans for tonight." Now she was playing "get me to tell you if you can." She may have learned that from Harold.

"If you don't mind saying, do you have a date?" Dorothy Faye asked.

"I guess you could call it that," she said.

"And if you don't mind my asking, who is your date?"

"Dennis." Dorothy Faye could have sworn her daughter blushed when she said his name. Surely not. She would never blush. She looked as if she was waiting for another question.

Dorothy Faye spoke softly, hoping the other two might not hear. "He's a good person, Elizabeth. I don't think he needs repair work."

"I think you're right, Mother. Getting to know him should be a pleasant change. Now, tell me what you're going to do for furniture. Didn't you get rid of what you had?"

Harold jiggled the pickup keys and looked at his watch. "If y'all can stop talking long enough, we'll go on over to our house, right now," he said.

As everyone trooped out behind Harold, Dorothy Faye said, "Yes, we did get rid of that furniture. We're going shopping tomorrow—you, Rubyjo, and me."

———◆———

Dorothy Faye trailed behind Rubyjo and Elizabeth as they examined every room, guided by Harold, acting like a proud new homeowner. Elizabeth lingered in the kitchen, gliding her hand across the shiny new countertop and staring out the window over the sink. Dorothy Faye didn't ask, but she wondered what her daughter was thinking.

Harold called them from the back door. "Y'all come on out here. I want to show you the garage and the apartment."

"Are you planning on moving into this apartment, Harold? It looks like a bachelor's place to me or a good doghouse for you if you ever get in trouble with Dorothy Faye."

"That's not what I had in mind, unless Dorothy Faye's tired of seeing me every night and every mornin'. But you're right, it might be nice for some bachelors. We'll see."

Elizabeth caught up with them in the apartment. She had lingered in the backyard, studying the contents of the flower beds. "There are some nice plants in those beds. About furniture, Mother, what style are you thinking of?"

Harold held up a hand, traffic control style. "Wait, before you get into furniture. Elizabeth, we're gonna want a computer. Can you tell us what to buy?"

"I can. And I know Dennis would be pleased to set it up for you. He thinks Mother is the best person he knows, other than his own mother, of course."

"Isn't that sweet of him," Dorothy Faye said. Elizabeth and Dennis must have talked about more than the weather yesterday.

"What about the furniture?" Elizabeth asked.

"Something plain, tailored. Not that fancy, floral, overstuffed style. I don't know much about furniture or decorating. I'll recognize what I don't like, though."

Elizabeth said, "I'll get some design magazines tonight and put some ideas together. This is going to be just beautiful." She hugged Harold. He held on to her. "I'm so glad you got the house, and I'm glad you got rid of the furniture you had, especially that ugly Mediterranean end table."

"Looks like I need to find my suit and tie if I intend to listen to your presentation," Harold said when R.J. and Maia stepped into the trailer, dressed in business clothes.

During their twenty-minute presentation, Maia and R.J. addressed everything from their vision and mission through personnel policies and budget. Harold played the banker to the hilt. He asked several complex questions about different parts of the plan, looking serious the entire time. Their answers were clear and concise, all business. Dorothy Faye asked a question about comparable programs and research on parents' interest. Harold said, "Good question, Mrs. Bell. Thank you." And then they were all out of questions. Harold stood and said, "Thank you for bringing us this opportunity. Our board will discuss it at the Thursday meeting. I will be in touch on Friday with our answer." Then he offered each of them a handshake. They played their roles, shaking hands firmly and gathering their material.

Dorothy kept a straight face until the handshaking was finished. Then she laughed. "Harold, you should consider a career in banking. You did a good job as the loan officer." He looked embarrassed when she nudged him with her elbow.

"Do you think we're ready, Dad?" R.J. asked.

"Son, I think you two are ready. I sure do. You make me proud, both of you." Harold sounded like the man from Whaley again.

Day 50 Friday, July 7 8:00 p.m Rubyjo's driveway, Lubbock

This afternoon I had been working a puzzle to keep from telling our secret to everyone. I stopped puzzling long enough to change into my dress for the trip to the real estate signing. Harold still wasn't back and there was at least an hour more before we needed to leave for the lawyer's office on Broadway. What happened to that woman who used to wait so patiently? She's gone forever, I think.

I went back to the puzzle. A fourteen-letter word, "having no depth or scope." _ N _ D I M E _ S I _ N _ _ had all been filled in by solving other clues. "Having no" might be U N. I tried it and then stared at the five blank spaces that remained. Maybe it's—

U N I D I M E N S I O N A L. To be thorough, I checked my new dictionary for the definition of unidimensional. There it was, "having no depth or scope; seeming to have only one dimension."

That could have described me before this trip. I might never have realized there's more to me if Harold hadn't changed things by getting me out of Whaley and leaving me with nothing to do. If you only allow others to see one side of you, eventually that's the only side you or they can know about. All the rest—your spirit, your talent, your hopes—diminish until that one side is all that's left. And I have to hand it to Harold. Nothing I have done lately, none of the things I've shown of my other sides, have seemed to upset him. Just the opposite; he's taken them all in stride.

The next day they were all busy all day long. Harold and O.D. and R.J. and Maia went to Whaley and filled O.D.'s utility trailer and the pickup bed with the things from the storage unit. After they returned, they spent a couple of hours arranging the garage. They situated all of Harold's tools and equipment neatly, ready for the next project.

When Rubyjo, Elizabeth, and Dorothy Faye got back from their furniture expedition, they all sat out on the back porch talking about what to do next. O.D. said he'd better get home because Janiece might need something. They had invited her to go shopping with them, but she said her irritable bowel had flared up. Rubyjo said she was pretty certain they didn't need to know all the details Janiece had furnished on that subject.

"Where's the furniture?" Harold asked. "Y'all were gone a long time not to have anything to show for it."

"Just you wait, Daddy. You're going to love it," Elizabeth said.

"It will all be delivered tomorrow morning," Dorothy Faye said. "We should be able to sleep here tomorrow night." The queen-sized bed she had chosen for their bedroom was her surprise for him. And he'd be even more surprised that in addition to guiding her furniture choices, Elizabeth had also steered them to an electronics store. The computer would be delivered tomorrow too.

The next morning he was up early again, dressed and eating breakfast when she got out of bed. She hugged him from behind and said, "Good morning, Mr. Bell."

"Well, good morning to you too, Mrs. Bell." He finished his cereal, looked at her, and asked, "Did you get furniture for the apartment yesterday?"

"No, I thought you would like to choose what goes out there."

He showed her his reckless grin. "I was thinking that maybe two twin beds would fit in that bedroom."

She said, "Well, now that I've been to all the furniture stores in Lubbock, I know where we can get everything we need to make that apartment homey."

"We can do that after the kids leave. Speaking of the kids, we didn't get a chance to talk about R.J. and Maia and their business loan." He rinsed his cereal bowl. "I was thinking—we could offer them the same deal they want from the bank, let them pay the interest if they're able, and then when the loan is paid, give them the interest back as a gift. Or we could give them part of the money they need as a gift and the rest as a loan. Or we could just leave it as it is and see if they can get the loan from the bank. We could still back them later if they can't. But they don't have any collateral except their ideas and hard work. Getting turned down by banks might take all the starch out of them. What do you think?"

She'd been prepared for the approach he used to use, where he would tell her what he thought and then ask if she agreed. Or tell her after he'd already taken action. She knew, though that she shouldn't have been surprised. She had changed and so had Harold. She said, "If you were in their position, if you were R.J., which would you prefer?"

"Now that's a good question," he said. "Let me think about that a while. We can decide later on today. If we plan to do anything, we ought to tell them before they leave."

They only had to wait for two deliveries after they got to the house. All the furniture came from one store. With Elizabeth's expert advice, they had the deliverymen place the large items where they would stay. After a couple of moves, the placement of the end tables and the new recliner looked right. Even though he helped a lot, Harold rested at least three times. He made it a joke, saying he needed to break in his new recliner.

The second delivery, the computer equipment, desk, and desk chair, got his attention and had him up out of his chair. He unpacked and began assembling the desk. "You can thank Elizabeth for that chair," Dorothy Faye said. "She bought it as a present for you. She thought you should have an executive model, rolling casters and all."

"I hope she didn't spend too much, but it sure is comfortable." He rolled all the way across the room to the doorway where she was standing. "If you're real nice, I'll let you sit in it later," he said, giving her his version of a leer. She swatted him on the shoulder. He said, "Here, you can try it while I go find Elizabeth to thank her." He turned around after a few steps and said, "Dorothy Faye, I told you years ago if you'd just agree, we'd buy ourselves a nice house like this."

"Well, you know how hard it is to get me to agree with you."

"Yeah, you've always been hard to get along with." They both laughed. He said, "Seriously, I'm glad we bought the house. Are you?"

"I am." She didn't trust herself to say anything else.

------◆------

An hour later, they were alone. Elizabeth and Rubyjo had left, promising to bring back lunch for everyone. R.J. and Maia would arrive by noon. "Do you like this bed, Harold? It's wider than the one we've always had."

He stretched out on his back on the bare mattress and spread his arms. "It's a good firm mattress," he said. "I'm a little concerned you might be too far away clear over there on the other side."

Lying down from the other side, she spread her arms and reached out a hand to hold his. "See, I won't be far away."

"If you promise me that, then I like it fine."

"Okay, we'll keep it. I'll go after lunch and buy linens to fit it."

They were both still lying on their backs, looking up at the ceiling fan twirling slowly above. "I've been thinking about R.J. and Maia," he said. "If I was R.J., I'd want to try to do this on my own, no gifts. If we tell them we'll furnish the line of credit and set up the loan with a legal contract, just like at the bank, I think that would be the best way."

"I think you're right; he'd like staying independent. He's a lot like you."

"That's what we'll do then," he said. "And after we get that settled, I'll tell them about the other."

"Let's go out to the apartment and measure to see if twin beds will fit," she said. "If they will, I'll buy sheets for those too, when I go shopping for linens this afternoon."

"This room is bigger than I reckoned—eleven by thirteen. That's plenty big for twin beds and a chest of drawers," he said. He reeled the tape measure into its case with a flourish and stood in the doorway to the bedroom.

"There's room for a couple of comfortable chairs and a little dinette and a television set in this other room," she said.

"Two recliners?"

"Two small-framed ones would fit. Who did you see sitting in them?" she asked.

He came out of the bedroom smiling, looking like the first time he asked her for a date. "I was thinking maybe we could invite Elmer and Bill up for a visit. It might do 'em a world of good to get out of that prison. What do you think?"

"I think you're just full of good ideas, Harold."

———◆———

R.J. and Maia left Friday afternoon after the four of them signed the contract for their loan at the same lawyer's office. "Those kids were both awful quiet when they left," Harold said. "Why do you think they turned so serious?"

"Your news about cancer treatment," Dorothy Faye said. "And I think they were still a little shocked that their money worries are over. Now they have a lot of hard work ahead of them. They were so cute, the way they thanked us so formally." She didn't mention hoping they would decide to be more than business partners.

Before she left for Dallas on Saturday, Elizabeth said, "I nearly forgot to mention that I have dibs on that second bedroom. I'll be coming back out here more often, now that you have an address."

"Your daddy will appreciate your coming when he has his treatment. I hope you'll be able to come often after he's well again too."

"I will." She did blush that time.

Dennis came over Sunday afternoon to set up the computer and printer. As he put the pieces together and started it, he explained each step to Harold. He demonstrated the word processing program, how to connect to the Internet, the e-mail, and several games. Then he handed Harold a book and told him not to worry about breaking the computer, just to explore it and read the book. Before he left, they showed him the house, and Harold took him out to see the garage. It was quite a while before Harold came back in. "He's a real nice fella. He's interested in my idea for the Pumper's Pal. Had a couple of suggestions. He said to tell you thanks again for introducing him to Elizabeth."

Day 54 Tuesday, July 11 Our house, Lubbock

I've spent most of my morning thinking. We left Whaley on May 19. That seems like years ago, not fifty-four days. I had another dream last night, the first one in a while. I don't remember much about it. But I do know it was about the future, not the past. Harold was with me and looked happy. I know that may just be me hoping, but having hope is important. I have to have it myself if I am going to give it others.

One other thing I remember: in the dream, Elizabeth walked in and the first thing she said to me was, "Mother, you're taller!"

I can't wait to see Mrs. Ottley and tell her how much she had to do with all the changes in my life. And I'm going to figure out a good way to explain to Harold, and to other people, about my listening and the hospital visiting. As soon as I get my plan straight in my mind, I'll tell him. I know now that whatever I do, it will be fine with him. It took me fifty-four days—and all those years before—to figure that out.

Harold was staring at the computer screen so intently that he didn't look up when Dorothy Faye stood in the doorway to his now-favorite room. "I'm going to the shoe store to buy some new walking shoes," she said.

He stopped typing and looked up, his big grin showing again. "Did you wear out that other pair?"

"Not yet, but I need to be prepared. I have a long way to go."

www.ingramcontent.com/pod-product-compliance
Lightning Source LLC
Chambersburg PA
CBHW050713180626

46814CB00002B/410